UNDER
THE
WATER

OTHER TITLES BY PAUL PEN

The Light of the Fireflies

Desert Flowers

UNDER THE WATER

PAUL PEN

Translated by Simon Bruni

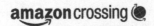

Previously published as *Un matrimonio perfecto* by Plaza y Janés in Spain in 2019. Translated from Spanish by Simon Bruni. First published in English by AmazonCrossing in 2019.

Published by AmazonCrossing, Seattle

www.apub.com

Amazon, the Amazon logo, and AmazonCrossing are trademarks of Amazon.com, Inc., or its affiliates.

ISBN-13: 9781542042062
ISBN-10: 1542042062

Cover design by David Drummond

Printed in the United States of America

UNDER
THE
WATER

1.

The young woman appeared with the rain. Luis saw her turn the street corner the moment it began to pour down, when the drops were visible in the bright halos of the streetlights. Soon puddles formed, reflecting the light from the same streetlights, from the green traffic lights, and from the burger-shaped neon sign above Luis. The woman walked along the opposite sidewalk, skirting a large block of apartment buildings. At this time of night, the lights were off in almost every window. Even the bars that occupied the ground floors had closed a while ago. Her pace was slow. She didn't bother to take cover from the rain under a roof or protect herself with an umbrella.

"You're gonna get soaked!" Luis yelled from where he stood at the counter under the neon burger sign.

Beside him, with a spatula in his hand, Ray laughed when he saw her jump. She put her hood up, as if she'd just remembered that her sweatshirt had one. The light gray of the cotton darkened as the rain soaked it. The woman looked at them from the other side of the street. Her silhouette was bent over, her hands in her sweatshirt pockets as if she was holding on to them to stop herself from falling. They couldn't make out her face in the shadows under the hood—only a bright spot that emerged from them that could have been her nose.

"Drunk or high?" Luis asked in a low voice.

"Drunk," Ray guessed, his elbows on the counter. "And a little crazy. But fuckable, and that's what matters."

The neon, or perhaps the smell of the onions on the grill that seduced the hungry drunks who came out from nearby bars, must have caught the attention of the woman, who turned to cross the street. She did so without looking. A car avoided her with an angry blast of the horn. The driver yelled an insult at her through the window, stopping under the traffic light whose reflection in a puddle dissolved when the girl trod in it in her black Converse shoes.

Seeing her approach, Ray straightened.

"Good luck," he whispered, before escaping to the grill.

From there, the cook would shoot his mouth off about customers who couldn't see or hear him. The idling generator, the hum of the neon, and the music from the radio on the counter insulated them from him, so they could hear none of the offensive remarks Ray made about them for Luis's supposed enjoyment. In reality, Luis did not find them very funny. His coworker sometimes forgot that he was a son of Mexican immigrants.

Before the young woman reached them, Luis turned a wet handle to unroll the awning that covered the bar and two stools on the street. Water that had gathered on the canvas trickled onto a power strip on the counter, to which the neon sign and the radio were connected. Yellow and blue sparks crackled and gave off a burning smell, different from the one coming from the grill.

"Welcome to the best food truck in Seattle. Those were fireworks to celebrate your arrival," Luis joked to play down the dangerous wiring. "Little wet, huh?"

The woman didn't respond. She sat on one of the stools without drying it. Luis wiped the counter, the bar, the laminated menus, the ketchup and mustard bottles. She sat looking at the ground with her

2

hands between her knees. She was clutching her sweatshirt's cuffs with her fingers, hiding her hands as if she was cold.

"You all right?" asked Luis.

The light inside the van softened the shadows under her hood, revealing her face. She was much prettier than he'd expected. The neon created an optical illusion on her pale skin, like makeup outlining her cheeks in orange and accentuating the curvature of her top lip, the volume of her lower one. Her pronounced nose didn't make her ugly in the least—it only added character. Luis guessed she was around his age, about twenty-five.

"Told you she'd be fuckable," Ray declared from the privacy of the grill at the back of the truck.

The stream of obscenities had begun. The sound of the rain would hide Ray's off-color commentary even more, but to make sure the girl didn't hear it, Luis turned up the radio. In the early hours, they tuned it to a station that played melodic soft classics that helped make the atmosphere more relaxed and dampened the spirits of passersby wanting to carry on the party. Now it was playing something by the Carpenters. On tiptoes to reach the set above him, Luis's eyes flicked to the open zipper on the woman's sweatshirt. He discovered that she had nothing on underneath. Her hair, divided into two parts on either side of her neck, dripped water onto the material over her breasts. The way the wet cotton clung to her nipples confirmed her nudity. Her hair seemed wetter than the rain would have made it—it hadn't been raining long enough to soak it this much.

"Hey, seriously, you OK?" he persisted.

"Amigo," said Ray, showing that he did in fact remember Luis's Mexican heritage. "You need to stop worrying so much about everyone else."

Luis could easily imagine a group of the girl's friends wetting her head in the bathroom of one of the bars that had closed an hour ago, to sober her up. Then they would've dried it for her with her own T-shirt and put the sweatshirt on her so she didn't have to wear wet clothes. Of course, if they were such good friends, they could have walked her home instead of letting her go on her own, at the mercy of a ravenous alcoholic stomach.

"Hungry." It was the first word she said, almost confirming Luis's thoughts. "I'm hungry."

The young woman looked at him with eyes of a blue so light it seemed gray. Luis wondered if that was how she saw the world right now: *gray* and plunged into some profound state of gloom. Luis could smell a few beers on her breath as she spoke. A few chasers, maybe. Some shots of tequila. A year serving late-night burgers on the street refined one's ability to detect alcohol. No wonder she was acting so strange, if she'd had that much to drink.

"Then you've come to the perfect place," Luis said.

He offered her two laminated menus, one with pictures of burgers and the other of milkshakes. She gestured at the former without letting go of the sweatshirt's cuff. She didn't let go to pick up the menu, either, preferring to let Luis leave it on the bar. After glancing at the options, she chose the regular burger.

"You can't go wrong with the classics," he said.

He informed Ray of the choice. Ray had already chucked a disc of meat onto the hot plate.

"Always one step ahead of you, buddy," he boasted with a smile. "I told you she was drunk, and she is, because if she was high she'd have gone for something sweet. I also told you she was crazy, and you can see I was right."

He gestured at the girl, who at that moment was wringing her cuff out onto the power strip, watching new sparks crackle.

"Hey, hey, stop that." On tiptoes behind the counter, Luis held her wrists. "Behave. My boss will kill me if the neon blows."

She freed herself from his grip as if it bothered her a lot that she was being touched. Ray flipped the burger on the grill, pressing it down with the spatula, making it hiss in its own juices. The smell of cooking meat filled the food truck.

The girl rested her sad gaze on Luis. "Are you a good person?"

"Huh?"

"I said, are you a good person?"

She was the first customer to ask him such a question. He doubted even his mother, or his girlfriend, had asked him something like that.

"Er, well, I think . . . I'd say so."

"What's the worst thing you've done in your life?"

Luis gestured toward his greasy clothes and then toward the inside of the truck, and Ray at the grill, and the clock that showed three in the morning. A gloomy summary of the only job he'd managed to find in the last three years.

"Probably leaving school," he explained.

"Have you ever hurt anyone?"

Luis thought about it for a few seconds. "Yeah, I guess so. I've let one or two girls down, for sure."

The tiniest hint of a smile appeared under the hood, as if that was precisely the damage she was referring to. In the story Luis was forming in his mind about the stranger, he imagined that this was why she was drunk—a breakup. The worst pain anyone feels, that of abandonment. A pain that was as much a classic as the regular burger she'd ordered.

"And the worst thing someone's done to you?" she asked.

Ray emerged from his hiding place to interrupt the conversation.

"Hey, you, I have an easier question for you: Do you want cheese on the burger?"

She looked at him as if she was surprised to find there was another person in the truck. Her eyes scanned the cook's plump anatomy, but she didn't answer the question. She dried her face with her sweatshirt's sleeves, closing her eyes.

Luis pushed his coworker back toward the grill.

"With cheese," he whispered. "Let's give her something filling."

Ray expressed his disapproval with a snort. He grudgingly laid the cheese across the meat.

"Are you sincere?" she asked when she'd finished drying her neck. She'd also wrung out her hair. "Truly honest?"

"Quite the philosopher when you're drunk, huh?" said Luis. "My coworker here's kind of rude, but he's right: we're here to serve burgers, not have these deep conversations. Overdo it on the tequila shots, or what?"

The woman lowered her head, rubbed her hands together between her knees. A tear or a raindrop rolled down her cheek, and she dried it with a finger. Luis suddenly regretted his comment.

"All right, all right, I'm sorry. Please forgive me. But what's happening here is you're coming down from a night of partying hard, right? You've done something you regret? Don't worry, we've all been there. Message your ex, fight with a friend, make out with a stranger in a restroom . . . something like that, yeah? Well don't worry, in a couple of days all you'll remember is what a good time you had. And there's no better remedy for the blues than a good burger."

"Chicks don't know how to drink," was Ray's contribution.

Luis rested a hand on the woman's shoulder.

"Seriously, there's nothing to worry about. Everything's fine." He massaged the wet cotton of her sweatshirt. "It's not like somebody died."

Another tiny smile visited her face, and she fixed her eyes on Luis's.

"It's just that really I am dead," she said without blinking. "I should be."

A cold tremor ran down Luis's back, and for an instant he thought it was in fact possible he was talking to a ghost, squeezing the shoulder of a woman who would now disintegrate, leaving a puddle of wet clothes on the ground and etching into his soul the supernatural memory of the girl who appeared with the rain.

"What the fuck?" he heard Ray say. "Now we're in an episode of *The Walking Dead.*"

The comment pulled Luis from his phantasmal trance. He let go of the shoulder of the girl who was still in front of him. A normal shoulder, of muscle and bone.

"Yeah, right." He gestured at her from top to bottom. "I'd say you're pretty alive."

"Although now that she mentions it," Ray broke in, "she does look like the typical girl who'd cut her veins open in the bathtub because some guy dumped her—"

Luis was about to challenge Ray's statement when he realized it was quite a reasonable explanation for all the strange things about the girl. Her hair being so wet. The fact that she was naked under her sweatshirt. The way she didn't let go of her cuffs for a second, perhaps to hide the cuts she made on her wrists. The night out getting drunk with her friends that Luis had imagined had really been a solitary intake of alcohol to give her the courage to use the blade she would've left on the edge of the bathtub.

"Do you want us to call someone?" he asked, fixing his gaze on her eyes so she knew he was being serious. "I know there're numbers you can call if you're feeling depressed. Or you can stay with us tonight if you need company."

"Great, let's have every lunatic in the neighborhood here," Ray chimed in again.

"Do you need a phone?" She didn't seem to have one. "Take mine." He took it from his pocket and offered it to her.

"She'll swipe it," Ray warned him.

But the girl didn't even take it. She shook her head. "I just want to eat. Really."

Luis could hear her tapping her feet on the stool's footrest. He sensed her unease. She obviously didn't like being told how to behave, or the patronizing tone that Luis's voice had taken on—a tone that even he found unpleasant. He put his cell phone back in his pocket and laid the burger Ray had just finished on the bar.

"Then eat is what you'll do." He moved the sauce bottles and a pile of napkins closer to her. "And it's on the house, so you can see that the world's a happy place worth being in, with friendly guys who buy you dinner."

"Hey, shithead, you're paying for that—I'm not working for free."

The girl neither smiled nor thanked Luis for his kind gesture. She just picked up the burger, using her little fingers to keep the bread in place. She bit into it with her mouth wide open and bit again before swallowing the first mouthful. Luis almost told her to slow down but stopped himself. The rain fell harder, and the images reflected in puddles resembled pointillist paintings. The pitter-patter on the awning was as loud as the generator. Dolly Parton's *Jolene* was playing on the radio.

The girl continued to eat, slowing down. She paused to take in air and sniff. Luis didn't know whether she was cold or really crying. He couldn't decide whether the drops running toward the corners of her mouth were tears or rainwater. And her irritated eyes, red around the edges, could have been the result of either silent sobbing or the early onset of a hangover, now that she was filling her belly. Luis turned to the hot plate.

"What should we do?" he whispered. "We can't let her leave like this."

"What do you mean, what should we do?" Ray raised his eyebrows. "Burgers, compadre, that's what we do. And as soon as that chick's finished hers, she can go back where she came from. She probably lives in one of the apartments over the road if she got here so quickly after . . ." He mimed cutting his wrists with the spatula.

Luis grabbed his hand to halt the performance, which surprised both of them because he never stood up to Ray, who was the food truck owner's son. That was also why Luis tolerated the constant abuse directed at the customers. But making fun of a girl who might be suicidal was too much.

"You're too good, buddy. You should never trust people." Now Ray used the spatula to scrape the burned cheese from the grill. "We're all selfish pigs deep down."

The girl finished her burger. She folded up the greaseproof paper with drops of ketchup and the remains of a pickle inside and left it in the plastic basket in which it had been served.

"Did you like it?" asked Luis.

"It tasted like soap." She clicked her tongue, as if unsticking an unpleasant flavor from the roof of her mouth. "Everything tastes like soap to me."

"Come on, hombre." Ray's spatula scraped harder against the hot plate. "Get her out of here now."

A drop of water from the awning landed on the adapter, making a spark float in the air before disappearing. The girl followed it with her gaze.

"Have you ever felt so sad you no longer feared pain or death?" she asked, without taking her eyes off the wiring.

"Hmmm . . . no?"

She smiled, her lips outlined in neon pink.

And she took the plug adapter in both hands.

She began to shake, seized by a violent electric shock. So violent that she looked as if she would collapse from the stool to the ground, but the current kept her hands clamped to the adapter. The neon sign blew, exploding like a broken lightbulb. The music on the radio turned to smoke. When the girl finally managed to take a hand off, she held it out to Luis. He grabbed it without thinking. The electricity passed through his body in a brutal spasm. With his eyes lost in the young woman's brokenhearted gaze, Luis couldn't work out whether she had stretched out her arm wanting help or with the perverse intention of sharing her pain with him. Of passing the pain to him, in some way, albeit transformed into electricity.

"What the fuck are you doing?" he heard Ray yell. Their hands separated.

Luis fell to the floor. He trembled, unable to control his body. Everything was darker. He had the cook's feet right in front of his nose. He tried to keep his eyes open, focusing his attention on one point, which turned out to be a hole in Ray's sock where his rubber Crocs left the heel exposed.

"Luis!" Ray knelt down and gave him a few slaps. "See what happens when you're nice to people? Can you hear me? Luis! Luis! Luis!"

2.

The water on the stove was about to boil, and a light curtain of steam emanated from the small pot—the kettle was already in one of the boxes. Grace saw her husband stick his thumb in.

"Damn!" He snatched his arm back to his chest, then sucked his thumb. "It's burning hot."

Grace stifled a laugh. "There're better ways to check the water's temperature. See those little bubbles?" She pointed at them at the bottom of the saucepan. "That means it's almost boiling."

Seconds later, a loud bubbling sound broke out in the water.

"See? It's ready."

Grace pushed Frank aside with her hip and turned off the heat. The fluorescent orange of the glass-ceramic cooktop faded.

"I knew that," he said in his defense. "I was just getting my skin ready for the hot springs."

Frank pulled his best naughty-boy face, and Grace had to kiss him. She felt an impulse to do so every time she saw that expression of innocent childish mischief on the face of the attractive forty-something her husband had become. Sixteen years married to him and the trick still worked.

"I hope those hot springs aren't quite *that* hot," Grace murmured against his lips. "I want to relax, not scald myself."

Frank locked his hands together at the base of her back, turning the peck she'd wanted to give him into a longer kiss. In that same position, a few years ago, he would have put his knee between her legs and lifted her in one motion onto the kitchen island to make love to her right there, both of them with their clothes still on, crumpled at their ankles and shoulders, their tongues lost in each other's mouths. Now his tongue remained on the threshold of her lips. It was how they'd kissed for years, perhaps since they'd had Audrey, or, more likely, since Simon was born. It was, probably, how every couple who became parents ended up kissing. Or maybe in every marriage after the seventh or eighth anniversary.

"Come on, let me be so I can finish up—I've got to seal up all the boxes from the studio."

Grace separated herself from him, thinking that it might be interesting to make a video on the subject of waning passion between long-term partners. It would certainly generate discussion among the eight hundred thousand mostly female subscribers to *Gracefully*, her YouTube channel, and that always livened up the comments section. Hearing Frank pour the water into two cups, she weighed some arguments she could put forward in the video. For instance, however much books and movies suggested otherwise, she was certain that it wasn't passion that kept a marriage going beyond the first few years, but everyday affection. Kissing Frank every time he gave her his naughty-boy look, making her heart melt—that was love. Her subscribers would like hearing that. It seemed to be mostly millennials who'd learned to make a living sharing videos, but there she was, a member of Generation X, bringing in a more than decent second income for the family by recording her married life with her camera and offering relationship advice to help her subscribers achieve the happiness she herself enjoyed.

"Coffee's ready," Frank yelled from the kitchen.

In the entrance hall, she put two tripods and a ring light in the last of the cardboard boxes where she'd packed the gadgets from her studio.

She sealed it with the moving company's tape dispenser and stacked it on top of the other three. With a marker, she wrote her name on the boxes' sides. She checked whether Audrey had done the same with hers, which formed several columns next to an empty cage.

"Yes, I wrote my name on them," she heard her daughter say as she came down the stairs, her fingers tapping frenetically on her cell phone.

"And you've packed everything. Are you sure?"

"Everything except my soul and my social life. They're staying here, not that you care."

Audrey was generally mature for her age and usually surprised Grace with near-adult reasoning and values, but she sometimes showed herself to be the just-turned-sixteen girl she really was.

"Aren't you the one who says it's good to evolve, that change makes you grow and revives the spirit?" said Grace.

It was what Audrey had told Grace when she'd had her hair cut in a pixie style, an act of self-expression that made her stand out from so many of her classmates who competed to have the blondest, longest, and straightest hair.

"If I ever said that—I can't remember right now if I did, but I might have—I was referring to changes that come from within yourself, not your parents telling you all of a sudden you're going to live on the other side of the country."

Before Grace could respond, one of the men from the moving company arrived to carry more boxes to the truck. He pointed at the cage.

"What's this, some kind of mansion for hamsters?" The cage had several levels, with ramps and staircases connecting them, even little hammocks hanging from the bars. "These guys live better than I do." The young man turned the brim of his company cap to the back of his neck, ready to crouch down. "Can I take it like this, as it is?"

Grace held her daughter's hand. She gave Audrey a few seconds so she could be the one to decide what to do. If she wanted to keep the cage, they would take it, even if it took up a lot of space in the truck.

Saddened, Audrey shrugged. "No, just throw it out—or donate it," she told the man. "It's empty."

The squatting young man gave Grace an apologetic look, understanding that he'd touched upon a delicate subject for the girl.

"Oh, I'm sorry. Really. Hamsters don't live that long, do they?" he said to try to make amends. "Not even in such a cool house."

"They were ferrets," Audrey corrected him. "That's why the cage is so big. Come on, I'll help you."

Audrey picked up one side of the cage, the man the other. They left it against a wall in the living room, where the things that didn't make it through the selection process were accumulating.

Grace returned to the kitchen, which smelled like coffee. She positioned herself next to Frank, accepting the cup he was holding out to her. They sipped at the same time, resting against the worktop, looking around the empty kitchen. Grace felt a deep melancholy when it occurred to her that it was the kitchen where her children had had breakfast all their lives. It had been their first home, the only one that's really a home forever.

"How about we take it down together?" asked Frank.

Immersed in her nostalgia, Grace didn't understand what her husband was referring to until he went up to the photo hung near the wall clock.

"It's the last thing," he said.

He beckoned her over. They took a corner of the frame each, like two art restorers taking down a painting in a gallery. The photo had followed them to every house they'd shared: the little studio in downtown Seattle where they lived together for the first time, the two-bedroom apartment where they moved as soon as Frank got his first promotion at the hotel, and this single-family home the company arranged for them after his third promotion, where the suburban dreams they shared of a perfect family life came true.

"Look how gorgeous we were," said Grace.

"And *are*," he said back.

In the photo they were sitting in the backseat of a car. A friend took it from the passenger seat. They were laughing with their foreheads pressed together, looking at a cassette Frank was rewinding with a pen inserted in one of the holes. While they both remembered the tape and the significance it had in their relationship, neither of them recalled why they had laughed so much at that moment. The friend produced the picture using some technique that left it all in black and white except for the jeans they were both wearing, which stood out in bright blue. It was an effect their daughter described as tacky twenty years later, but it had still been a surprising look at that time in the late nineties when they began their relationship.

"We'll take this one with us in the RV. I don't want it to get lost during the move," Grace said.

Frank raised an eyebrow. "You've just put your studio worth six thousand dollars in boxes and you won't pack an old photo?"

"This photo's worth much more than all that money."

He smiled at the comment. "The hotel's paid for the best moving company. Nothing's going to get lost."

But Grace left the photo on the worktop. She wanted it to travel with them.

"Your tacky photo," said Audrey, walking into the kitchen.

With her iPhone, she took a picture of the framed image. Her fingers tapped on the screen as she returned to the entrance hall. She would be sending the image to a friend, laughing at how ancient her parents were, with their paper photographs and antique contraptions for listening to music.

A deep sigh overcame Grace.

"Are we doing the right thing? I feel sadder than I thought I would. I'm sad to leave the city where we started our family, where the children were born."

She remembered the night they found Simon, when he was little, asleep in front of the open refrigerator. He was afraid of the dark but couldn't yet reach the light switches—the fridge light was the only one he could turn on. In no other house would Grace be able to relive that moment, the tenderness of which had made her cry. She felt her eyelids moisten.

"Hey . . . honey." Frank pinched her chin.

"Ignore me, I'm just being stupid."

"You're not stupid, you're beautiful." He kissed her on the cheek. "But this city's stopped being good to us."

"We've been through a bad patch, is all. It happens to everyone, everywhere. And not everyone leaves like this, just like that. People don't just move so easily."

"Sure, but we have the chance."

"You begged your boss for the chance, it didn't just come up."

"It doesn't matter how it came up. What matters is that we have it. And we're seizing it, which is what any smart family would do in our situation. You can work from anywhere, and it's a great opportunity for me—there aren't that many opportunities for hotel managers out there, you know."

"I know, I know . . ."

Grace didn't even know why she was discussing it with Frank at this stage. The decision was more than made, both of them agreed. She clutched the cup in her hands and took a sip.

"The change will be great for the kids—it'll open their minds," Frank went on. "If only they'd gotten me out of my hometown much sooner."

"First off, Seattle isn't a small town like yours was." Audrey had reappeared, waving her cell phone in the air as she gesticulated. "Second, my mind's already very open because I've seen *Girls*, believe it or not. And third, please stop including me in the word *kids*—I don't identify as a

16

kid anymore. I'm a young adult now. Haven't you seen me reading John Green?" She left the kitchen without giving them the chance to reply.

Frank laughed, seeking Grace's complicity, but she was fighting to shake off her sadness. She just smiled with her mouth on the rim of her cup, felt the drink's heat on the tip of her nose.

"Honey"—Frank turned serious, a profound look in his eyes—"we need the change. I need the change."

Grace caught sight of the bad memories housed behind her husband's eyes, the same ones that were housed behind hers and that would always inhabit this place. Frank's face darkened as if he'd just heard the explosion again, and his nose wrinkled as if he could still smell the gunpowder. She relived the vibration in the ceiling, as if the walls were shaking.

"We've waited the three weeks the doctor recommended for Simon, but we can't delay it any longer," he went on. "The job and the house in Boston won't wait for us forever. We have to be grateful and feel very lucky." He must have realized how inaccurate that sentence was to describe what had happened to them recently, because he quickly corrected himself. "I mean with my transfer. We've been lucky with that, at least."

"Yeah, it'll be good for us," Grace admitted. Her last sip of coffee tasted more bitter.

"OK, but just one thing." Audrey was there again. "Did we have to get up so early? Who am I, Ariana Grande performing on *Good Morning America*?"

She laughed at her own joke and typed frantically on her phone, no doubt passing it on to her friends. Grace reflected on the fact that physical distance no longer made communication more difficult. Her daughter would still be able to exchange messages with her friends from coast to coast. The move didn't have to be so traumatic. The idea made her feel better. "Come on, let's go."

All at once she felt full of energy to face the change. She put her cup in the kitchen sink next to the remains of what had been their final breakfast in the house.

"Let's see—the dishes, who's going to wash them?" There were just a couple of plates, some flatware, some cups. "Is it your turn or Simon's?"

"Mine," Audrey quickly replied. She didn't try for one second to foist the work onto her brother. Grace's daughter was sometimes prone to typical teenage outbursts but could also make reasonable gestures like this one.

"Leave them there," said Frank with a wicked expression. "We're not going to use them again. Or are you going to dry them and put them in a box now?"

"Finally. Something good had to come out of moving."

Audrey dropped the scourer before Grace could counter the idea.

"At any rate, there's no time. It's after seven." Frank checked the wall clock that wasn't going with them, either. "We should've left five minutes ago. We've got a lot of driving to do."

Grace went to look for Simon, who'd gone up to say goodbye to his bedroom after breakfast. She saw him from the hall, with his knee on the floor, searching through the contents of a box. As she approached she was able to see the various fabrics, the various patterns that danced in his hands, coming out of the box and returning to it because of the boy's indecision. Like Frank choosing a tie for an important meeting. If only her son were choosing ties.

"What's up? Can't decide?" she asked, inside the room.

"Which one's best for moving?" Simon showed her two eye patches he'd set aside. "This one with a monarch butterfly because we're migrating like they do? Or this Red Sox one because we're going to Boston?"

Grace was touched that he was making the decision with the same joy with which another boy would choose which pair of socks he liked best.

"It's going to take us ten days to reach Boston," she said, rummaging through the box in search of a specific motif. "And it isn't just any move. It's a road trip. Put this one on."

She took out a patch printed with a road map. She had chosen twenty different fabrics and made the twenty patches with them, wanting to minimize the trauma of wearing them as much as possible for Simon.

"Great choice," he said.

"Take all three anyway," said Grace, "so we can wash and change them."

Simon smiled with his whole face, as he always did. The left eye narrowed normally, the eyelids responding in harmony with the stretching lips, the iris brightening in response to his joy. The expression wasn't reproduced in the right eye as it would have been a month ago, because the right eye was no longer there. Behind those eyelids, which had healed but hadn't resumed normal behavior yet, there was just a void and a wall of red flesh, almost completely healed over. The eyelashes and eyebrows would grow back.

Simon stretched the patch's elastic, pulled it onto his head, and covered the eye that was no longer there with the disc of fabric. Grace could smell the ointment applied to the wound.

"OK?" she asked her son, stifling a moan in her throat. The wounds and the healing process had hurt her more than they had Simon himself.

"Perfect," the boy answered.

The same man who'd helped with the cage came into the room. He turned his cap back from the nape of his neck to his forehead. He took a baseball out from a box.

"Hey, kid, one last throw?"

Before Grace could say anything, her son turned around and the man threw the ball to him. Simon's hand missed it by some distance, and the ball rolled along the floor.

"It's my depth perception," Simon explained. "I'm still getting used to seeing the world with one eye, I see everything in two-D."

The man gave Grace another apologetic look, worried he'd been insensitive with the boy now, too. First the elder sister's ferrets and now this.

"Well, two-D's much better, buddy," he said to Simon. "I hate those three-D movies, all those glasses do is make you dizzy."

He picked up the box the ball had come from and held it out toward the boy like a basket.

"Let's see if you can make a basket."

Simon recovered the ball from the floor. He calculated the shot and threw. The man had to take a step to one side to make the ball go in.

"Perfect two-D shot!" He showed an open hand without letting go of the box. "High five!"

Simon high-fived. Grace smiled at the young man, thanking him for the spontaneous way he resolved the situation. She closed the flaps on the box for him and put the box of patches on top.

"These're the last ones," she said.

"Want to come with me and I'll show you the inside of the truck?" he suggested to Simon. "If you're older than eight, I'll let you go inside."

"I'm nine!"

With his eyes, the man gestured to Grace at the lines marked on the doorframe, recording Simon's growth. The last measurement was labeled 9. Grace smiled at him. The boy went out with him, asking him how many boxes he could carry at the same time, whether he'd ever slept overnight in the truck, and something about the possibility of moving to Europe by road. Grace didn't hear the last question clearly, since Simon asked it as they went down the stairs. She left the room, stopping herself from looking back to avoid sad thoughts about the only bedroom where, for his entire life, her son would ever play with two eyes. She closed the door with more force than intended.

"Hey, what's the matter?"

Frank, who was coming up the stairs, quickened his stride.

"It hurts," explained Grace. "It hurts seeing the wound. Physically." She squeezed her fingers on one hand to illustrate the feeling. "It actually hurts."

Her husband lowered his head.

"I'm sorry," Grace said. She stroked his face. "I didn't want to make you feel bad."

He emptied his lungs with a sigh. It took him a few seconds to recover his voice. "See why we need the change? I could never erase that memory from this house."

"I hope the prosthetic eye really does change everything," she said.

"Sure it will." Frank forced a smile. "I'm certain of it."

He handed Grace the framed photo she'd left in the kitchen. When he held out a hand to one side, Grace took it. They went down the stairs together, leaving the past behind, step by step. They walked down the long hall toward the front door they would now use for a final exit. Grace picked up her purse from the floor. She'd left it ready in the usual place, though today it wasn't sitting on the long sideboard that had occupied the hall for years. It was where they had left the folder containing the ultrasound scan confirming their first child would be a girl. And where they left bags of diapers while they got the stroller ready to take Simon out for a walk. The children had cast their report cards there at the end of each school year, dashing upstairs toward a new summer. And on the same sideboard, they finally signed the papers that handed the house back to the hotel chain that employed Frank, while securing them a new one in Boston. Grace examined the outline of dirt on the bare wall, hypnotized by the ghostly presence of a piece of furniture that could summarize their family's story.

"Come on, don't make a big thing of it," said Frank, reading her thoughts. "Keep walking—that sideboard's going to be in our new home, too."

Outside, Simon's squeal of excitement stood out amid the birdsong as he leapt from the moving truck down to the street. The young man in the cap climbed down after him. He and two other men, all dressed in the same company polo shirt, yelled things to one another about distributing the weight of the boxes evenly and securing the cargo.

Audrey crossed the front yard to one of the side paths. When she waved goodbye to the wooded area behind the house, Grace knew who the farewell was for. The girl then pulled out her cell phone and took a selfie in front of the house, exaggerating her sad face.

"Right, enough drama!" Frank yelled to everyone. "We've got much better things ahead! Starting with Idaho and the hot springs!"

Grace caught up with her husband, who was signing moving-related documents on a clipboard held by the young man in the cap. Frank was explaining to him that a representative from his own company would receive the shipment at the destination address. He and his family would take it easy and make the most of the move, getting to know the northern states better. He reeled off the names Yellowstone, Mount Rushmore, the Badlands, Niagara Falls.

"What did we buy one of these for if not to see the sights, huh?" Frank pointed with the pen at the motor home parked right behind the truck. "Now that the weather's improved at last, it's the best time to travel with it."

It was one of the big RVs, the size of a bus, painted in various tones of gray with undulating maroon lines. They'd bought it a year ago but hadn't found the time to break it in with a big trip. In the end, the big trip became a move to the other side of the country.

"Oh, sure. A Class A," the young man said. "You're going to be nice and comfortable in there. I bet it has more space than my apartment. You know how to do things right, huh?"

He looked at Grace cautiously in case he'd made a third misstep, but she responded with a smile.

"Done," said Frank, marking a loud dot on the last of his signatures. "We're off!"

The man retrieved his pen. "Enjoy your trip." Then he yelled to the boy. "And you, Simon! You have a great time, OK?"

"I'll have fun in two-D!"

They both gave a thumbs-up. The gesture put Grace in such a good mood that she sent a kiss into the air with her fingers to say goodbye to the young man.

"Drive carefully, it's a long journey," she told him in a maternal tone. "And stop to rest all you want, there's no hurry."

Frank laughed and took her by the elbow to lead her to the RV. "I love how you're so friendly with people," he said on the way. "Even some kid from the moving company."

3.

It was the first time she'd manned the desk alone. She'd been with the company just three days, but the boss had decided she was ready to serve customers by herself. He told her not to worry, that first thing in the morning there would be hardly any rentals and that at eight in the morning a coworker would begin his shift to help with the rush. For the time being, the boss had been right: no one had turned up at her desk since she opened up at six.

She adjusted her shirt cuffs for the umpteenth time so that they protruded slightly from her jacket's sleeves. Every five minutes she checked that her name badge was straight on her pocket. Each time the screen saver came on, she moved the mouse to make it disappear. She was terrified at the idea of the system freezing. Bored, she invented a pastime that consisted of drawing a dark blot with her pen on a piece of paper and pressing her thumb against it to reproduce her print all over the rest of the page. She'd almost filled it when the first customer arrived.

A lone woman. Pretty. Dressed in a stretched sweatshirt, her hands barely visible. She now wished she hadn't stained her thumb with ink. She tried to clean it on the page before the woman reached the desk.

"Good morning, welcome to Emerald City Car Rental, where your best journeys begin. I'm Holly. How can I help you?"

She heard the nervousness in her voice. She'd sounded too high-pitched, too cheerful. More like a college student doing an internship than a real professional.

"You can help me rent a car," the woman replied.

She said it in such a way, stressing the obvious, that Holly knew she hadn't made a good impression. The woman must have disliked the anxious high pitch in her voice. It was to be expected. Starting on such a bad note made her even more nervous.

"What type of car would you like?"

Now her voice was at least deeper, but her lip had trembled. For goodness' sake, she had to calm down. She gestured at two large cards on the counter showing the various car models. The young woman ran her finger over them.

"I don't know, I don't care."

Holly saw that some fingers on the woman's left hand had blackened skin, like an old burn of some kind. An electrical burn, maybe. As a child, Holly had stuck her hand in an electric heater and her hand had been black for weeks.

"This one here," said the woman.

"A standard size, then—perfect. When do you need it?"

"Now?"

Again, she used the dry tone that invalidated the question as too obvious. And she was right. When would she want the car if not now? Holly's lip trembled again. Her gaze escaped to the computer. She entered the details, leaving ink on the spacebar with her thumb.

"And will you return it here?"

"I don't know. I'll decide later. I'm going on a, let's say"—she searched for the right word—"an emotional journey. More internal than external, if that makes sense."

"Sure, sure, of course it does," Holly said, though in reality it didn't.

"I've been having a rough time, and I think a trip on my own is just what I need. I've never been to Idaho, and it's so close. Have you?"

"No, to be honest, I haven't."

"Well, it's right there."

"Yes, very close." She would have agreed with anything the woman said. "You don't know the return date, then?"

The woman shook her head. Holly smiled but her back was beginning to sweat. Could she log a rental without a return date? It hadn't come up in the first few days of work, nor could she remember having covered the situation during her training days. On the screen, a box on the registration form required the information. She clicked with the mouse several times to try to leave it empty, but an error message appeared.

"I'm going to need a return date," she said, full of doubt. "I could change it later, I guess."

"Well, I don't know, say I'll return it"—she waved her hand in the air—"in five days. On July fourteenth."

"Are you sure?" Holly asked, and regretted the question right away. How could she have done that, questioned the customer? Her job was to process the car rental, enter the details the customer provided. If the information proved to be false, that wasn't her problem anymore—the boss, or the insurance company, or whoever, would have to deal with it.

"I'm sorry. You seemed undecided. I asked to know whether you were completely sure, not because I thought you were lying."

Fabulous. Now she'd called her a liar as well. But the woman wasn't offended. Her lips formed into a strange smile.

"Can we ever be completely sure about anything?" she said. "Will I still be alive in five days to return the car? Will you still be alive?"

OK. Now it was clear: there was something unusual about the woman. Her response wasn't normal, whichever way you looked at it. Maybe that was why Holly had felt so uneasy from the start—her intuition was warning her of something.

"I hope so," Holly replied. Her heart had accelerated. "Both in five days and in fifty years, I hope!—I'm pretty young. Would you like me to tell you about the insurance?"

"Add all the insurance," the woman answered. Then she deepened her voice: "Just in case." She said it with exaggerated darkness, verging on parody. So perhaps what she said before was also part of some joke. Maybe the woman simply had an unusual sense of humor and Holly was more nervous than she needed to be. Drops of sweat appeared on her forehead, and one rolled down the side of her face.

"Are you sad?" the woman asked.

"Sad?" Holly dried her brow with her jacket sleeve. "Not at all. I'm just nervous—it's the first time I've been left on my own here and I want to get everything right. I was hoping for a normal rental."

"And I'm not normal?"

"Sorry, sorry. See how nervous I am? I think it's best if I just stop talking."

"Don't say that. Don't let anyone silence you, ever. We women have had plenty of that already. In any case, I like honest people. And that's what you've been since I walked through that door."

At what moment had the woman gone from wanting to frighten her to valuing her deeply as a fellow female? Holly thanked her for her words with a smile but endeavored not to say much more. The customer was always right, and she was going to give her the car, just as she asked. If the car was then found burned out after a drug feud or driven off an embankment with the seats full of bullets, it wasn't Holly's problem. Her boss could deal with it.

She followed the steps to complete the rental procedure. As she scanned the woman's documents, she saw that the name on the driver's license was Mara Miller. She also took payment from a credit card. The woman's signature was rounded, clean, with no lines through or under the name. The simplicity of it made her think of a woman at peace with herself, an image at odds with how troubled she seemed right now.

"I'll show you to your car."

At last her voice sounded confident, professional. She took an envelope from a drawer containing the keys, went around the desk, and asked the woman to follow her. A door at the back of the hut led straight to the parking area. From there, she pointed at a row of standard-size cars.

"See the red car with SKY on the plate?"

"I see it."

"Well, that's yours."

Holly handed her the envelope. A print in black ballpoint ink was left on one corner, almost imperceptible because the ink had dried on her thumb. The nervous Holly wanted to say something about the spiritual journey the woman had said she was embarking on, that she hoped she would find whatever it was she was searching for, but the professional Holly of the last few minutes asserted herself and, with a businesslike absence of emotion, just wished Miss Miller a pleasant drive. The woman thanked her and crossed the parking lot in the car's direction.

"*Please* bring the car back," Holly whispered when she was out of earshot. "I'm still in the probation period."

4.

Frank loved driving in the high motor-home seat. He felt as if he were flying over the road, seeing what was happening on all six lanes, calculating the consequences for them of a vehicle maneuvering far in front. In the distance he saw a rest area that was still several miles away. In the passenger seat, Grace was also looking ahead, but her eyes were out of focus. Frank had seen his wife go in and out of this absent state several times as they drove. Now she was also rubbing the pointed hairs at one end of her eyebrow with her fingertip.

"Come on, honey." He pinched her elbow to interrupt the habit that always manifested itself when she was worried. Later she would complain that her eyebrow looked sparse in her videos. "We're doing the right thing. We need to change our luck."

In the rearview mirror, Frank saw Audrey move her cell phone away from her face. She'd spent the last hour lying on the sofa, typing away, disobeying her parents' constant orders to sit at the table and put her seat belt on as Simon had. Now she sat up and moved to the part of the sofa nearest them, behind Frank's seat.

"And why do you think our luck will change on the other side of the country?" she asked.

"For starters, because your father's going to earn more money," he replied. "That's important."

"You must know I'm not materialistic," said Audrey, before returning her attention to the iPhone X her father had paid for.

"We've only been driving a few hours and I already feel too far away," Grace whispered. "It's too soon. I feel like we're running away."

Frank let out a guffaw. "Nonsense. We're not running away."

"That was our home . . ." Audrey gestured at some indeterminate place behind her, at the three hundred or more miles between them and the house they'd left behind.

"In a month, Boston will be our home. Just like the old one. Or better. And Boston's that way." He gestured ahead, to the future.

"All I'll say is, my ferrets won't come back however many times we move. And Simon won't grow a new eye."

Frank let his shoulders drop. Every time Simon's eye was mentioned, he felt his heart stop. His blood stopped running and stagnated, then putrefied, turning into guilt. Grace tutted. She wanted to give Audrey a smack on the knee but couldn't reach.

"Don't say that," she whispered. "What if your brother hears you?"

Frank searched for Simon in the rearview mirror, running his eyes over the inside of the vehicle in its reflection. Behind the driver's seat, against the wall on the left side, was the three-person sofa Audrey was occupying. Next, perpendicular to it, was a dining table with two benches facing each other. Beyond that was the bathroom and, at the back, the master bedroom. On the other side, behind Grace's seat, was the main door, the kitchen—which had a double-bowl sink, three burners, a pantry, an oven, and a refrigerator—a large closet space and, at the rear again, the bedroom. Both the living room and the bedroom were modules that extended to create more space when the vehicle was parked. On the road, with the modules retracted as they were now, the motor home's interior was compressed in such a way that the sink was close to the sofa on the opposite side and the refrigerator almost touched the dining table. That was where Simon was, oblivious to Audrey's comments, munching on a pack of Flamin' Hot Nacho Doritos. The entire RV smelled like chili peppers.

"Dad!" he yelled right then. "The license plates, Dad! They're changing! Now they're red and blue. And they say"—he sucked a finger as he pressed his nose against the glass to read—"Famous potatoes?" He wrinkled his nose, doubting his imperfect eyesight, but moments later he confirmed it. "Famous potatoes! Dad, they say famous potatoes." Simon burst into laughter, then noticed Frank looking at him in the mirror.

"Look how well you can read even from a distance, Gizmo," he said. "Of course the plates are changing, we're approaching Idaho."

His son looked back out the window, the patch covering his right eye.

"It says it on all of them! *Scenic Idaho. Famous potatoes.*"

"Each state has its own plates, son. On the ones from here, like ours, it says *Evergreen State*"—half the cars surrounding them still bore the Washington state design—"but on the Idaho ones it says the potato thing. And wait till you see what's on the Wyoming ones."

Simon's healthy eye opened wide, intrigued, ready to be surprised, as expectant of life as he had always been.

"What's on the Wyoming ones?"

"You'll see," Frank replied. "You'll have to wait till we arrive."

"What is it?"

Frank shrugged, maintaining the intrigue. Beside him, Grace smiled. Like him, she was happy that Simon was still the same boy he had been a month before.

Frank saw Audrey in the mirror, showing her cell phone to her brother. And in the reflection of a window, the screen with an image of a Wyoming license plate. Simon opened his mouth when he saw it, amazed. *Wow, a cowboy*, Frank read on his lips. Audrey shushed him so their dad wouldn't know she and Google had given away the secret. The conspiracy between siblings touched Frank.

31

"Look, Dad, a hitchhiker." Simon pointed toward the windshield.

On the roadside, a young man with dreadlocks, walking boots, and a large backpack was holding a piece of cardboard with a message written in black marker: **GOOD GUY.**

"Should we pick him up?" Audrey suggested. "There's plenty of space. It'll be interesting to talk to him. I bet he's traveling the country, he must've seen a lot of things."

"And he's a good guy," Grace read.

"If he really was a good guy, it wouldn't occur to him to announce it with a sign."

"Let him in!" yelled Simon.

"Come on, Dad, pick him up."

"Don't be silly. You can't just go around trusting people and picking up strangers these days. He could have explosives in that backpack, for all we know."

"Yeah, right . . . a hippie with a bomb," said Grace.

"Why not? You can't even trust the ones that dress normally, let alone that guy, with that hair and all the rips in his pants."

"Dad, that's so awful and snobbish I don't know where to start."

"Then don't. And forgive me, everyone, for not wanting a stranger near my family. The next serial killer we see, we'll let him in." Then he lowered his voice so that only Grace could hear. "And you: unbelievable. As if we haven't had enough of strangers already."

She rubbed his thigh by way of an apology.

Concentrating on the discussion inside the motor home, Frank didn't see the red sedan that moved into their lane. When he looked back at the road, they were already on top of the vehicle—so close that he could only see its nose, the car's body eclipsed by the RV's dashboard. Though he was certain they would hit it, his foot pressed on the brake and a hand turned the wheel. Frank braced himself for the impact, locking his elbows, hunching his shoulders. But they didn't crash.

By some miracle the motor home changed lanes in time, earning itself nothing more than a horn blast from some car behind them. Frank also honked his horn, hard, the urge he'd contained while maneuvering to optimize his reaction time now concentrated in the palm of his hand.

"Moron!" he yelled at the windshield, at the little car. "Learn to drive!"

He hit the horn as rapidly as the pulse in his neck, aimed at the red vehicle that was now moving away as if it had nothing to do with the honking. The letters on its rear license plate read *SKY*.

"Yup, the sky's where you'll end up driving at that speed. Drive faster, go on, drive!"

"Stop, Frank, he can't hear you," Grace said.

"God, what a scare! Are you two all right?" he asked the children.

He saw Audrey sprawled on the floor, wedged in the space between the sofa and the sink.

"Audrey!"

Frank steered into the shoulder and stopped the RV. He released his seat belt, as did Grace. They both rotated in their swivel seats to face the vehicle's interior.

"Are you OK, honey?"

"Yeah, yeah, I just fell." She got herself up with knees and arms.

"See?" Grace scolded her. "No more lying on the sofa without a seat belt. We've been saying it since we left. Go sit with your brother at the table, right now. Are you all right?"

Simon nodded, still gripping his bag of Doritos. "But this fell." He picked up the framed photo of Frank and Grace from the floor. The glass had broken, as if the happiness in the image it protected had cracked.

"What a dope I am, I just left it on top there." Grace tutted. "I forgot to put it somewhere safe."

Audrey gathered her legs in on the sofa to let her mother pass. Grace reached Simon at the table, warning him to be careful with the glass, which she threw in the trash can. She blew on the photograph and showed it to Frank. It wasn't scratched, and the frame had withstood the impact.

"No big deal," she said to him with a smile.

"This *is* a big deal," Audrey cut in.

She showed them her cell phone. A cobweb of cracks had formed in one corner of the screen. She ran her thumb over it, she typed, she opened the camera app, she played a song.

"At least it works," she said with relief. "But see what I'm saying? It doesn't matter how far away we move, things won't get better. I bet we're jinxed."

"Don't say that." Frank turned back in his seat, facing the front again.

In the distance, almost at the rest stop, he could see the car that had almost ruined their trip. Luckily, he'd dodged it just in time. Now it was just a red dot in the distance, a long way ahead of them.

"Everything's going to be better from now on," he said to himself, as his wife made sure the children had their seat belts on at the table.

5.

The mother guided the little girl by the hand. Seeing her walk with her knees together, containing the urge to pee, made her want to laugh. She didn't, so she wouldn't upset her daughter—the girl had reached the point where her need to urinate was no longer a laughing matter. She pushed open the door to the public restroom at the rest stop and allowed the girl to go in first, without letting go of her.

"Next time, tell me as soon as you need to go. Don't wait till the last minute, because look what happens, you—"

She broke off when she discovered a young woman at the first sink. She was looking at herself in the mirror with the water running, gripping the washbowl, her fingers white from the pressure she was exerting. Her face was also pale, her hair stuck to it with water or sweat. The dark patch on the back of her cotton garment made the theory that she'd been sweating seem the most plausible. The mother's first instinct was to keep her distance from the woman, to get her daughter away from her, but she hid her feelings to avoid offending her.

"Oh, I'm sorry. Look at me, coming in here yelling like there was no one. Like the restroom was all ours," she said. "We have a little emergency."

She spoke without stopping, guiding her daughter to one of the cubicles. She cleaned the seat with some toilet paper.

"Don't move or touch anything, OK? When you've finished, wipe yourself with this and you're done." She gave her daughter another length of toilet paper. "I'll wait for you out here."

She left the stall door ajar as she went out. From there she observed the young woman, who was splashing water on the back of her neck. She took a deep breath and let it out slowly. Seeing her now, it seemed ridiculous that she'd been frightened. She was a harmless young woman having a rough time, not some drug addict going cold turkey or an armed fugitive, two of the options her prejudiced brain had weighed when they'd walked in. The bag the young woman had hung from the hand dryer was a good brand.

"I try to leave her alone in the toilet," she explained, gesturing at the half-open door. "So she starts getting used to the idea that peeing is a private thing she'll have to do by herself sooner or later."

The attempt to strike up a conversation was as much an apology for her bad thoughts as a way to distract the young woman from her own.

"I'm Brittany!" the girl yelled from inside the stall. "And my mom's called Bree. Brit and Bree. Brit and Bree."

Bree laughed, hoping to engage the young woman with the funny way her daughter was repeating their names, but the stranger barely looked away from the sink. The two women's eyes met just for an instant in the stained, broken, scratched mirror. A graffiti artist's tag crossed it from corner to corner. Bree could see that the young woman would rather be left in peace. She watched her hold her mouth under the faucet, rinse it, and spit.

"Mom, somebody's puked in here," said Brittany. The young woman stopped what she was doing, aware she'd been caught.

"It's in the trash, Mom. Ugh, how gross! Somebody threw up in the trash can."

The young woman stooped over, trying to hide behind her own shoulders. She looked guiltily at Bree, as though she were being accused of a crime.

"There's corn," the girl added.

The shoulders hunched even more. Bree felt sorry for her.

"Well, it doesn't matter, sweetheart," she said. "Just hold your nose. And don't touch anything."

Bree continued to study the young woman. She saw tears on her face. They could have been the tears that come with intense vomiting or those of the deep sadness that she radiated. This sadness touched Bree, who could recognize a suffering soul.

"There's always a way out," she said. "Try not to make it worse. Whatever it is."

The young woman turned off the water, as if she needed silence to reflect on the words Bree had said. Bree felt satisfied that she'd helped her. At her own worst moments, she would have appreciated some words of encouragement like those, even if they came from a stranger.

The young woman turned her head. "You don't know anything," she said over her shoulder.

"I'm not your mother nagging you, honestly. I'm just trying to make you feel better. I know how powerful it can be to find that someone cares about you. And I care about you. I've suffered, too, I've done awful things to myself." She took a step closer to the young woman and lowered her voice. "I've found myself lying on the floor in some rest stop bathroom, too, and no one even bothered to check whether I was alive or dead. I don't want that happening to anyone else."

"Do you see me lying on the floor?" the young woman replied.

In the silence, they heard the girl's last drops fall into the toilet water.

"I'm wiping myself, Mommy," she said in the cubicle. "Geez, this barf stinks."

"I just want to help," Bree whispered.

"But you don't know anything about me. You don't know anything about what's happening to me."

Bree just observed the young woman's eyes, taking pity on her for the confused state she seemed to be in.

"Don't hurt yourself anymore," she said. Then she raised her hands in the air, bringing her attempt to help the young woman to an end.

Brittany came out of the stall pinching her nose.

"Did you wipe really well?"

The girl nodded.

"Then let's wash our hands."

On tiptoes, Brittany reached the soap dispenser next to the faucet where Bree had stationed herself, two sinks away from the young woman. Bree wrapped her daughter's hands in hers and they rubbed them together, forming a lather. While they rinsed, she sensed her daughter's intention to say something and squeezed her fingers to stop her. They both dried their hands with paper towels. On the way out, the girl stopped next to the young woman and tugged on her pants.

"Don't worry, I've been sick a few times at school. One time, milk came out of my nose."

Bree was moved by her daughter's gesture.

"Can I please have a little privacy?" The young woman didn't even bother to look at the girl, to thank her for her good intentions. Bree pulled her daughter away from the young woman, no longer caring whether she offended her as she had when they'd come in. She didn't care whether the young woman was rude to her—there wasn't much that could hurt her at this point in her life—but she wasn't going to let anyone be rude to her daughter.

"Next time, be sick in the toilet, not the trash can next to it," she spat out at the young woman, without a trace of compassion, "and flush it. Just because the world's crappy for you doesn't mean you have to make it crappy for everyone else. We all deserve a clean restroom. My daughter deserves one."

The stranger didn't reply, nor did Bree expect an answer. She left the restroom satisfied that she'd defended her daughter, while knowing how much the judgment might have stung the young woman.

Outside, the girl pointed at an RV the size of a bus.

"What a huge car, Mom."

"It's called a motor home, honey. It's like a house on wheels."

"I want a house on wheels! Like a snail!"

"Snails have wheels?"

"Oh, no!" Brittany burst out laughing.

As Bree hugged the girl, the young woman in the sweatshirt came out of the restroom and ran to a red car with its windows open. She threw her purse on the passenger seat before climbing in, starting the vehicle up, and driving off.

"That lady's mean," her daughter said.

"No, sweetheart. She's just sad."

6.

Grace had given the driver's seat back to Frank. They'd begun to take turns once they left I-90 and, four tradeoffs later, they had covered more than five hundred miles in around ten hours. The sun had gone down behind them, the ever more oblique rays now filtering through the motor home's rear window. The evening light turned the bedroom orange and spilled down the corridor to the main compartment, where Audrey and Simon were both entertaining themselves on their cell phones. The number of lanes had decreased each time they turned onto a new road, until the last exit they took led them onto the single lane on which they now traveled. On both sides, a thick conifer forest had replaced the urban landscape from which they had set off. Western white pine, ponderosa pine, Douglas fir, western hemlock . . . Grace could name the conifers of the Northwest by heart after studying them at school and refreshing her memory with Simon in the last school year. She was going to ask him whether he was still able to identify them, because to her they all seemed the same however well she remembered the different names, but Frank spoke before her.

"Look how beautiful it is here," he said. He lowered a window and took a deep breath. "It smells of earth, of life. It smells of the future."

Grace recognized the same optimistic excitement in her husband's face that she had seen the day he gathered her up to carry her through the front door of the house they'd left that morning. If the expression had translated into so many years of happiness for the family, perhaps the bright future that Frank saw with such clarity awaited them now. Grace looked him in the eyes, peering into his rosy image of what lay ahead of them and allowing his enthusiasm to infect her.

At that instant, notes from a guitar sounded on the motor home's speakers, which were playing a Spotify list from Grace's smartphone. The music of those chords lifted Frank's spirits even more, his mouth opening by itself as if there could not be a better moment for that song to play, as if he couldn't believe they were experiencing one of those rare moments in life when everything's perfect. Grace turned up the volume to amplify their joy.

"Your phone's ringing!" the children yelled at the same time.

"Very funny," Frank answered.

They'd said it because it was the song both spouses had set as their ringtone for when the other called. Jewel's guitar played several times a day in their house.

"It's weird hearing the whole thing," said Audrey. "You always take the call while the guitar's playing. The woman doesn't even start singing."

"Oh, it's an actual song?" asked Simon. "I thought it was just one of the ringtones that comes with the phone. Seriously."

"It's much more than that," Frank said.

He smiled sidelong at Grace, another of his gestures that made her melt.

"It's the song I recorded for your mother on both sides of a cassette so she knew we were made for each other." His eyes sparkled the way they did in the photograph in which they were rewinding the very same tape with a pen. Without taking his eyes from Grace, Frank waited for Jewel to reach the end of the chorus before whispering a slight variation of the lyrics to her. "You are meant for me, and I am meant for you."

"And you were right." Grace took his hand on the armrest. With her other one she stroked his jaw, as robust as it had been so many years before. "You're amazing."

"How many songs could you fit on a cassette?" Simon asked. "A hundred?"

"Don't be silly," Audrey said in response to his stupid remark, though she'd never even held a cassette in her hands. "A lot less. In the ones in *13 Reasons Why*, I don't think they could take more than an hour of music. And the question you should be asking our parents is how they can be so darn mushy at their age."

"Hey!" exclaimed Frank. "Isn't that one of those discriminatory comments you complain about so much? Isn't it wrong to demean your parents because of their age, taking advantage of the privilege of youth?"

Audrey thought about it for a moment.

"You're right, Dad," she said after an inner debate. "And sorry to you, too, Mom."

The parents smiled at each other, both proud of how they were bringing up their children. They listened to the rest of the song without interruption, Grace running her fingers over the topography of her husband's knuckles, Frank looking at her out of the corner of his eye as he had from the bench outside Starbucks where they had coincided every morning before they'd known each other.

"I'm hungry!" Simon yelled as soon as the song ended.

"Me too, Gizmo," Frank said, turning the car radio down, "but let's eat when we get to our destination—that's why we've got a house with a kitchen in the back. It's a spectacular spot, you'll see. We're going to eat hot dogs under the stars—Idaho's skies are incredible. And ketchup tastes better outdoors. Seriously, this place is going to blow your mind. And I bet there'll be no one else there. We'll have it *all* for us."

"How long will it take?" asked Audrey.

"About two hours."

Simon unbuckled his seat belt. He walked forward gripping the table, the kitchen worktop, the sofa, his sister's knee, the door. When he reached his father's seat, Grace smelled the ointment under his eyepatch. The boy asked them to listen carefully. His belly rumbled at such a volume it sounded like it was digesting itself.

"I can't wait that long," he said.

Another rumble lent force to his words. Grace laughed.

"I'm hungry, too, to be honest," she said. "And I'd rather not have to do anything when we stop today—we're going to be worn out when we arrive. Let's stop and eat so we can just go to sleep when we get there. We can always make a big breakfast in the morning. We can still see the stars when we get there, but with a full stomach. And we won't have the noise from this kid's belly disturbing us."

"I second the motion," Audrey agreed. "Let's have dinner—it's almost night."

Frank directed an exaggerated pout at Grace, lamenting the unanimous rejection of his proposal.

"You know what? I'm starving, too," he admitted.

Simon gestured ahead. "Well, there's a restaurant coming up."

The yellow and green of capital letters at the top of a post stood out from the purple tone of the twilight landscape. They formed the word **DINER**. Underneath, *Danielle's* was written in a more informal type, as pink as the color that tinted the clouds at dusk.

Frank hit the blinker.

"Will they have vegetarian options?" asked Audrey.

7.

The bells above the door rang. Then she heard laughter. There was nothing worse at the end of a hungover day than a happy, noisy family. Until now she'd been lucky with one of the quietest evening shifts she could remember, as if the heavens had heard her prayer as she walked through the restaurant's back door. She'd prayed for an easy shift. For an empty restaurant. And for the few people who did come to be completely alone. Single men, widows, truck drivers. She'd taken a Tylenol from the first aid kit next to her locker, washed it down with a swig of Pepto-Bismol, and gone out to serve the tables. As if the heavens really had granted her wish, she'd had almost no customers. She was two hours from the end of her shift, and there was only an elderly couple occupying a table at the back. They were sharing their third portion of pie. Without speaking, just holding hands. They'd sat there that way all afternoon. Aniyah wanted to grow old like that with someone, and silently she awarded them the prize for best customers for a hangover, even if the hangover had almost subsided. Until the sound of the little bells over the door brought the headache back. And the laughter returned the discomfort to her stomach.

Aniyah looked up from the bar, where she was drying flatware with a dish towel. It was a family of four that came in. White. With two kids. Kids who would order dessert—an extra twenty minutes of service. And they would order ice cream. Everyone ordered ice cream in July, and she'd already cleaned the syrup bottles. How lazy she felt. She made herself focus on the fact that, if they had dessert, the check would be bigger and so would the tip. She'd be none the worse for it— she'd hardly collected any tips today, and at least it was an American family, not the European tourists who pretended they didn't know how much to leave. Aniyah mustered her strength, left the towel on top of the flatware, and came out from behind the bar. She felt the corners of her lips fight against the rest of her face to paint the fakest smile she was able to force.

"Hi, beautiful family! Welcome to Danielle's," she said in a singsongy voice, her face feeling almost deformed. As she always did to win over the children and, in doing so, the parents, she searched for some detail on the little one to personalize the greeting. "I'll bet the road's made you all hungry—especially you, little pirate," she said on account of a patch the kid wore on his eye.

"Really hungry!" he replied.

Despite the boy's enthusiasm, there was an uncomfortable exchange of looks between the parents. Perhaps mentioning the patch hadn't been the best way to earn their affection, after all. While she showed them to their table—for her own benefit, she offered them a booth near the kitchen and bar so she'd have less walking to do—she asked what they'd like to drink and memorized it.

"Great, I'll go fetch those drinks while you decide what you'd like to order." She laid menus in front of them. The parents had sat nearest the wall, opposite each other. The children were at the outer end of the table.

Back behind the bar, Aniyah took four glasses and began filling them under the soda fountain's valves. She'd almost finished filling the mother's Coke Zero when she heard the bells above the door again.

Her shoulders dropped as the hangover grew heavier. "I don't believe it," she murmured.

Everything had been going so well, and now she had two new arrivals in quick succession. She prayed it would be just one person, maybe a hiker on the way to the hot springs—she was in no state to deal with another family. The Coke Zero overflowed the glass, and she wiped it with a cloth and placed it on a round tray with the others. She watched a young woman walk in, her sweatshirt's hood covering her head. Without waiting for anyone to receive her, she headed to a table of her own accord. Aniyah picked up four straws. She cursed the young woman's bad manners—the least you can do when you arrive at a restaurant is wait for the server to offer you a table. Now the girl would sit on the other side of the room and she would have to walk ten miles just to serve two tables. She'd done so well with the trick of positioning the family near the bar, and this young woman was going to ruin her night and make her hangover worse. She peeled the paper wrapping from the straws, leaving one hood-shaped end as proof that they were unused. The girl didn't choose a table, she went into the restroom. Maybe it was a sanitary emergency and that was why she'd gone in there in such a hurry. With luck, she wouldn't stay for dinner. In which case, Aniyah would forgive her for everything.

She was about to pick up the tray of drinks when the young woman came out of the bathroom. She'd been quick. Again, she appeared to search for a table—she would stay to eat. Aniyah considered rushing out to meet her and redirect her, but the girl approached the bar. When she ended up sitting in the booth next to the family's, Aniyah began to like her much more. In fact, the girl was pretty. The kind of white woman she liked—small, but with character. She could see it in her face. With renewed energy, she picked up the tray of drinks and balanced it on the palm of her hand, her bicep swelling.

"I'll be right with you," she said to the young woman as she passed her.

Trying hard to put a friendly mask on her exhausted face, Aniyah took the family's order. The mother had straight chestnut hair, worn down with a part in the middle. She had sunglasses on top of her head, acting as a hairband. She barely wore makeup, sure of herself or comfortable among her loved ones. She was wearing jeans and a baggy checkered shirt, the buttons open to give an everyday garment a sexy cleavage. On one wrist she had a hair tie, and on the other she wore a gold watch. She'd left a brown leather purse on the seat. She ordered a Caesar salad, smiling with both her mouth and her eyes, exuding warmth. Aniyah was attracted to her natural manner and simple charm, but she looked too much like a good girl for Aniyah to really like her. She was more into women who could give her a tough time.

The father ordered a double burger with bacon and cheese. The height and width of the man suggested he would've played football at the private college where he'd probably studied. And where he no doubt met the woman opposite him, with whom he must have spent twenty years and made their beautiful family of four, with two children that had, of course, been a girl and a boy. Straight couples were always perfect like that. And conventional. She also thought it was no surprise that the father, with his physique, had ordered such a high-calorie dish without thinking twice—unlike Aniyah, whose butt grew bigger if she even looked at the desserts she served. The polo shirt he wore was tight on his chest and shoulders even though it was as baggy as his chino pants, the classic outfit of a father at the wheel. Four-day stubble rounded off his relaxed appearance—in his professional life he was almost certainly obliged to shave.

Aniyah liked the girl's hairstyle, short and asymmetrical, it reminded her of a rocker girlfriend she'd once had. And the fact that she ordered a veggie burger also matched her memory of that girlfriend. Were she able, Aniyah would do more with her hair, but she'd tried chopping most of it off a few years ago and the convenience of not having to comb it was hard to beat. It also gave her a virile look that proved a winner. Finally, the boy with the patch ordered chicken fingers with french fries. Lots of french fries.

"More than you can eat, don't worry," Aniyah said. "If that's everything, I'll be back with the food real soon."

Before taking the order to the kitchen, she stopped at the next table. The sweatshirt girl's eyes were a blue color that seemed grayer. Aniyah felt a flutter in her stomach, and the palms of her hands broke out in sweat.

"Thanks for not sitting on the other side of the room." She winked without intending it.

The girl frowned. "Huh?"

"Don't worry, just a waitress thing."

The furrows on the other woman's brow remained. She didn't seem friendly. There was some torment in her expression, or perhaps it was shyness that made her a little uncomfortable to look at. Aniyah thought about Kristen Stewart—she had a few photos of her in the locker from which she'd taken her uniform a few hours ago, before swallowing the Tylenol. She'd begun to like the actress when she came out of the closet on *Saturday Night Live*.

From the other table, they heard the father comment: "We're the kings and queens of a country called Our Family."

Hearing it, the girl in the sweatshirt snorted.

Aniyah lowered her voice. "I can't stand these regular families, can you?"

The girl shook her head, raising her eyebrows, as if it was obvious and no one in the world could stand them. Aniyah wanted the response to give her a clue as to whether she had a chance with the girl. She looked for a trace of masculinity in her demeanor but found nothing.

"Too heteronormative for my taste," Aniyah added.

She introduced the term on purpose, to make her inclination clear. That way she made it easier for the girl if she was timid. Aniyah was rarely wrong when she set eyes on a woman, as difficult as it may seem, but this one showed no particular reaction to the unusual adjective.

"I can't stand them," the girl whispered.

"You're lucky you can't see them." With her pen, Aniyah pointed at the back of their seats, which reached the ceiling, giving each table complete privacy. "And if you put some music on your headphones"—a cell phone was on the paper table cover—"you won't have to listen to them. I've got an hour of forced smiles ahead of me, all for a couple of dollars. I think I'd do better as a stripper."

Aniyah laughed but the girl didn't join in, as easy as it would have been to go along with a joke like that. How hard it was picking up customers in Idaho. In California it was much simpler.

The girl turned her attention to the menu on the table and ordered one of the all-day breakfasts. Aniyah returned to the kitchen assuming she'd been wrong. It would be one of the rare occasions when her intuition failed her. Or perhaps the girl didn't like black women, or she had a girlfriend, or a boyfriend, or she was just unfriendly. She finished drying the flatware while the chef prepared the five dishes. The smells of french fries, butter, meat, and oil alternated in her nose.

After serving the family, she took the pancakes and scrambled eggs to the girl. She noticed that she hadn't put on her headphones as Aniyah had suggested.

"I see you like to suffer." She gestured at the family with her chin. "How's life for the *nuclear* family?"

The girl shot herself in the head with a pistol formed from two fingers. The gesture amused Aniyah and she smiled, though she'd just promised herself she'd stop flirting. She looked at the family's table.

"Well, they've calmed down a little," she said. "They're all on their cell phones. And if you need anything—anything at all—I'm right here."

She bookended her words with another wink, so that the sentence could take on whatever meaning the girl chose to ascribe to it. Clearly she wasn't going to be able to control herself. What else could a bored waitress do when a girl as beautiful as Kristen Stewart walks through the door?

8.

Frank observed his family. Opposite him, Grace was sliding her thumb over her cell phone, no doubt reading a long list of comments on one of her videos. She'd left her fork in her salad bowl a little while ago. Next to her, Audrey was typing on her phone like a centipede in a hurry. She'd eaten all of her veggie burger except the top half of the bun. She was drinking through the straw in one side of her mouth. The boy was also entertaining himself with his cell phone, matching the colors in a game to make lines disappear. On his plate, there was a circular brushstroke from french fries soaked in the last remnants of ketchup.

"Seriously?" asked Frank. "Everyone in their own little worlds? Don't we have anything to say to each other anymore?"

Five eyes looked up from their screens at him.

"This is supposed to be a family trip," he added, "and families talk to one another."

"All the time?" asked Audrey. "We spoke while we ate."

"As much as possible, yeah. Let's call it a day with the cell phones."

First he took Simon's, since he was sitting beside him. Grace thumbed hers faster before he snatched it as well.

"Dad, just because you're a digital dinosaur who hasn't got a clue about technology doesn't mean you have to drag the rest of us down with you," Audrey argued. "I'm a digital native and I need to stay connected."

Seeing that Frank had no intention of giving in, she finally handed her phone to him when she'd finished typing her message.

"That cell phone's my only contact with the life you're making me leave behind."

Frank rolled his eyes. "Give me one of your ziplocks," he said to Grace.

His wife always carried the hermetically sealable transparent bags in her purse, separating her cosmetics from her keys, her food from her billfold, her accessories from her pens. It was a system she recommended to all her friends who complained they could never find anything in theirs. She'd even made a video on the subject. Grace lifted her purse onto the table. She took out a bulky guide to Idaho and some of the used bags. She passed an empty one to Frank. He put the three cell phones in it and closed the zipper.

"There we go."

"And yours?" asked Audrey. Simon laughed.

"Busted!" said Grace.

"Not at all, I'll do it gladly. I'm the one who wants to make the most of the time I have with my family."

He took his cell phone from his pocket and added it to the ziplock. He set the bag aside on the table, beside the wall. It was so full he struggled to close the zipper again, but managed it.

"Confiscated until further notice."

"This is scary," Audrey said, slumping forward. "I already feel so disconnected . . ."

"We're an eighties family now," Grace added.

"Cool," said Simon. "We're in black and white."

He looked at his hands as if he'd traveled back in time to an era in grayscale. The anachronism made Frank roar with laughter, though it also made him feel old. Grace opened the Idaho tourist guide.

"We could read in the eighties, couldn't we?" she asked with an arched eyebrow. She flicked through several pages, reacting to some of the photographs, reading some titles. "So, what's this spectacular place we're stopping at tonight?"

"It's a secret."

Examining the pages, Grace started suggesting possibilities. She asked whether it was Rocky Canyon Hot Springs, and Frank shook his head. Or Kirkham Hot Springs. No. Red River Hot Springs? Not there, either.

"Goldbug?"

"That's still a long way away. And you can quit with that list, it's of the state's most famous hot springs. The place we're going isn't even in there." He tried to close the book but she resisted, making her fingers strong. "We're going somewhere out of the way that no one knows, only the locals. Carl in Reservations recommended it to me. He came with his family, and he said they spent the three days they were there alone. The places you mentioned will be full of people. Everyone reads the same guides."

"And how're we going to get to this place if it isn't in the guide?" asked Audrey. "We'll have to search for it on Google Maps."

She stretched out her arm, trying to reach the cell phones. Frank gave her a tap on the hand to interrupt her ploy.

"We have to turn down a road marked with two fat tree stumps. It's just after a Super 8 motel we're going to pass soon. Once we're on that road, we'll be there in two hours. People found places before they had cell phones, you know."

"It seems so." Audrey slumped back on the bench. "When life was in black and white, like my little brother says."

Grace read out loud: "While there are few experiences as pleasant as taking a warm bath surrounded by nature in hot springs, some of them are fed by currents that come from inside the earth at temperatures exceeding the boiling point. They are, therefore, incompatible with life.

Visitors must also take great care to avoid locations with high sulfur, sulfuric acid, or hydrogen sulfide levels, which are capable of breaking down a human body." She closed the book on the table. "I think I've read enough."

"That's disturbing, Dad," said Audrey. "I'm not going in anything like that."

"I will!" yelled Simon.

"Hang on, hang on." Frank made a dampening gesture with his hands to calm his family. "Carl went in with his four children, and one was a baby. Anyway, it's easy to take precautions: if there's no steam coming from the water, then it's not boiling, and if there's sulfur, it'll stink of rotten eggs so we won't feel like bathing in it. In either case, I'll be the first to stop us from going in. But you'll see, these thermal waters are perfect. Like a spa in the mountains."

Four long spoons appeared on the table.

"Here're your tools," the waitress said with a wide smile, "and the sundaes are on their way. I warn you, they're big. And very deep. That's why the spoons are so long. Have you seen spoons like that before?" She directed the question at Simon.

"Similar ones." He inspected the flatware. "But these are better."

"Everything's better in Idaho."

The waitress winked at the boy, gathered up the plates, and went away to fetch the sundaes.

"See? Even the waitress says it—everything's better in Idaho. The world's on our side, giving us a new opportunity," argued Frank.

"Yeah, sure, what else is she going to say if she lives here?" Audrey grouched. "But I love her look, with the nose ring and tattoos. It reminds me of a character from *Orange Is the New Black*."

"I was a little unsure, to be honest, but we've only crossed one state line and I already feel like we're leaving all the bad stuff behind us. I even think my hair's started growing at the normal rate again."

Grace ran her fingers through her hair, giving it a volume that she hadn't felt for months. She'd missed it so much she had even cried. There was no trace of the two worst bald patches.

Frank found his wife's hands on the table, among glasses in which the last ice cubes were melting. "Honey, everything's going to be just great," he said to her. "We're indestructible." He held her palms to his mouth and kissed them loudly.

The clatter that rang out in the restaurant hunched their shoulders. There was a series of crashes. Glass smashed. A woman's scream preceded a noisy metallic drumroll. Frank's mind pictured a tray spinning on the floor. The bells over the door shook, as did the windows at the entrance after the door slammed.

"What happened?" Penned into the booth, Frank couldn't see beyond their table.

"Not much." Audrey gestured at the floor with her chin. "As was only to be expected, our sundaes have fallen on the floor. I told you all we're jinxed."

Grace got up to take a look. Her mouth opened. She pushed past Audrey as the two of them came out of the booth. Frank did the same with Simon, who also made way. The waitress was on the floor, on her side. Her elbow was resting in a pinkish milky pool, her hip in a chocolate-colored puddle. Scattered all around her were the four thick glasses, wafers, cherries, straws, and a little paper umbrella. Simon let out a guffaw. Frank held his hand over his own mouth to contain his laughter. Grace and Audrey started to help the waitress up.

"She must've been in a real hurry," said the waitress. Then she gestured at her own backside. "Lucky I've got cushioning."

She got up onto one knee, then the other. Once on her feet, she discovered the scratches on her elbows, the ice cream on her uniform. She swore without considering that there were children right in front of her.

"What happened?" Grace asked, interrupting her expletives.

"The girl that was here"—she indicated the nearby table—"she dashed off and pushed past me. I couldn't keep my balance with the tray and I ended up on the floor. And I bet she left without paying."

Frank checked the table. A folded twenty-dollar bill was poking out from under a maple syrup bottle.

"Actually, she hasn't," he informed the waitress. "She paid. And I thought we had the restaurant to ourselves. Have we been very loud?"

A crabby voice reached them from the other side of the room.

"A little, yes."

It was an elderly gentleman sitting with a woman about his age. They were sharing a piece of pie or cake from a plate in the middle of the table.

The waitress shook her head. "Ignore him. You haven't bothered anyone," she whispered through the teeth of her extremely broad smile. "What bothers me is being thrown to the ground at the end of my shift. You can't trust anyone." She brushed the blobs of ice cream from her uniform. "Well, except you ladies," she said to Grace and Audrey, "coming straight to help me. Women helping women, as always, while the men stand there watching without doing anything."

She aimed a reproachful look at Frank and also gestured at Simon. The severity in the waitress's eyes, framed by a cropped head of hair that gave her an intimidating look, suggested that she was being deadly serious. But then she widened her eyes and burst into laughter, admitting it was a joke. She told them not to worry, that some fresh sundaes would be ready in a moment.

9.

"No, put on your seat belt," said Grace.

She spoke facing into the motor home from her passenger seat. Frank settled into his, left the bag of cell phones on the dashboard, fastened his own seat belt, positioned his feet on the pedals, and started the vehicle. The restaurant's luminous sign was reflected on the parking lot's surface. The night's darkness made it even brighter. After her fall, the waitress had returned with four more sundaes as if nothing had happened. Frank felt so bad for not helping her himself that he left a much higher tip than the usual 20 percent. As they went out through the door, he heard her singsongy thank you, as well as an invitation to return whenever they wanted. Simon had run to the RV.

"We all ready?" Frank asked with his hands on the wheel. The children, sitting at the table, yelled that they were. Grace nodded and stroked his forearm.

"Please, let's get to this fabulous spot you keep telling us about." She smiled at the theatricality of her own tone. "I'm burning with the desire to see it."

His wife's mood had gradually improved the farther they traveled from Seattle. He sensed her doubts and fears dissipating like the fumes from the exhaust pipe. She'd started the day with half-closed eyes, but now they were so wide and bright that it was easy to imagine her with a glass of wine in front of the fireplace.

"I love seeing you like this," he said to her before stepping on the gas.

Before long they passed the Super 8 motel Frank had expected, with its giant luminous yellow-and-red sign. He slowed down and put the high beams on. He asked Grace to keep her eyes on the right side, where they were looking for the two thick tree stumps Carl had said marked the entrance to the road they had to take.

"Here it is." Frank hit the brakes and turned on the hazard lights. "It's wider than I thought."

Grace stretched her neck. "Is it paved, or not?"

"Doesn't look like it. But it's a firm road, it's been graded very recently. And look at how wide it is. Almost like this highway. It's perfectly safe."

She lowered her window and stuck out her head to inspect the area the headlights were illuminating, also tinged orange at intervals from the turn-signal light.

"Nothing's safe for us, remember," Audrey said from behind.

"Stop saying that." Frank's words sounded more severe than he intended.

"What if we stay at the Super 8 and finish the drive in the morning?" suggested Grace.

"Oh, sure," said Simon. "So what did we bring a motor home for?"

Frank gestured at the boy, at his unbeatable argument. "Exactly. Anyway, the guy in Reservations used this road with a Class A just like ours, even a little bigger. Look, we'll try it, and if the road gets more difficult than it seems, we'll stop right there."

"All right, all right." Grace raised both hands and sat back in her seat. "You're the one who knows about these things. And, actually, I'm dying to see this place now."

"Let's go!" Simon threw his arms up in the air.

As Frank had predicted, the road was as stable as if it had been paved. What's more, another vehicle could come in the opposite direction and there would easily be enough space for them both. The most frightening thing, as soon as they left the streetlights and reflectors of the highway, was the darkness that enveloped them. Outside the bright halo of the RV's headlights, the blackness was total—the edge where the light ended was not a gradually fading band but a sharp line. Such dense darkness was not a consequence just of the night: the tall conifers that lined the road also eclipsed the moon and starlight with their trunks, branches, and crowns. To Frank, the bright light of the yellow-and-red motel sign they had just passed seemed to belong to another world. The fake world humans had created, ignoring the majesty of nature. Without warning, or without realizing what she was doing, Grace lowered the volume of the music, bending to the surrounding silence.

They climbed successive slopes that then descended only a little, so that they reached ever-higher altitudes each time. Frank forced a yawn to unblock his ears. There were bends, though not many and not very sharp. Around one of them, the road ran along a ravine or precipice and the trees suddenly disappeared on one side, revealing a starry sky that prompted expressions of amazement from the whole family.

"Wow, how lovely is this?" Grace sat up in her seat and held a hand over her mouth. "I don't think I've ever seen so many stars."

"Look at the moon, it's so small," said Audrey.

It was a weak gray slit in the firmament—the new moon was on its way. Frank enjoyed the views without taking his eyes from the road, which resumed a straight, flat course.

"And it smells so good . . ."

Grace had left the window open since she'd lowered it to watch the road. There was a touch of cold in the air, but much less than Frank had expected in Idaho's mountains—the summer was making its mark on the night. Grace breathed in, filling her chest, the cleavage under her open shirt becoming more pronounced. When she exhaled, Frank sensed her letting it all out, giving herself up to the aroma of the pine trees, to the immensity surrounding them.

"I have a good feeling about all of this," she said. "I really do."

Grace looked back at the forest. She surfed the air with an arm outside the window. The innocence in her face made her as beautiful as the sky. When she closed her eyes, Frank felt proud to have been by her side as time painted the wrinkles that now extended toward his forty-something wife's temples. In the rearview mirror, he saw his children also spellbound by the scenery. Audrey was resting her cheek on her brother's shoulder. A moisture that had nothing to do with the landscape condensed in Frank's eyes. Because he was certain that leaving Seattle had been the right thing to do, moving even if they'd had to do it in such a rush and even though Simon would have to complete his treatment in a different city. At that precise moment, inside a motor home where all the members of his family were happy at the same time, everything was back where it should be.

Everything was again how it should always have been.

It was when he looked back at the road that the figure appeared in front of the headlights. Frank's brain wanted to play a trick on him, make him believe it was a deer, that the smartest thing to do was nothing, to run it over, because the lives of the four people in the vehicle were worth more than a wild animal's. But deer don't have arms. Or wave them in the air requesting help like people do.

Because the figure was a person.

Frank turned the wheel to the left, certain it was too late to avoid a collision. He also hit the brake. His instinct was to search for a gear shifter that didn't exist in this vehicle. First he felt the sudden jolt of his seat belt on his chest, then came the pain in his neck and back.

A cupboard opened in the kitchen and things fell out of it. A scraping sound skittered across the dashboard. Audrey and Grace's screams merged into a single howl. Simon shrieked *Dad* several times, turning the word into a siren. *Dad-Dad-Dad-Dad-Dad.* The RV shook, the wheels slid instead of turning. The rear and front fought against their inertia, generating a circular movement that twisted Frank's elbows—he was gripping the steering wheel as if he could still control the runaway vehicle. In the short time the accident lasted, his brain considered so many variables and consequences that it was left exhausted, as if the braking had ground him down.

With a mechanical gasp more likely to be heard in a train station, the motor home finally stopped. The headlights were no longer lighting up the road, only the trees on one side of it. The human silhouette the light had outlined was now just a blotch on his retinas—the body must have been smashed into a jumble of flesh and bones under the vehicle.

"Grace! Audrey! Simon!"

Frank yelled their names with the last of the air in his lungs, his temples pulsed with pain. Another pain, in his ribs, told him he had almost been lifted onto the right-hand armrest, which was pressing into his side, burying itself in his sternum.

"What . . . what . . . what was it?" asked Audrey.

"Dad . . ."

Hearing his children's voices enabled him to breathe for the first time since he saw the figure in the beam.

"Are you all right?"

They confirmed they were, gripping the edge of the table, their faces as wrinkled as when they were babies. Simon's patch had moved toward his ear.

"Grace."

Her hair had fallen onto her face, hiding it. Frank grabbed her by the shoulder. A frightened eye looked at him through locks of disheveled hair. Grace had both hands on her chest, the right one under the left. Remembering that she'd been holding her arm outside the window the moment they swerved, a dreadful image gripped Frank's stomach, of a branch cutting off his wife's hand, the entire arm. That was why she was covering the bleeding stump that resulted from an amputation. Then a second hand, unharmed, sprouted from under the visible one. It was trembling. Grace looked at it with horror.

"I . . . I touched it . . ." She held her hand out to Frank as if showing him something repulsive, some roadkill she'd picked up from the side of the road and wanted to get rid of. "I touched his face. Frank . . . it was a mouth, a tongue . . . I have his . . . saliva on me."

She pushed herself back in her seat, holding her own hand away from her, her heels trotting on the floor as if wanting to go through the back of the seat to run away from what was beyond her wrist, to have nothing to do with those fingers plagued by the sensation that had distorted her face. She shook them as far away from her body as possible, spattering something imaginary on the windshield.

The seat belt pressed against Frank's chest when he tried to stand up without unbuckling it. He relived the neck pain the first impact had caused. Releasing the clasp, he went to Grace. He brushed the hair from her face and made shushing sounds, calming her.

"Frank . . . what . . . what happened? We . . . we hit someone."

These last words remained inside the vehicle. They echoed around the front cab and bounced off the ceiling above the table, the fridge door, the shower base, the bedroom, refusing to disappear. Then there was a silence that revealed that the forest that had at first seemed noiseless was actually a symphony of owls hooting, crickets chirping, and pine cones crackling as they opened with the change in temperature, just as Frank, his wife, and their children were shaking in the motor home. The four of them looked one another in the eyes, in the reflections in mirrors, in panes of glass.

"What just happened?" asked Audrey.

"Dad—"

Simon's throat had gotten stuck on that word.

"Everything's fine, son, we're all fine."

Frank slumped back into his seat. He sank his face into his hands, his elbows on the steering wheel. He took a long breath that brought to the surface more pains from the accident and another, deeper, pain from the soul. He couldn't believe it. Just when everything was beginning to go well, what bad luck. At the moment when he'd felt most confident that accelerating away from the past was the right thing to do, something had happened that had forced them not just to stop, but to look back. Unless . . .

"What should we do?" he asked his wife. He did so in a low voice, the volume they used when they had to say something and it was best not to involve the children. "What should we do, honey?"

His whisper had a gravity to it that frightened him.

"What?" Grace asked. "What do you mean, 'what should we do'?"

Frank sharpened his look, forced his whisper even more.

"What're we going to do?"

He wasn't even sure what he was suggesting. Drive off? He was seeing flashes of the silhouette waving its arms and a blood-soaked body under the wheels. Leave the body behind like a problem that could just be forgotten? His heart accelerated until it hurt in his chest. Could they? The way Grace's eyes refocused, the slight change in the angle of her chin, rekindled Frank's memories of severe criticism in the past. The smell of gunpowder. Simon's sobs.

"What're you saying, Frank?" Her upper lip rose to produce a grimace. "There is only one thing we can do."

She turned her seat with the force of her disapproval. While he asked cowardly questions about how to react to hitting a person, Grace jumped into action, driven by the adrenaline of feeling responsibility, more powerful than her fears. Just as she had been the first to get up to help the waitress on the floor, it was she who opened the door to go in aid of whoever was on the road.

"Of course," murmured Frank. "Let's go."

He asked the children not to move. They both nodded in silence. Frank jumped down over the retractable steps. Grit crunched under his shoes.

"Honey, wait." He reached her right shoulder from behind. "Wait. Where is he?"

"I don't know, but we have to find him. Help him."

The motor home had ended up diagonal across the road, with the front encroaching on the other lane. Frank swallowed, preparing himself to look underneath. He knelt down with his eyes closed, opening them when he rested a cheek on the ground. His imagination threw up a mutilated body under the chassis, but in fact there was nothing. Relieved, he rested his forehead on the earth, as if kissing it.

"Frank?" Peering around the rear corner of the vehicle, Grace was pointing at something in the road. "Frank, here."

"I'm coming. Let me. Don't look."

He searched over her shoulder. The darkness was impenetrable beyond the reach of the RV's lights, but at the border between the two, he could make out a shape on the ground. A body. A human body. Not even the most powerful delirium would turn that form into a deer.

"Oh, Fra—" The rest of his name was reduced to a groan in Grace's throat. "He's dead."

"He just appeared in front of us," Frank said, showing his palms. "On this dark road where no one should be walking. In a split second. I couldn't do anything. It's not my fault. We'll just have to explain what happened."

An accident. That was all. Frank made himself believe it. He had suffered too much, blaming himself for recent events, and he couldn't carry any more guilt on his shoulders or his knees would buckle. He asked his wife to stay where she was, but she gripped his hand. Without letting go, behind him, she started walking again—short, slow steps.

"Oh my God, oh my God . . . ," she murmured.

He heard her sniffing in snot.

"Hello?" Frank yelled at the body, at nothing. "Can you hear me?"

His arms broke out in goose bumps, and the cold of the Idaho mountains now seemed more intense. He heard activity inside the motor home. The children were moving around in the bedroom. They poked their heads out of one of the two side windows at the rear. Frank swiped the air to tell them to stop spying. He turned back to the body.

"Are you all right?"

"How could he be all right? Please, Frank, I don't know . . ."

The next step took them close enough to see that the oval shadow that resembled a shoulder was, in fact, a purse. They also discovered the victim had long hair, spread out like a fan on the earth.

"Oh no, a woman."

Frank asked himself whether that was worse than running over a man. It sounded absurd, but the alarm and sadness with which Grace had said it made him really wonder.

Then something scraped on the earth. A groan cut through the darkness. The body moved, and black-painted fingernails scratched the ground.

"She's alive," whispered Grace. "Oh my God, she's alive."

Frank didn't hesitate this time. He reacted with the same feeling of responsibility that Grace had shown immediately after the accident. He patted the pockets of his pants. The front ones. The back ones. He was searching for his cell phone to call for help. His chest pocket was empty, too.

"Go get a phone," he said to Grace. "Hurry, it's inside. We need help. Call nine-one-one!"

This last cry sounded too much like another recent cry, when it had been Simon who needed assistance. Frank's pulse quickened, and the blood throbbed in the bruise the seat belt had left on his thorax. Grace also remembered that cry, because her eyes widened, her body tensed up. She was left immobilized as if it were her son who was in danger again.

"Go!" Frank ordered, to make her react. "Run!"

10.

The motor home's retractable steps creaked under the force with which Grace climbed them. Though she could feel her entire body trembling, her hands remained steady. She kept the fear contained, as if some emergency protocol had taken control of her nervous system, enabling her to act with precision during the crisis. With her knee on the driver's seat, she groped the dashboard, the crevice where it met the windshield. She expanded the search to the other end.

"Did Dad kill someone?" asked Audrey, standing next to the kitchen.

"No, honey, of course he hasn't."

Grace stuck her hand down the sides of each seat, and underneath. Down on her knees, she combed the cabin's carpeted floor with her fingers. She caught crumbs, a coin, a pen lid.

Simon came out of the bedroom.

"But he's really hurt," said the boy.

"*She* is," Grace corrected him. "It's a woman."

She stood and held her hair up with both hands, her elbows raised on each side. She looked around the front compartment.

"Where are they?" she mumbled before spinning around. "Honey, give me your cell phone, quickly."

Audrey shrugged. "I don't have it, Mom."

"Come on, Audrey, I need the phone." She took a step forward and held her hand out. "Give it to me. Now. This is more important than your friends and your Instagram. Right now, please."

"I didn't take it, Mom, honestly. I haven't had it since Dad put them in the ziplock at the restaurant."

Grace's throat tightened. She turned back to the front. She remembered the transparent plastic that was close to tearing open, and the zipper forced shut, curving. She also looked at the open window that had given her liberating blasts of air that smelled like damp earth. Then Frank had swerved left. And the dashboard would have acted as a launch pad to propel the bag out. Through the right window.

"Oh, no."

"I knew that bag was a bad idea," Audrey pointed out.

Grace climbed out without answering her daughter. She combed the illuminated part of the road with her feet, lifting dust into the air.

"No, no, no . . ."

As soon as she ventured outside of the lit area, the ground disappeared. She couldn't even see her feet. She searched the sky for the moon, but all she found was a ghostly claw.

"Brilliant, Frank," she said through her teeth. Then she yelled while she walked toward him. "Great idea you had to confiscate the cell phones! Just great. They've all gone flying through the window. And it's impossible to look for them now, you can't see anything outside the—"

She found Frank on his feet, covering his mouth with his hands, his eyes fixed on the body on the ground. Words gurgled in the victim's throat, which seemed to be blocked with some kind of fluid.

"Help . . . me . . . Hel . . .p . . . He . . ."

The woman tried to sit up but spasms shook her injured body. The air smelled like fresh wounds.

"Frank?" asked Grace. "Are you all right?"

He shook his head in silence, unable to take his eyes off the ground. On the victim's blood-soaked face, a hole formed—the mouth opening to try to speak. To breathe. It coughed dark liquid on the road. Grace was torn between tending to the woman or to her husband.

"Are you all right, Frank?"

His hands were climbing his nose, trying to cover his eyes, to insulate him from reality. Grace took his elbow and massaged his arm. She understood her husband's shock—it was one thing seeing the back of a body lying on the ground, it was quite another looking into the eyes of the victim pleading for help. Especially for Frank, who had never dealt with the guilt of what had happened with Simon.

"Frank, this isn't your fault. You said it yourself. Not this time. It was an accident. And she's alive. You dodged her in time. That's why I hit her in the face with my hand." She showed it to him as if it was evidence. "And what happened with the cell phones is just bad luck. Sorry for yelling. That wasn't your fault, either."

"He . . . Hel . . . p."

"Come on, Frank. We have to help her. We have to think. We have to find the cell phones." She shook him by the shoulder. "Do we have a flashlight in the RV?"

"We have four."

Graced sighed with relief.

"One on each cell phone," he added.

"Frank!" she berated him. "Come on, I need you to be OK. Frank!"

He squeezed his eyelids shut and suddenly opened them, as if waking up.

"What? Right, yeah. The cell phone, have you brought the cell phone?"

"Frank, they're not there. They flew out the window. In the bag you put them in. They'll be lost out there, in the trees."

The thick forest caught Frank's eye, and he gazed at the pines. On the ground, the woman choked, her coughing ending in a retch.

"Goddamn it, Frank!"

Grace pushed him aside, realizing he wasn't helping and it would be up to her. She knelt next to the woman although she didn't know what to do—whether to touch her back, sit her up, lie her on her side, face down, face up . . .

"Do you have a phone?" she asked. "We need a phone."

The eyes on the dark face looked at her without reacting, as if the woman couldn't hear her or didn't understand the language. Grace repeated the question in mime, pointing at the woman, stretching out her thumb and little finger on one side of her face.

"Do you have one?"

The answer was a cough that spattered Grace's face with snot, blood, and saliva. She dried herself with her shirtsleeve without showing her disgust.

"We need a phone so they can come help you. We've lost ours and we can't search for them because we don't have a flashlight, either. Our flashlights were the cell phones." She smiled as if it was a joke. "I bet you have one on you. Can you give it to me?"

The woman remained silent. Grace moved closer and identified a sour odor of sweat that the smell of blood had covered up until now. She began to search in the pockets of the sweatshirt the woman was wearing. Nothing. Then she delicately patted the jeans—she didn't want to put pressure on any fractured bones. Finally, she pulled on the purse's strap to investigate its contents. The woman let out a scream that carried over the treetops. Grace gave a start.

"All right, all right, I won't touch your purse." The trace of anger in the scream made Grace feel as if she had been trying to rob the young woman. "Just tell me whether you have a cell phone."

There was a spark of comprehension in the woman's eyes—at last she was listening. A pitiful gurgle came from her throat.

"It hurts . . ."

"I know, I'm sorry. But I need a phone and I think there might be one in your purse. Tell me if you have one on you, please."

She accompanied her words with a pleading gesture, pressing her palms together. The woman cleared her throat, swallowed something thick.

"I . . . I was carrying it in my hand . . . I don't know where it is . . ."

A feeling of dangerous isolation overcame Grace. She saw herself trapped in a glowing bubble floating in a void, surrounded by a darkness that stalked them, that was hiding their cell phones like an evil big brother. She undid another button on her shirt so she could breathe. She sought Frank's support, but he was walking around in circles a few yards away, hands on his waist. He moved in and out of the field of light, disappearing at intervals as if he truly did not want to be there.

"Frank!"

With an absent expression, he moved into the darkness.

"Don't worry." Grace stroked the woman's face with her thumb, spreading blood across her cheek. She feigned calm, although she was so frightened she could vomit. "Let's think, we have to think."

She felt dizzy. She sat back on the ground to stop herself from falling.

"Frank!"

He emerged from the shadows.

"Stop that now, Frank. Pull yourself together, we have to do something."

Her husband looked at her from the semidarkness, without approaching.

Grace made a noise of frustration at his inaction.

"At least bring me the first aid kit," she ordered.

Frank headed to the motor home without taking his hands from his waist.

11.

Audrey was at the door.

"What're we going to do, Dad?"

Frank stood there, a hand resting on the back of the passenger seat, pinching his bottom lip with the other hand.

"Can we help?" Audrey persisted.

He heard his daughter's voice articulating words, but his thoughts were louder than her words and he couldn't pay attention to both things at the same time. It was why he hadn't been able to continue the conversation outside with Grace.

"Yeah, yeah, all right," he replied to something that sounded like a question.

"So what should we do? Search for the cell phones?"

"We hit a woman."

Audrey blinked, confused. "Are you OK, Dad?"

She touched his elbow just as Grace had. His daughter reminded him more and more of the girl he'd fallen in love with. He felt jealous of all the boys who would succumb to her charms, and it hurt him to think how much he loved his daughter. His wife. His family.

"I love you all so much," he said.

"Calm down, Dad, we're all fine. Look, Simon's fine."

The boy was still sitting at the table with his back too straight for him to appear calm. He looked at Frank with his eye wide, and he didn't smile.

"He's scared like you, but we're OK. Nothing hurts. Someone will have to come help the woman."

"That's why I came in here," Frank suddenly remembered. "Go get the first aid kit. Where was it? I can't think."

Audrey leapt into action with the energy of a nurse receiving instructions from the emergency-room doctor. She searched in the bathroom. Frank heard drawers opening, cupboards closing, the toothbrushes shaking in the tray the four of them shared—a cup wasn't very practical in a house on wheels. The girl came out with a plastic case with a red handle.

"Here it is. But hang on, Dad, your hands are shaking."

He felt Audrey's fingers folding his own around the first aid kit's handle, just as he had done with hers on the handlebars of her tricycles.

"Should I get towels, too?"

Frank identified the intonation of a question again but forgot its contents as soon as Audrey finished asking it. He said nothing, preferring not to invent an answer.

A sob broke through the silence. It was Simon, crying at the table. "I'm scared . . ."

He pressed the patch against his eye to dry a tear.

"Hey, Gizmo, no," Frank said. "It's nothing to worry about."

"Yeah, right. Even you are scared," the boy blubbered.

"It's the shock, I'm not scared. I'm just a little"—he searched for the right word—"a little punch-drunk."

Audrey sat next to her brother.

"Si, you're in shock from the accident, and that's perfectly normal." She kissed his shoulder. "Dad had to brake really hard. Cry if you need to, it's healthy to get all the tension out. Even Dad should cry if he feels like it."

If only he could. Sit down, cry, and do nothing else.

"Thanks, sweetie," he said, holding up the first aid kit.

He stood looking at his children, at Audrey consoling her little brother just as she had by his hospital bed when he left the intensive care unit.

"Are you going?" she asked. "Do you want me to take it? Should I give you some towels?"

Frank turned around to go out but his feet stopped on the first step. He couldn't move.

"Dad." Audrey hardened her tone. "It's not a hitchhiker or a stranger you can decide not to pick up, it's a woman who needs your help."

"I'm sorry, sweetie. I'm going."

He walked along the side of the motor home, searching for the fasteners on the case with his fingertips. He thought he could hear laughter in among some whispering, but that made no sense. It must have been his exhausted mind manufacturing the illusion of the most inappropriate sound for that situation. When he turned the vehicle's rear corner, where the hazard lights blinked, the supposed hallucination became real. He recognized Grace's chuckle, seeing her now sitting with her legs crossed. Beside her, the woman had also managed to sit up as well, resting on an elbow. She was holding her sweatshirt, rolled into a ball, against her forehead, using it as a compress. They both looked at him, Grace grinning with relief.

"Good news," she said in a deep sigh. "She's feeling better. It looks like the blood's only coming from a cut on her eyebrow."

"I am better," the woman confirmed.

Her voice sounded solid, with no choking or grating.

"But I need the bandages, quick," Grace pressed him.

The first aid kit fell onto the ground. The bandages, the roll of surgical tape, some blunt-tip scissors, and dozens of other items scattered around Frank's ankles.

"Shit!" he yelled.

He crouched to pick up bandages, antiseptic wipes, syringes. He returned them to the case, open on the ground. The roll of surgical tape rolled off toward the motor home. Grace leapt after it.

"For God's sake, Frank, you can relax now."

She snatched the bandages and some sample-sized packets of disinfectant from him. "I'm going to need a towel."

"Sure, Grace, I'll go right now." He remembered that Audrey had thought of this, too. "Let me pick everything up."

The needle on a loose syringe pricked his hand. Frank howled with pain.

"Look, seriously, step aside," Grace ordered. "Better to do nothing if you're going to do it like that. I'll take care of it." She picked up the case and closed it, not caring that some of the things hadn't been put back in. "She seems to be OK, so stop worrying. She just hit my hand and then fell on the ground. A big scare for everyone, especially for her, but she can move her body. It'll all just go down as a scare." She rested a hand on his face. "That's good, right? Now relax, breathe, and let's all calm down. I'm going to tend to Mara. Her name's Mara."

Frank sank down on the road while Grace went back to Mara to dress her wound.

"Audrey!" Grace yelled. "Audrey, come give me a hand! And bring towels!"

He felt ashamed that his wife preferred the help of a sixteen-year-old girl to that of her inept husband, defeated by the situation.

"What have I done?" he whispered.

12.

Making two trips, Audrey brought towels and a couple of pans full of hot water. Grace had embroidered Frank's or her own initials at the corners to differentiate between them when they hung both behind their bathroom door at home. Audrey returned from a third trip with a kitchen lighter, like a long-barreled cigarette lighter that produced sparks when its button was pressed. Bending over, she held it near the ground to search for the bag of cell phones, unfazed by the weak and fleeting light each spark offered.

"Simon's inside seeing if he can connect to someone's Wi-Fi on the laptop."

"Out here?"

Grace regretted the tone of her question, which betrayed the lack of confidence she had in her children's solutions to their situation, whether it was using a lighter in the dark of night or searching for an internet signal in the middle of the forest.

"I know, I know, but it's worth a try."

"You're right, sweetheart. Good thinking."

While Audrey sparked away in the darkness and Frank remained sitting on the road doing nothing, Grace used a damp towel to clean the injured woman's face. She had lain her on her back using her sweatshirt as a pillow and had asked her to press a bandage against her left eyebrow.

To make things easier, she had put her own hair up in a ponytail using the band she'd had on her wrist. The white towel gradually darkened as it absorbed the blood. Grace felt calmer as she uncovered a neck, chin, nose, and pink-skinned cheeks free of bruises. Cleaning the eyelids made her think of Simon's disfigured eye, and her protective maternal instinct set in, as if this stranger deserved all her care and attention. She wrung the towel out over the pan with a comforting dripping sound.

"We're doing good, Mara." She repeated her name more than was normal, as if it helped to keep her conscious even though she was showing no sign of fainting. "It all looks fine."

She finished cleaning the blood from the forehead and found no other wounds there, either. The face was largely unharmed. Then she asked Mara to let go of the bandage she was pressing against her eyebrow, near the temple. As soon as she eased the pressure, the bleeding began again.

"Well, it's definitely this cut the blood's coming from." She cleaned it with the corner of the towel. She pressed the fabric against the wound several times, at ever-shorter intervals, checking the stream of blood each time she lifted it off. "But it's nothing—eyebrows always look worse than they are."

She picked up a vial of antiseptic solution. She tipped the contents onto the wound, dissolving the last remains of blood. Mara sucked in air to brave the stinging. Grace continued to wash with a wipe until she could see a clean cut.

"Just as I said, no big deal. It's not even bleeding anymore."

She called to Audrey to find some butterfly bandages in the chaos of the first aid kit—asking Frank would have been a waste of time. Just a couple of strips were needed to close the wound nicely, though she used a third to reinforce the first two where the eyebrow hair made it difficult to stick them down.

"How do you feel, Mara?" Grace asked, repeating her name again as if she needed waking from a concussion.

"Um . . . all right, I think."

She tried to sit up, pushing her elbows against the ground.

"No, no, wait, stay on your back." Grace held her shoulder. "Come on, Audrey, help me check the rest of her body."

Between the two of them, they felt their way up Mara's anatomy, from the feet to the neck, pressing each area with their fingers, asking her to move her ankle from side to side, to bend her knee, to open and close her hands. They asked whether she was hurting anywhere, but aside from bruised knees and elbows she only complained when Audrey pressed above her waist. Lifting up her T-shirt, they discovered an inoffensive scrape. Grace finished with an examination of her head, exploring with her fingertips amid hair still spattered in blood. She found nothing out of the ordinary, not even a bump.

"To be honest, I don't really know what I'm doing, but I'd say everything's fine," she admitted. "At least on the outside."

Audrey let out a sigh of relief, as did Grace, who blew her daughter a kiss, passing on her thanks for the help. Mara watched the gesture with eyes gray like an alley cat's, and Grace saw something in them that might have been envy. Or sadness. She guessed that, lying on the ground surrounded by strangers, the young woman would be longing for her mother to be there with her, to comfort her with her affection as Grace had just done with Audrey. Maybe Mara didn't feel much older than Audrey right now. At the worst times, people still need their mothers as if they were children. Without stopping to think what she was doing, Grace kissed Mara on the cheek.

"Grace," Frank intervened from where he was still sitting, his voice as firm as it was alarmed, "what do you think you're doing?"

Grace flushed—it really wasn't normal to kiss an injured stranger on the ground. Mara herself frowned, taken aback.

"He speaks when he wants to complain," Grace said in a low voice, diverting the attention onto Frank. Then, seeking her female audience's complicity, she added, "Men, huh? Always messing things up, and then it's us women who have to pick up the pieces while they sit and watch."

"That's sexist, Mom," said Audrey. "We've just had an accident and Dad was the one driving. It's no surprise he's in shock. I'm going to give him some emotional support—men need it, too, you know."

As soon as she was far enough away, Grace repeated the joke. "Teenagers, huh? They think they know everything."

A hint of a smile appeared on Mara's face for the first time.

"Feel better?"

"Much better. But I need to get up. I can't stand lying here like I'm dead."

Grace tried to stop her.

"Honestly, I can do it," the other woman insisted. She turned onto her side to go up onto her knees. "I'm not hurting anywhere. I was paralyzed by the fright, but I'm fine now."

"I don't know if you should—"

"Come on, help me."

Mara was so determined that Grace gave in.

"How many times must I have heard that you shouldn't move someone who's been in an accident . . . ?"

She took Mara's hand to help her up. When she was on her feet, Mara held her hands to her head, seized by a moment of dizziness that she overcame by taking a step back. Then she stretched her neck, brushed off her shoulders, stroked the scrape on her abdomen. She ran her fingers over her face, checking that everything was still there. She paused at the butterfly bandages, appreciating Grace's work. She bent down without difficulty to pick up her purse, and hung it on her shoulder as if ready to go to work. Finally she gathered up her sweatshirt from the ground, pinching it at the hood to spread it out. In addition to the large bloodstain, there were holes in the elbows. The friction against the ground had also torn the knees of her jeans.

"This is all the rage now, right?" she said, indicating the ripped pants.

Grace laughed. "You don't know how happy I am to see you on two feet." Her shoulders dropped, unburdening themselves of a great weight. "When we saw you lying there like that, we thought . . . just imagine, a motor home this size hitting someone . . . luckily what you hit was my hand. My husband reacted in time. He reacted well."

They both noticed how she emphasized the last words.

"And you, what were you doing walking down the middle of this road at night?"

Grace felt proud of herself for the quick and astute way she'd managed to absolve Frank of any responsibility. Adding the question after her previous sentence had made it clear how she viewed the accident: Mara had been reckless and Frank had reacted as well as he could. But Mara didn't bother to argue with her or blame anyone else.

"My car broke down up ahead. I was on my way to some hot springs I was told were at the end of this road. Apparently almost no one knows about them and there's never anyone there. I needed some time out. I wanted to spend the night alone, under the stars, thinking . . ."

Her gray eyes now brought to mind a stormy sky, both melancholic and dangerous. The hairs stood on end on the back of Grace's neck, but she blamed it on the cooling air. .

"Looks like those hot springs aren't the best-kept secret in Idaho, hey, Frank?"

"But my car broke down," Mara went on. "Stopped dead. So I started walking back toward the main road, trying to find a signal on my cell phone. That was when I saw your headlights approaching. I thought it was a miracle that there was another car in these parts. I was afraid you wouldn't see me, so I went in the middle of the road, waving my arms so you'd stop."

"Next time, stay with your car and turn the hazard lights on. Much safer," said Grace. "And if your car doesn't work, we'll take you to the hospital. You might be fine on the outside, but who knows what you could've broken in there. They'll have to che—"

"I feel fine, honestly," Mara cut in. "I was more shocked than anything at first, when I was on the ground. My eyes filled with blood, and I imagined things a thousand times worse. I saw myself being paralyzed or something like that. But I feel fine now, seriously."

She did a few little jumps to prove it, and shook her body the way Grace had seen actors in improvised theater groups do in some documentary.

"It wasn't a suggestion. We'll take you to the hospital," repeated Grace. "Or do you intend to get up, brush your knees off, and act as if nothing's happened after a motor home ran you over?"

"We didn't run her over," Frank corrected her from afar. "I swerved out of the way and you knocked her down with your hand. It's not the same thing."

"Just the fall's enough to have them take a look at you," Grace insisted.

"Seriously, it's not necessary. I . . ."

Mara's hesitation, the way she scanned the surroundings searching for something to seize upon to construct an excuse, worried Grace. She rubbed her arms, the back of her neck, as if she still believed the cold was the only thing giving her goose bumps. But it wasn't the friction's warmth that Grace needed to calm her—what she needed was to find out why someone would refuse medical attention after an incident this serious. She considered whether the story Mara had told her made sense, whether a person really would leave her car and head off alone into the middle of nowhere. Grace clutched her elbows. Her next thought had frightened her: Was Mara really alone? Several pairs of eyes opened among the branches of the dark forest, an image her mind borrowed from dozens of fairytales, so powerful that she had to contain her urge to check again that nobody was stalking them.

"I'm unemployed at the moment," Mara confessed, looking down at the ground. "I don't have insurance."

Grace let go of her elbows. She wanted to laugh at herself and at the phantom eyes hidden in the trees. There was her explanation, much more horrifying and real: the inadequate healthcare system of the world's most powerful country.

"I see."

She rubbed Mara's shoulder to comfort her, but a new fear darkened her thoughts. Some instinct working hard to keep her alert reminded her of cases of people who threw themselves in front of vehicles on purpose to claim millions in compensation for the accident.

"Our insurance wouldn't cover anything, either, of course, because it's clear this wasn't my husband's fault." She increased the pressure in her massage. "That's clear, right?"

"Yeah, sure, it was my fault. I shouldn't have gone in the middle of the road."

Grace eased the massage. She attributed her unfounded fears to letting Frank's paranoia about dangerous hitchhikers infect her.

"So you don't have breakdown coverage, either, I guess?"

Mara shook her head. "And even if I did, we don't have a cell phone to call them on."

A corner of her mouth curved upward. It was a subtle invitation to recognize the funny side of the situation, an invitation Grace accepted without reservation. She erupted with laughter, allowing fears, suspicions, and worries to melt away with each guffaw, persuading herself that this would be one of those experiences that ends up as a fun anecdote to remember forever. She saw herself and Frank recounting it endlessly to guests at future dinner parties at their home in Boston, her barefoot, kneeling on the rug, her chin resting on his legs while he sat on the sofa. The terrible darkness of the forest, the smell of antiseptic, and Frank's state of shock were details they wouldn't even remember when they recalled the incident for their dinner guests, who would have made themselves comfortable by this time, having undone a button on their shirts, and who would listen to the story by the firelight among empty cocktail glasses. Mentioning that the woman they'd hit had said there were no phones to use to call AAA would be one of the story's attractions, the amusing moment leading up to the punch line of a joke that would make one of the guests choke on her martini, trying not to spit it out as she laughed, just as Grace was choking now on saliva from her own laughter.

"Do you know what?" she said when she regained her composure. She dried her tears with her fingers. "You can stay with us tonight, Mara. Under observation." The medical terminology almost made her burst out laughing again, and her abdomen hurt as it contracted once more. "We have a house on wheels and plenty of space for one more. And tomorrow we'll take you to the first town we find with a free clinic—someone's got to see you whether you like it or not."

The smile on Mara's face broadened while she nodded.

"Grace?" Frank had stood up. He spoke with his neck stretched, his hands pressing against his waist. "Can you come here a second?"

13.

"Are you crazy?" Frank whispered as soon as she was close enough. "She's staying with us?"

He saw the girl throw her torn sweatshirt into one of the pans that Audrey had brought out, now empty. Then she took a few unsteady steps toward the motor home. The effort of her short walk exhausted her or made her dizzy, because she rested her back against the side of the vehicle and slid down until she was sitting on the ground, near the rear wheels on the left side. Audrey approached her, offering a hand.

"Audrey!" Frank yelled. "You keep looking for the cell phones. Get your brother to help you. Go on, leave the girl alone."

When their daughter went off, he turned his attention back to Grace.

"Why're you telling her to stay here?" he complained in a low voice. "I would've preferred it if we'd picked up the hitchhiker. At least he advertised that he was a good guy. This girl might've thrown herself in front of us intentionally, or she's bait for a gang—we don't know anything about her. But if there's one place that's perfect for robbing a defenseless family like ours, this is it."

"You know, I thought about some of those things, too."

"They're things we have to think about. They do happen. And not to people we don't know or friends of friends—it could happen to us.

Right now, this is our house," he said, indicating the motor home. "Do you want a stranger in there, too?"

"Oh shut up, Frank, don't bring that up."

He immediately regretted doing so. Grace took a deep breath, fighting against recent memories. Then she turned around to look at the girl, only her legs protruding from behind the wheel. In his wife's eyes Frank recognized the warmth that always defeated her other thoughts, the kindness with which she faced life. People who are truly good struggle to understand how bad intentions exist in the world. They're unable to even process the idea that other people exist who are the very opposite of noble.

"She's a good girl, I'm sure of it." Her generosity had won again. "She's not from a gang or anything weird. She's sad, I noticed. She says she needed to be alone in a place like this to get things straight. That's a very human thing, Frank."

"Alone? A woman? On a road like this?"

"As your daughter would tell you, that's sexist. Would you ask the same questions about a man traveling alone?" Her arched eyebrows left no room for reply. "Anyway, what else can we do? Are we going to dump her out here on her own?"

"No, with her gang."

Grace gave him a gentle punch on the shoulder. Audrey and Simon came out of the RV. They announced that it hadn't been possible to find a connection on the computer, and they continued the search for the cell phones.

"Listen," Grace resumed, "I'd rather call an ambulance, or a tow truck, or a taxi—anything to take her somewhere. But since you decided to put all the cell phones in the same bag and leave them on the dashboard . . ." As soon as she said it, she rested a hand against the angle in his jaw as an apology. She, too, regretted opening up recent wounds. "Look at it another way. We would've spent the night with her at the hot springs anyway—we were going to the same place tonight. What's she going to do to us?"

Grace scraped the tip of her thumb against his stubble, giving him time to consider it. Then she stroked his neck, scratched the back of it with her fingernails—she knew that relaxed him. A pleasant tingling ran down Frank's spine. Until he looked at Mara, still crouched by the wheel.

"I don't want her here." He trapped his wife's fingers. "If we're going to help her, we'll take her to the nearest town. But now. Or we'll leave her at the restaurant, I don't care. We'll sleep at the motel we saw, like you said, and tomorrow we'll get back on the road, and there'll be other nice places to stop at farther on. We've only just started the trip."

"But you were so eager to see this place . . ."

"That was before we got into this mess. Now all I want is for us to get rid of a strange woman who appeared in the forest."

He gestured at her with his entire hand in the way one gestures at a nuisance, at overflowing trash containers. Grace caught it and hid it as if she was the offended party.

"And what if we treat her badly and she decides to report us?" She squeezed his fingers with the force of her concern. "Up till now she's been very understanding—she hasn't made any threats or anything. Don't you think we'd better be nice to her? Let her spend the night with us, so she can see we care, and tomorrow we'll drop her off somewhere. Then everyone's happy."

Frank considered the situation once more, weighing up a thousand variables.

"We're taking her now," he declared.

He freed himself from Grace to bring the conversation to an end. She tutted behind him.

"Frank!"

He headed toward the motor home and stood in front of the young woman, who'd gotten to her feet when the sound of his footsteps alerted her. She was clutching her purse to her stomach. She touched the cut on her eyebrow and let out a yelp.

"Can your car be fixed?" he asked.

Grace caught up and hooked an arm around Frank's, as if he needed to be calmed down.

"I don't think so," she replied. "I tried starting it a ton of times until the battery went. It's dead."

"Then we'll take you to the junction at the beginning of the road. There's a restaurant and a motel. A Super 8. You must've seen it before you turned off, there was no other way to reach this road. If you don't have any money, I'll pay for your room at the motel. I'm very glad you're all right and that it was all just a scare. Luckily, I reacted in time and my wife's been able to dress that wound." He felt Grace interlock her fingers with his to make him relax. "But we have our plans and we don't want to change them just because you appeared so carelessly in the middle of the road. Now let's go."

"I'd like to find my cell phone, at least," she said. "I don't want to go without it."

She indicated the place, some distance away, from where a recurring clicking sound was coming. The children were talking to each other, the touch of irritation in their voices suggesting they hadn't found anything yet.

"If you had yours in your hand, it would've broken with the impact. It could be lost in the bushes. There's no point in staying for that—it's more important that you get some rest and see a doctor. You can call one from the motel or restaurant."

"I don't have insurance."

"So I heard," said Frank, "but that's your problem, not ours."

From the sudden flash in her eyes he knew his words had hurt her. Grace squeezed his forearm twice, the number of syllables in *Be nice*, but all he did was point at the front of the motor home, instructing her to walk toward the door.

"Kids!" Frank yelled at the children. "Come on, get in! We're going!"

"Should we search for the cell phones or get in the RV?" Audrey's face was little more than a pair of intermittent eyes in the orangey halo from the sparks. "Make your mind up, Dad."

Frank scraped his tongue against his teeth. They could hope they would find the cell phones and then wait for help to come, or they could just take the girl away and get it all over with.

"Get in," he said.

"And leave the cell phones out here? Dad, I have photos from the Twenty One Pilots concert on there I haven't uploaded yet."

"And I finally made it past level three-fifty-six," said Simon.

"Get in."

The children sought their mother's empathy, but she shook her head and tipped her chin at the door. Audrey climbed onboard with her arms crossed, leaving a trail of little hollows in the sand behind her, dug by her heels with the furious impact of her footsteps. Simon's anger tended to veer toward melancholy, and he got in the vehicle with his shoulders slumped. His mark on the road was two parallel lines from his feet dragging themselves along. Letting Grace go ahead of him, Frank followed them on without looking at Mara, who was standing by the retractable steps like a shy guest.

"Get in, girl," Grace said from inside, after asking her if anything hurt or if she needed help. "Have you ever been in an RV?"

"No, never," came the voice from outside. "And I've been really curious to see one."

Frank shut the laptop he found on the sofa with such force that Audrey warned him he was going to break it. He pushed the children ahead of him toward the bedroom at the back. With the remote control, he switched on the television. He played the first thing that appeared in the list and turned up the volume, then ordered his son and daughter to sit on the bed and stay where they were.

"Is she dangerous?" Audrey asked.

Frank went out without answering, wishing there was a door to the room that he could shut. At the motor home's entrance, Grace was inviting Mara to sit on the sofa. Mara observed the vehicle's interior with fascination.

"This opens up to make more space," Grace explained about the extendable living room module, "so you don't have to walk sideways like we are now. Do you like it?"

"It's amazing. It's like a real house."

"Or even better. A lot of people spend their entire lives in worse houses than this."

Mara looked serious. While Frank knew there were no bad intentions in his wife's comment, he also knew the face their guest was pulling would make Grace think how offensive her remark might seem if the girl was one of those people who lived in a house that wasn't as nice as their motor home. Grace squeezed her ponytail in an embarrassed gesture. With her eyes, she asked Frank if she'd put her foot in her mouth. He shook his head, but Mara's gloomy expression must have disturbed his wife, because she examined her from top to bottom with renewed surprise. Her eyes, suddenly filled with suspicion, stopped on the purse. A silent alarm went off around them, as if she'd imagined it contained a handgun.

"Come on, let's go," she blurted out.

Frank welcomed Grace's urgency—at last they agreed they needed to get rid of the girl. The family would be much safer without an intruder in its midst. Everything would be better without her.

Frank sat at the wheel and put on his seat belt. From the passenger seat, Grace turned toward the sofa.

"Ready, Mara?" Her voice had recovered its usual innocence. "Great, just wait till you see how lovely the views are from up here."

14.

The motor home rocked as it reversed. The lurching repeated when it went forward. The rear of the vehicle seemed unstable, leaning too much to the left.

"No . . . ," said Frank.

"What is it?" Grace asked.

A premonitory fear knotted his stomach. He replied that he didn't know, he had to check something outside. He headed to the rear wheels on the driver's side, where Mara had just been sitting. He hoped he could throw out the suspicion growing in his belly, but as he crouched down, his fears were confirmed. Both wheels were flat on the ground. He ran his finger over a wound in one of the tires, a cut through which the air had escaped. While he wanted to persuade himself that a sharp stone could have caused a flat like this when he jammed on the brakes, he soon discovered an identical cut in the adjoining tire. The same length, the same serrated appearance. He felt both of the slits, imagining what kind of cutting edge, knife, or penknife could have made them. He knew who owned the hand responsible for them.

"So?" Grace had stuck her head out through the driver's window. "What is it?"

"The wheels are totally deflated, as if they exploded."

"From braking so hard?"

"I guess so. And swerving. A lot of pressure on the tires."

He lied to Grace to avoid frightening her. Her or the children. He climbed back into the RV, brushing brake dust from his fingers. Inside, Grace asked him if it was normal for a pair of tires to give way under pressure like that. Suppressing the tremor that was rising in his throat, Frank suggested that it was possible. He tried not to look at Mara, who was watching the scene from the sofa.

"So where do we have the spare?" Grace asked.

"This isn't a car. It's not so easy to change a tire, and most RVs this size don't have one onboard."

"Seriously?"

"Even if we'd brought one, I wouldn't have been able to change it without getting help. So why bother?" His voice was firm again because this, at least, was true. Before buying the motor home, he had read that a driver had been seriously injured trying to change a tire, and since then, most companies avoided potential accidents and lawsuits by not including a spare with the largest and heaviest vehicles. It meant users were obliged to call for professional help. "And both have blown on us."

"Just great, Frank." Grace crossed her arms.

"It's an RV thing. Look it up on your cell phone. You'll see I'm right."

"Very funny, Dad. With what cell phone?" Audrey said from the bedroom.

Frank breathed in. He steeled himself to confront Mara without revealing his fears to Grace.

"As you heard, our tires are flat." He studied the cold reaction in her eyes. "So if we want to move from here, we're going to have to fix your car. Where did you say it was?"

"A little way ahead. But there's nothing we can do, it won't start."

"We'll both go. Maybe we can push it back here. If it's just a battery problem, I have jumper cables. And I have gas."

"I don't think . . ." Mara was getting up from the sofa slowly. She appeared to need some time to think. "We're not going to be able to push it uphill."

"There was a slope?"

"Yeah, quite a big one."

"Well, we're going to take a look anyway," Frank insisted. "We're certainly not going to fix anything sitting here."

He narrowed his eyes, challenging her to make up another excuse.

"Maybe . . . I don't know . . . maybe we can try."

Frank smiled.

"Shall I come with you?" Grace was rolling up her shirtsleeves. "It'll be easier to push between the three of us."

"No, honey. You stay here with the kids."

"The kid and the young adult," Audrey corrected him.

Frank led his wife to the back of the motor home as if she were a third child. Simon and Audrey watched from the threshold of the non-existent door, ignoring the television show on the screen.

"And lock the door when we're gone."

"Here we go again," whispered Grace. "Don't frighten the kids as well."

Simon pointed to the front.

"Dad, something's up with her."

Frank heard the convulsion before he turned around. When he did, he saw that Mara was holding her hands to her throat, squeezing it as if she were trying to strangle herself. From the sofa, she looked at them with tears in her eyes, guttural sounds emanating from her throat. Her body shook with spasms.

"What's wrong?" yelled Grace.

She ran to help, and slapped the other woman's back as if she were choking on food. Mara slapped her own chest, a desperate action that alarmed Frank. He stood in front of Mara without knowing what to do. Her neck was enlarged and her face had turned a bright red color that was beginning to purple. She was really suffocating.

"What's going on now? What . . . what do I do?" asked Frank.

Frank grabbed Mara by the shoulders, shaking her. Grace lifted her by the waist. Neither of them knew how to help her until she hugged herself, reminding them of the Heimlich maneuver. It was Frank who performed it, imitating what he'd seen in movies. Instead of something flying out of the mouth like in those films, Mara's throat cleared itself inward. First she swallowed, and then air flowed through lungs that contracted and expanded at a frantic rate. Each breath sounded painfully rough. She wriggled out of Frank's arms as if they were dangerous snakes and lay down on the sofa.

"What was it?" Grace asked her.

"I don't know." Mara dried her eyelashes, her nose. "Something that came from inside got stuck in my throat. It was like wanting to throw up and not being able to."

"Like I said. Who knows what you've broken in there."

"You need a doctor, that's for sure," said Frank. "Take a few minutes to recover and we'll go get your car."

He wasn't going to let up in his efforts to get her out of there, away from his family.

"I don't think I can walk . . ."

"Sure you can."

Grace pinched his back twice to disapprove of his comment. *Be nice.*

"Now that you mention it," Mara added, lying face-up on the sofa, a forearm on her brow, "I don't have the key."

"What do you mean you don't have it?"

Frank didn't fail to notice that she remembered this detail right after almost choking to death.

"I had it in my hand, like the cell phone. When you hit me."

"When you appeared on the road," Grace elaborated.

"It must be out there on the road, in the dark." Mara aimed her next remark at Frank, repeating an argument that he had used against her before and that was now convenient for her. "It could be lost in the bushes."

He clenched his teeth, containing his rage.

"Fuck!"

He turned around to avoid looking at the intruder. Grace held him by the waist and guided him to the bathroom. At the entrance to the bedroom, Audrey had her hands over her brother's ears after the swear word.

"Frank, seriously, it's nothing to worry about," his wife whispered. "Let's do what I said and that's that. We'll take her in for one night, she can have a good sleep, and tomorrow when the sun comes up, when there's light, we'll search for the cell phones and her car keys. Don't make things more complicated than they need to be."

His wife's words exuded calm, trust in the goodness of strangers. Frank wondered whether to tell her about the wheels. Let her know that the woman she was so keen to help had gashed their tires for the sole purpose of keeping them there. And that in her purse, right near the kids, she must still have the knife she'd used. That everything was part of some sinister plan to stay with them tonight.

Frank looked at his children. Simon was clinging to his sister, rubbing one foot against the other, frightened like the small child he was. The moment they and Grace knew about the wheels, terror would flare up. Frank would no longer be able to control the situation. And things would happen that he could still prevent if they kept calm. If he managed to think with a cool head.

"You're right," he said, stifling other words.

He ruffled Simon's hair, pinched Audrey's chin with his knuckles. He would never forgive himself if anything harmed his son and daughter.

"I love you so much," he said. "More than anything in the world."

They both looked down at the floor, embarrassed.

Mara coughed.

"It's decided." Grace took a set of sheets out from a compartment above the sofa. "You'll stay with us."

Frank snatched the sheets from her hands and returned them to their compartment. Without giving an explanation, he went outside. From the window over the kitchen, Grace followed his movements. Mara also peered out. Frank opened the side trunk at the rear—the space the people at the dealership had called the *basement*. From amid the luggage, he pulled out a long bright-green bag by its handles. He also took out another, fatter, bag. He emptied the contents of the green bag onto the ground on one side of the road, in view of the two women, and started to put up a tent.

Grace quickly went out, and Mara followed her.

"She can sleep on the sofa, Frank."

Without answering, he fitted some poles together.

"Come on, she needs a good rest," Grace insisted.

He continued with his work, spreading out the fabric.

"She has to recover."

Frank inserted tent pegs into the holes in the fabric, one by one.

"Frank!"

He dropped the rings he was holding. He approached Mara and pointed a threatening finger at her.

"You're not going to sleep near my family. I'm very cautious with strangers."

Frank returned to his task, ignoring Grace's complaints. When his wife accepted that the tent was going to be the only option, she changed tack, worrying as ever about keeping others happy.

"It's a very good tent, to be fair. It cost us a ton of money. The sleeping bag, too," she said. "You'll sleep very comfortably, you'll see."

Frank shook his head, unable to believe that a day that had started with the promise of a great trip and a better future had turned into a disaster. He howled with pain when he pricked himself with a peg.

15.

Grace twisted the string on a teabag around a spoon, which she used to squeeze the last drop of chamomile out. She breathed in the aroma, which made her think of a sunny field, so different from the wooded darkness that surrounded them. She had prepared the infusion using the kettle, considering whether they should start limiting their use of the most power-hungry appliances. As a precaution, she had turned off the device as soon as she heard the first bubbles, though she remembered they had enough self-sufficiency for several nights. Frank had made sure of it because their trip included overnight stays in isolated places where they wouldn't have a chance to connect to power at a campsite, just as they wouldn't have tonight even if they had reached the hot springs. There would be nights when they'd be *dry camping* or *boondocking*, terms that Frank used to show he'd learned some RVer jargon. In any case, tonight they might not even have to spend the whole night on the road. With a bit of luck, another car would drive past in the early hours and they could ask for help before dawn.

She took the infusion to Mara, who was sitting on a folding chair on the road. Before taking the first sip, she wrapped her hands around the cup to make the most of its warmth. She was wearing some paja-mas that Grace had lent her. The clothes that were dirty and torn from the accident were in a heap next to the chair, her purse weighing them down.

"Ha, they look better on you than on me," Grace said about the pajamas. "They don't fit me like that at the top."

Returning the compliment, Mara remarked how nice Grace's hair was.

"You don't know how much I appreciate you saying that," she admitted as she unfolded another chair. "I almost lost it all."

Frank, still pitching the tent, let out a disapproving snort—he probably wasn't liking the fact that they were getting along—but she really was grateful for someone saying something nice about her hair after so long. Grace also was clear in her mind that being good to people is the best way to make sure they're good in return.

"Don't mind my husband," she whispered. "He does it to protect us, me and the children. It's not that there's any danger, I know you're harmless, but he does it to set an example for the kids. It's true that we're alone, at night, in the middle of nowhere . . ."

She looked into the abyss of darkness beyond where the light died. Pine branches swayed in the wind, rubbing together in a whisper, as if the forest were revealing some secret to her. Or warning her of some danger.

"He's not at his best," she said, casting out the gloomy thoughts the surroundings evoked. "Well, not him or any of us. I won't bore you with our life story, but we're not on vacation. We're trying to make it seem like we are, but really we're moving. We're leaving Seattle. We've been through a difficult time, especially my husband, so please forgive him."

She hoped Mara would take over, respond with some kind of understanding, but she didn't. Some subtle changes in her expression were insufficient for Grace to be able to interpret her emotions. Fear, anger, sadness, helplessness. All or none of them were possible in the depth of her peculiar gaze. When the trees breathed their indecipherable message again, Grace thought she saw a flash of hatred in those eyes. It quickly went out—it must have been a reflection from what remained of the moon in the sky.

"The idea was that by moving we'd leave behind all the bad things that've happened to us recently," she went on. "Everything was going so well today . . . until you appeared."

Mara looked away and blew on her cup.

"Sorry, that came out wrong. But you know what I meant."

A few more seconds passed before Mara accepted the apology.

"Sure, don't worry. I'm not having a great time, either. Is anyone?" She narrowed her eyes in the steam from the tea. "I've even thought about taking more extreme measures . . ."

Grace thought she understood what Mara was referring to. In her mind, the profound sadness the young woman exuded, her aura of loneliness and abandonment, and these extreme measures she said she had considered taking all flowed toward a simple explanation. She took one of Mara's hands in her own, offering support.

"You're not going to tell me you threw yourself in front of us on purpose, are you?"

She was surprised at herself for asking the question without hesitation, but it had suddenly seemed logical to her that Mara may have intended to take her own life.

"No."

The denial was so emphatic that Grace felt ashamed that she'd imagined the story without enough consideration, giving in to her caring instinct as if deep down she enjoyed other people's dramas because they enabled her to help and feel fulfilled. She released Mara's hand, not knowing what else she could say to excuse her audacity.

"It's ready," Frank broke in, indicating the tent he'd put up on the road. "All yours."

He said the words into the air, without looking at Mara.

"Frank, is it really necessary?"

Joining her husband, Grace could see the inside of the tent through an open zipper in the fabric.

"Well, to be honest, it's not bad." She invited Mara over. "You should get some good rest in there. The bag's thick and comfortable, and it won't get much colder than it is now. Oh, and wait a second." Grace disappeared into the motor home. She returned with three cushions she threw inside the tent. "So you're even more comfortable. And if you need anything in the night, just ask. This is our house right here."

"The door will be locked all night," Frank said.

He caught Grace's hand before she could pinch his back.

"And if I need the bathroom?" asked Mara.

As she finished her tea, her eyes searched for Frank's. He shied away from her gaze. Without answering the question, he went back into the RV. Her husband's stubbornness, his impolite behavior, annoyed Grace. Then he returned with a roll of toilet paper in his hand. He threw it into the tent with more force than he used playing baseball with Simon.

"There you go," he muttered without looking at Mara. "And everything around us is the bathroom."

With an exaggerated, almost mocking arm movement, he encompassed the whole landscape.

16.

Frank finished stretching a bottom sheet over the sofa where the children would sleep. While they changed into their pajamas, he and Grace had discussed whether it would be safe to extend the living room module when the vehicle was less stable because of the flat tires. They concluded it wouldn't be, so the sofa was unfolded just halfway, until it met the kitchen sink unit. Even so, it was a decent enough bed for Audrey and Simon to share. Frank took a bedspread down from the top compartment.

"And this is to go on top of you."

He laid it out on the sofa.

The children thanked him from their seats at the dining table. Audrey was spreading an antibiotic ointment on Simon's absent eye, which still needed to be treated daily. Grace helped him some nights, too, but Frank couldn't bring himself to do it. Just the smell of the ointment made him feel unwell—it was the smell of his own guilt. Nor could he touch the wound with his fingers, or face the void behind the eyelids. He couldn't bear seeing the reddish color of the flesh in the place where his son's sparkling eye should be, full of life and innocence. The most Frank managed to do was blow on the wound when it itched. Without looking at the hole in Simon's face, he blew until the burning sensation stopped, the boy's hands gripping his T-shirt to fight the temptation to scratch himself.

"Done," said Audrey.

She screwed the lid back on the tube of ointment and rearranged the patch her brother wore to bed. The one he'd worn in the day had been left on the table.

"Come on, both of you to bed now," said Frank.

He waited for them to climb onto the sofa so he could get past. In the bedroom, Grace was pulling back the sheets on the double bed.

"Remember what we were thinking, about whether she threw herself in front of the RV?" she asked. "Talking to her, I got the feeling we might've been on the right track. But not to sue us or anything like that, more to . . ." She indicated to Frank to unfold his side of the bed. "She seems sad. Really sad, capable of doing something crazy, to herself, even."

"Suicidal?"

"Yeah, I don't know," she confirmed. "Seems it."

Audrey's voice interrupted them.

"Mom, that's prejudice," she said from the sofa. "What does seeming suicidal mean? That only exists in the closed minds of people who want to simplify others' pain instead of thinking about how we could help them."

Out of her sight, Grace nodded with feigned gravity in response to her daughter's rebuke.

"It's a serious problem we experience in school because of bullying, for example," continued Audrey. "What we have to keep in mind is that anyone, facing certain circumstances, could end up committing suicide. In fact, you have to be very brave to do it."

"Cowardly, more like," Frank said.

"No, Dad, don't associate suicide just with weak, crazy, or sad people, because it's not like that. If we think like that, we never help the people who need us—we only push them to the point of no return.

And Mara seems fine to me—frightened by what happened, but that's all. Did you hear me?"

"Yes, honey, we did."

Grace rolled her eyes. When she sensed Frank was about to laugh, she admonished him with a conspiratorial look.

"Either way, I'm not happy," she whispered more quietly, sitting on the edge of the bed. "What if something happens? I don't know how many times I've heard stories of people who seem OK after an accident but then they collapse and die from undetected injuries."

"That would happen even if she was in here."

He sat next to her.

"Oh, I don't know, Frank . . ."

Grace looked around the room as if she could find a solution on the shelves, mirrors, or cupboards.

"I'm going to take the iPad out to her," she finally said. "In case she gets bored, she can watch a movie."

Frank grabbed her wrist.

"You're not going anywhere. We're safe in here. Our children are safe. That's all you should worry about."

"You're a good father." Grace rested a hand on his face. "And you know what?" She moved her lips closer, as if to tell him a secret. "I find it very masculine and exciting when you protect your female and litter."

"Pleeeease!" yelled Audrey.

"What did I just hear?" asked Simon, as horrified as his sister.

Grace covered her mouth, and shame flushed her face red. She took refuge on Frank's chest while the children yelled on the sofa.

"Cover my ears!"

"Format my brain!"

"Cover them! Or pull them off!"

The two of them kicked their legs under the bedcover.

"Help, Mom, we can't unhear what you just said," cried Simon. "You're like a Taylor Swift song!"

"Hey, hey," Audrey cut in. "A bit of respect for Taylor Swift, please. She's a singer, songwriter, and supersmart businesswoman."

Simon responded by singing the chorus to "Shake It Off" at full volume until his sister, laughing, joined in. Grace came and sat with them on the sofa, guffawing as well, singing along with them but hiding her red face with the bedcover. Even Frank hummed the part of the lyrics he knew, forgetting the problem they faced for a second and enjoying his family's explosion of joy. Then he glimpsed the tent through the bedroom window, and lost the desire to laugh.

17.

An idea prevented him from sleeping. Or rather, an urge: to grab the steering wheel, start up the motor home, and drive away.

Escape.

Get away from the threat that was lying in wait for him and his family outside. Leave it behind them. Forget about it. Deny its existence. If only the threat hadn't been cunning enough to puncture the tires and thwart their escape.

Frank couldn't close his eyes for more than a few seconds. Beside him, Grace was asleep. Her breathing hadn't slowed as much as it did when she slept safely in their bed at home, but a subtle spasm under the sheets told him she was now dreaming. A few minutes ago, she'd stopped scratching the pointed hairs of an eyebrow. Simon had been snoring for a while, finally regaining his usual carefree state after the shock of the accident. It hurt Frank to see his son frightened—the child who'd coped so well with the loss of his eye, the hospitalization, the recovery that was still ongoing. His brave little boy. Audrey was sleeping in silence, as she always did, as if she didn't want to offend anyone with the sound of her breathing, as cautious in her dreams as she was in real life with her views and the way she treated others.

Frank closed his eyes again and concentrated on his family's hypnotic symphony. He tried to lose himself in it, to slip into sleep. The presence outside invaded his thoughts. The feminine silhouette in the headlights. An intruder on the road, an intruder in his head. He thought about her with such intensity that he began to believe she was inside. Hidden in a corner of the room. Watching them sleep. Waiting for the right moment. He imagined her crouching in a corner, crawling around the bed, climbing the sheets, climbing the walls. Dropping from the ceiling to end up sitting on his chest like an incubus, cutting off his breathing with her weight. As if Frank was the woman in Fuseli's painting. He saw her turn her neck to seek the approval of a dark presence that had appeared at the entrance to the room. Except that presence was also Frank, and it fixed its red eyes on him, hypnotizing him at once. Helpless, he watched the incubus savage his family while he could only beg for forgiveness and plead guilty to having caused the situation.

Frank opened his eyes feeling himself choke. He grated his throat as he took in air. He didn't know how long he'd slept, but he was waking from an endless nightmare. His back was soaked in sweat down to the elastic on his underpants, his T-shirt twisted around his body.

Then he heard footsteps outside, and he thought he was still dreaming. But the crunch of the gravel on the road sounded too real. As real as the crickets' chirping, as the whistle of the wind through the pine needles. And as real as the shudder that cooled the sweat on his back.

Frank got out of bed, listening to Grace's breathing. He went to the window, fearing he would come face-to-face with the intruder on the other side watching them from outside as she'd done inside in the nightmare he was beginning to forget. He peered out with his stomach tightening. He could still hear the footsteps, but he couldn't see Mara. What if it wasn't her walking outside?

Following the crunch of the gravel, he went around the bed to the window on the other side.

Then he saw it.

The flash.

A bright beam that turned into a circle of light on the ground, a few steps from the RV.

A flashlight.

It had to be someone else—neither they nor Mara had one. And they'd all lost their cell phones in the darkness. The bright spot slid along the ground, searching for something. Frank followed the beam of light from the bottom to the top, toward the source. It wasn't a flashlight, it was a cell phone. He stopped breathing when he recognized the black-painted fingernails that held it.

"It can't be . . . ," he whispered to himself.

In a flash, Frank also recognized the pink cotton of Grace's pajamas. It was Mara. He had to contain the urge to yell at her for not telling them she had a phone. All this time they could have made the emergency call that would have gotten them out of there, but she'd preferred to continue with her sinister plan, whatever it was. He imagined the inside of her purse, the phone lying next to the knife while she assured them she'd lost it in the collision.

"What're you doing?" Frank murmured to the glass.

Mara combed the ground with her beam of light, like a night creature sniffing its way forward. After searching for a few seconds, she stopped. She bent down. Frank strained his eyes so much his head hurt, unable to make out what she'd picked up. Out there, she must have felt the force of his gaze on the back of her head, because she turned toward the motor home. Realizing she was being watched, she stood there, watching as well. Until she illuminated her face from below. And smiled. Her grimace was as horrible as the one Simon had carved into a pumpkin last Halloween.

"What the . . . ?"

On the other side of the glass, Mara held up the object she'd picked up from the ground. It was the ziplock. With the four cell phones in it. She waved it in front of her face, creating new shadows that distorted her features. For an instant, Frank thought it was the end of their nightmare. The cell phones had been found. With a tiny signal from any network, they could call 911.

But Mara gripped her phone in her teeth, the light pointing at the ground. She opened the bag. She threw the first cell phone into the trees on the right-hand side, lost forever in the precipitous vegetation.

"Fuck. No," Frank whispered through his teeth, his lips brushing against the window.

He spent a few seconds calculating whether he would reach her in time to stop her if he ran out there. Whether it was worth waking the whole family and scaring them with the intruder's strange behavior. During those seconds, Mara threw the next cell phone in the opposite direction. It would fall among branches, rocks, dead leaves. She did the same with the third, which was Audrey's. The last one she threw still in the bag. When she'd finished, she brushed off her hands like someone satisfied to have completed a task. Frank hadn't even finished calculating—there was no point anymore. The light went out.

The sudden darkness stunned Frank, who found that he was breathing more loudly than Simon was snoring. He dried pellets of his saliva from the glass. In the same way that Simon grabbed his own T-shirt to stop himself from scratching his eye when it itched, Frank grabbed the window's handle, fighting against the desire to go out after the woman. He closed his eyes to banish the images of what would happen if he went out to confront her.

At that moment, he wished with all his heart that he had run her over. That she'd died from the impact so he wouldn't now have to face this situation.

A buzz in the darkness, the sound of the tent's zipper closing, reminded him that she was still alive.

Right there.

Right outside.

Frank scratched the handle, knowing he was going to let go of it. And he couldn't stop himself.

Suppressing the furious rush his legs were demanding from him, he tiptoed through the motor home to avoid waking his family. He opened and closed the door with the same delicacy. He trod barefoot on the damp road. The shiver that started on the soles of his feet intermingled with the tingling that emanated from his stomach, his neck, his lungs, the heart that accelerated as he approached the tent.

He lowered the zipper little by little to avoid making any noise. He fought against another tingling sensation that disgusted him, the one originating in his crotch. Each click of the zipper triggered images of other zippers, on pairs of pants, which had made the same noise as they were unzipped. He fought against the onset of an erection that made him feel ashamed, one of those erections that are filled as much with premature remorse as with desire. He hated himself for associating the sound with the memory of his penis trapped in the suit pants he would have worn to work that day, his desire about to explode, waiting to be freed and to feel the warm breath of the woman whose mouth awaited it.

Frank finished unzipping the tent, opening the door to his darkest secret tooth by tooth. Inside was the woman to whom the mouth of his shameful memories belonged. Seeing her, every trace of inappropriate excitement disappeared, and he went as soft as the flesh of a corpse floating in water. The stiffness moved to his neck.

"How long have you been following me?" Frank whispered.

"You haven't lost that scared look on your face since you realized it was me," she said. "I don't know how your wife hasn't noticed something's up, considering how tense you've been. But shut that mouth, I'm not an apparition. I'm flesh and bone, just like when you were fucking me."

Mara was kneeling on the sleeping bag, her legs bare. She'd taken off the pajama pants. Frank remembered other times when, like now, they'd been together in their underwear, just after leaving the rest of their clothes scattered around the floor of her apartment. Mara stood so that their eyes were level—she could stand upright in the tent. He spoke while bent over.

"Why did you throw the cell phones away?"

"Same reason I punctured the tires. To give you more time."

Frank pricked his ears, alert to any movement in the motor home.

"What is it you want?" he asked her.

"For you to confess." Mara adjusted the elastic on her panties before continuing. "For you to tell your wife about me, about us. And about you, tell her about you, most of all. So that poor woman knows she doesn't have the perfect husband she thinks she has. So she knows how you treat women who aren't her, how you walked out on me as if I was worthless."

A sudden sadness dulled her eyes. When they lit up again, they glowed with malice. She tried to grab his hand, make him touch the skin he already knew. "When you left me"—she paused, harboring thoughts that darkened her gaze—"nothing has ever hurt me so much. And now you're running off to the other side of the country to get as far away from me as possible, right? You didn't think I'd find out, of course. How would I? But, as you can see, I did. Your wife tells us everything on her channel.

"Did I not mention I subscribed?" she added with a smile. "You're not going to get rid of me this easily, Frank. The truth is coming after you, and you're going to have to face up to it. She was so nice, the server at the restaurant, wasn't she? I didn't mean to knock her over."

"That was you."

"Sitting at the next table. Listening to where you were going. I didn't intend for you to hit me, that was unexpected. I would've settled for you stopping to help a poor girl with a broken-down car . . . and seeing the expression on your face when you discovered it was me. I wanted to be with you, with your wife, with your happy family. All together in the RV. Making you come clean."

"Don't do anything to my family."

"I'm not doing anything to them. I'm doing it to you."

Frank pushed her aside and searched inside the tent. He shook out the sleeping bag, looked under the pajama pants on the floor, kicked the cushions Grace had brought out. He examined folds in the tent fabric.

"Where's your purse? The knife, the cell phone. Where are they?"

"I wasn't stupid enough to keep them in here."

"Don't you try anything." Frank spoke with the most authoritative tone he could manage in a whisper. Really, he wanted to shout with all the air in his lungs. "Don't you dare say anything."

"Are you going to tell her?" Mara asked. "Are you going to tell her everything?"

She grabbed the bulge in his briefs, not in the provocative way she had when it had been she who'd taken them off for him, but squeezing so that it hurt.

"If you have enough of these to do what you did"—she kneaded his testicles—"then use them to face up to what you've done. Because I'm staying right here. We're all going to stay on this road for as long as it takes for you to decide to behave like a man and tell the truth."

Frank shoved her arm away and grabbed her neck, so slender he could almost fit his hand around it.

"You can't hurt me anymore," she said. "You could've run me over completely and I wouldn't have cared. It would've been fun to sit in hell and watch you tell your wife that the girl you'd just killed on the road was your—"

Frank tightened his hand, strangling her words. He didn't even want to hear the name she was about to give to what had happened between them. Mara looked at him with defiance in her eyes. The muscles in her neck fought to expand her throat, to keep her breathing. She didn't look away even when her eyes began to swell under her eyelids, even when they filled with tears. The rest of her face was swelling up, too, the blood trapped in her head, her face purpling. Frank realized it would be very easy to keep exerting pressure. Just a little while longer and the problem would disappear. Grace had said it: accident victims who appear unharmed often die hours later from invisible injuries. Mara had already choked, so it wouldn't seem unusual if, in the night, she suffered another seizure like the one they'd all witnessed, only this time it killed her. Frank's hand began to tremble, alarmed at what could happen if it continued to squeeze, at how easy it would be to keep squeezing. He began to fantasize about—

"Dad?"

Simon's voice was deafening in the silence. Frank released his grip, ashamed. The father of the lovely boy who'd just spoken couldn't be the person who was fantasizing about strangling a woman in the night.

"Are you outside, Dad?"

Mara dropped to the floor, coughing into the sleeping bag.

"Yeah, taking a pee." His son wouldn't know where the voice was coming from. "I didn't want to make the tank dirty."

"Can you blow on my eye?"

Mara twisted on the ground, regaining her breath.

"I'll be right there," said Frank. "You go in, I'll be right there."

He waited for the click of the door. Squatting, he found Mara's line of sight.

"Leave," he said. "Disappear."

She was opening and closing her mouth the way Simon's fish had when they found it on the carpet the afternoon he accidentally smashed the tank with a baseball.

"When . . . when you confess," she managed to say.

Frank left the tent. He zipped up the door, wanting to close the entrance to a past he'd hoped to leave behind him when they moved.

He caught his thumb on the zipper's last tooth. He held it to his mouth. He hated the taste of blood.

Simon was waiting for him inside the motor home.

"Can you blow on me now?"

Frank smiled, and tickled his son's tummy.

"Sure thing, Gizmo."

He kissed the top of Simon's head and, kneeling in front of him, blew into the darkness to soothe the itching.

"I love you, son," he whispered. "I love you all so much."

18.

If only he'd killed her.

If only she'd died.

If only he hadn't swerved with the motor home.

Frank knew his thoughts were abhorrent, but he couldn't get them out of his head. His ex-lover's battered body under the wheels seemed less problematic than having her out there, sleeping right near his family. He pressed his tongue against his teeth, scraping it to censure that last idea with pain. He was so tense under the sheets that only his shoulders, backside, and heels touched the mattress. Beside him, Grace was asleep. A wife dreamed in the marital bed while her husband fantasized about how he would get rid of the secret that would destroy their marriage.

Frank shook his head on the pillow. He wanted to stop thinking about how believable the death of a woman would be when she had been in an accident and refused to seek medical attention. How innocent he would be in the eyes of any authority, having swerved to avoid her. How simple it would be to explain why he hadn't allowed a stranger to sleep in the motor home—he had a young son and didn't want her sleeping near the boy. The knife they would find in the victim's purse would also confirm that she was a dangerous person.

The family's behavior toward her had been exemplary after the accident. They had treated her injuries, given her a change of clothes, offered her accommodation in a good tent. An unexpected complication from the accident causing her death later would be a tragic but believable outcome. Unfortunate for almost everyone, convenient for Frank. Very convenient. So convenient that he dug his fingernails into his thighs to distract his attention from how tempting the idea was. Because he knew that the more tempting it was, the more dangerous it was, too, and he hadn't been very good at resisting temptations lately.

He focused on his family's breathing. The three people who made his home, the three people who were his whole life. Rocked by his wife's sleepy spasms, lulled by his youngest child's snoring, and touched by the mere existence of the daughter who was turning into a woman, Frank couldn't understand how he had risked destroying so much stability, so much love, just to have a stupid affair with the woman who was sleeping out there. The woman who'd also sold them this very motor home.

The idea to buy the RV had been Frank's. Grace had thought it an unnecessary expense, as well as an eccentricity unsuited to a man who'd worked in the hotel industry all his life. "Aren't these things supposed to lose you customers?" she asked. Frank had suggested it two years ago, when Simon was seven and Audrey was about to turn fourteen. The children were no longer little kids and were beginning to look like responsible people—it had been a while since traveling with them had stopped being the living hell of tantrums, fits of gluttony, and puking in the car that their family vacations had usually become. But it wasn't easy to persuade Grace. Frank had to make the argument a thousand times that an RV would be the best way to travel as a family, to explore the country, to make geography something more than just boring information in textbooks for the kids. That every week off would be an opportunity to hit the road, and every trip would be a factory of family memories they would treasure forever. He also tried to persuade Grace that she could make interesting videos for her YouTube channel, but she rejected that idea outright—taking her camera on their trips would make them the opposite of a vacation. Frank seduced her by describing idyllic scenes of the children toasting marshmallows over a fire in Yosemite, of the four of them watching shooting stars from the top of a rock in Joshua Tree National Park or telling ghost stories under a blanket—the ones Simon liked even though they frightened him—after a picnic of hot dogs on the sands of Carmel-by-the-Sea. They would have snow, cactuses, beaches, fireflies, meteorite craters, mountains, the Grand Canyon, the Mississippi, geysers . . . all on their doorstep. They could look out their bedroom window at the most beautiful landscapes of the United States, because with a house on wheels, they could take their bed wherever they wanted. And wherever they were, their house on wheels would be a twinkling light in the darkness of the fascinating places where they would stop to sleep, making any point on the map where the four of them were a cozy home. On several occasions, the picture-perfect scenes Frank imagined for Grace made her defocus her eyes as if she could see them, too. Sometimes she even smiled at the living room when Frank described details like the cackle Simon would let out when Audrey's marshmallow fell off her stick into the fire. But what finally persuaded Grace, almost a year after the initial suggestion, was Frank describing the way he'd hug her with his raincoat to protect her from the cloud of water Niagara Falls would spray on them.

He'd gone alone to choose the motor home, in the spring of the previous year. He wanted to avoid the comments Grace would make about the cost, her inevitable insistence on choosing a cheaper model. He also wanted to avoid Audrey's and Simon's impulses—unlike their mother, they would push for the more expensive models they couldn't afford. On the Saturday morning when Frank went to the dealership, the sun was reflecting off the silver, blue, and red bunting strung overhead. The breeze was blowing a gigantic Stars and Stripes hoisted in the middle of the site. While sales agents drove other customers around in golf carts, Frank wandered among the rows of parked RVs, waiting for someone to attend to him. He peered into the windows of several motor homes from the outside, examining their interiors like a nosy neighbor. He paid no attention to the young woman who positioned herself beside him, even when she cleared her throat for the first time.

"I know everyone expects their salesperson to be a man."

She said it when he was jumping to snoop through a high window on one of the vehicles. Realizing he'd been caught, he feigned innocence like a child, rearranging the polo shirt that had ridden up as he leapt.

"But you got me, the saleswoman with the best record in the dealership. I'm also the only saleswoman, but hey. My name's Mara Miller."

She held out her hand with a smile—the way Frank had tried to cover up his mischief seemed to have amused her.

"It wasn't because you're a woman." Frank indicated another sales agent passing in a golf cart. "It was because you're not wearing the same uniform as them."

"The men wear a jacket. They make me wear this dress."

She ran both hands down the garment, from the round neck to the skirt's hem. Her frown and sharp tone made it clear that her comment was a criticism of the sexism encapsulated in the gender-specific company clothing. However, from the way she positioned her body's curves to emphasize the femininity of the dress, Frank detected a hint of an actress doing a twirl on a red carpet. A very attractive actress. An actress with whom Frank couldn't help but establish instant, furtive eye contact, the automatic mode of a man wanting to confirm whether, despite being married, he was still attractive to women.

She held his gaze. Under other circumstances, Frank would have interpreted the gesture as subtle flirting, but now he suspected it was a sales ploy. He had come to the dealership well aware of salespeople's ability to manipulate customers, and he was determined not to allow himself to be influenced by anything they said. Not even when the sales agent was a good-looking girl with gray eyes who seemed to be paying too much attention to him.

"Can you tell me what kind of motor home you're looking for and I'll help you?" she asked.

"I've done all my homework online," Frank explained. "Don't take it personally, but I think the time when we just trusted a salesperson is well and truly over. In the months I've spent reading about motor homes, I've learned much more than you could tell me here in a few minutes."

"OK, no problem, then. I respect the decision you've made based on the opinions of those people on the internet who know so much but who probably don't know the promotions and special offers we have at this dealership."

The saleswoman gave him a slanted smile, a mixture of commercial tactics and teasing again. Frank held her gaze. When she wet her lips, the meaning of the looks they traded changed completely, they both knew. Neither of them was thinking about RVs or the dealership's special offers anymore. Frank worried that it was obvious he was becoming excited.

"But if you don't mind me asking," she went on, "what model did you choose after all your research?"

Frank revealed his choice with all the confidence instilled in him by hours spent on manufacturers' websites, user forums, and specialized YouTube channels.

"It's one of the biggest models," the saleswoman replied. "Do you have a large family?"

"Two children."

Frank could feel the seductive energy that had enveloped them until now fade. He also knew what her next question would be.

"And a wife, I imagine," the sales agent stated instead of asking.

Her voice had lost its flirtatious overtone, instantly respecting the other woman she must have begun to visualize in her mind. Her uniform was no longer the party dress of an actress strutting along the red carpet, just work clothes. The contrast, the change to a more boring register, seemed so tragic to Frank that he refused to accept it.

"No," he answered, thinking of Grace, "not really. I'm single. Divorced."

The lie escaped his lips easily. He didn't even have to worry about hiding his hand in his pocket because he never wore his wedding ring. At first he felt ashamed, imagining Grace hearing him deny her existence, but he soon persuaded himself that he was doing nothing wrong. Flirting isn't cheating. And he just wanted to play the game a little longer, prolong the stimulating twist to the encounter. What was supposed to be a cold commercial transaction had proved to be more fun than expected. And so what? There was no reason marriage had to deprive him of some harmless flirting in broad daylight.

"Free, then. Great," replied the saleswoman, who made her smile glow when she wet her lips with her tongue. "It's beautiful, a father traveling with his children in a motor home. And you made a good choice of model—it's a very good make. I'm not going to try to persuade you to change your mind. What I can offer you is an upgrade . . ."

"Here we go," Frank blurted out with a boldness that kept the conversation less formal. "This is where the price starts going up."

"It's an upgrade that'll enhance your RV but won't make it more expensive, because it costs the same as the ten percent discount we're offering today on all the class As." She winked, blurring the boundary between seduction and commerce even more. "Better?"

The upgrade she offered consisted of an improvement to the finish in the galley—the word she used to refer to the kitchen—and a better distribution of the basement—the name she gave to the exterior storage area that Frank would call the trunk. Accepting the offer must have sent the wrong message to the saleswoman, who, as they walked toward the model of choice, then set about trying to sell him more things, some of them completely absurd.

"And would you like to add a security system with surveillance cameras for your new house?"

"For this house?" Frank rested his hand on the chosen motor home. The saleswoman nodded.

"Yeah, sure," he said. "As if people buy stuff like that. I'm not going to add anything else that costs money, thanks."

"A lot of RVers install security systems," she insisted. "Keep in mind there're owners who live in them full time. They park in inhospitable places and leave all their belongings inside. Valuable things. If you think it's sensible to have security cameras in your home, then it's just as sensible to have them on your house on wheels."

"I don't even have any in my house," explained Frank. "As if I'm going to put them in a car."

"I'm the opposite. I'm a security freak. And the basic cameras are so cheap these days, I have them all over my house. Even on the balcony. The only place I don't have one is in the bathroom, out of respect for my guests."

Frank let out a disbelieving snort. He hadn't missed the saleswoman's insertion of the word *cheap* into her spiel. He admired how well crafted her lies were. "You're making it up to sell me a security system no one buys."

"Do you really think I have the power to make you do everything I want you to do?"

The question's double meaning was so forward that Frank stammered, unable to think of an answer to match it. It had been too long since anyone had teased him in such a way.

"Seriously, a lot of people buy this system," she went on, visibly satisfied at having unbalanced him.

"Yeah, yeah," he said. "You turn your house into Fort Knox if you want. I'll take the motor home without surveillance cameras or customized horns, thanks. And guarantee me that the upgrade I've accepted costs the same as the discount you're offering."

"I promise—don't you trust me?"

A quick bat of the eyelashes embellished the question.

"Not much."

They smiled at each other, making eye contact for much longer than any saleswoman would normally look at her customer. In silence. Then they both looked down at the ground, not knowing how to continue.

That morning, Frank signed the reservation and paid the deposit. The sales agent asked him for a period seven to ten days to complete the paperwork and prepare the vehicle. But before the week was over, on the Tuesday morning, Frank received a call from Mara Miller, as she introduced herself on the telephone. The saleswoman apologized for forgetting to ask him to sign an essential document. The dealership would send out the paperwork that afternoon, and if they didn't have everything in order, it would delay delivery for another week. Repeating her apology, the saleswoman advised Frank to visit the dealership as soon as possible, advice he accepted. Though he kept telling himself he was only going there to sign a document, a whirl of excitement began to revolve in his stomach that had nothing to do with a simple sales transaction. Denying to himself what his actions made obvious, Frank visited the bathroom next to his office and took out the deodorant he kept in the last drawer for when the days dragged on longer than expected. That day he still smelled like the soap from his morning shower, but he wanted to be sure. He also made himself urinate even though he didn't feel the need. And when he dried himself with the cheap toilet paper the hotel bought and some remnants were left on his penis, he removed them carefully, one by one, until no trace remained.

Mara Miller received him in a hut in a corner of the premises rather than in the central building where they'd finalized the sale. She was wearing the same uniform she'd worn on the Saturday, but a lowered front zipper turned what had been a round neck into cleavage. Frank's eyes flicked to the uncovered flesh. The saleswoman thanked him for coming so quickly as she got up from the desk. She was shoeless, and her tights brushed against the floor with each step toward the door. Frank had left it open, but she closed it. She resembled a woman receiving a visitor at home, or in her bedroom, perhaps. It was as if an open cleavage and stockinged feet had stripped her of her professionalism. The thought annoyed Frank because it was a manifestation of the internalized sexism of which Audrey sometimes accused him and which he denied. But his daughter was right, because there he was, thinking a saleswoman is less credible if she's made herself more comfortable during her lunch break, a conclusion he would never have reached had it been a salesman receiving him with his jacket off and his tie loosened. Of course, maybe it wasn't all internalized sexism—maybe in reality there was nothing professional about the way the saleswoman rested against the edge of the desk, stretching her back to accentuate the curves of her spine and breasts. Or the way she looked at him with her thumb between her teeth in a half-opened mouth.

"Have you come to sign the document?" Her tone had lost the polite distance she had maintained the last time. "Or was there some other unfinished business?"

Frank wasn't the kind of man who was presented with this kind of opportunity, never had been. Not for a lack of confidence, or because he didn't feel attractive—he knew he was—but because he had never given off the sexual energy needed to prompt women to offer themselves to him. Not before he was married, let alone after. Faithfulness and monogamy were fundamental values of his marriage with Grace, and they both honored them. Even now, when their sex life had stagnated to the point that they felt ashamed when other couples spoke about theirs at a dinner party. That was why Frank had been the first to be surprised at the exchange of looks between him and the saleswoman the other day. Maybe it wasn't that he was effortlessly honoring the pledges of monogamy and faithfulness but simply that he'd never been presented with such a clear opportunity to break them. Certainly, no woman had offered herself to him in such an obvious way as the saleswoman was now, looking him up and down with her gray eyes, pausing unashamedly at the hands he was using to try to hide what was happening in his pants.

"We both want it," she said. "And there's nothing stopping us. I'm single, too, if that's what's worrying you."

Frank removed his hands from his groin to show Mara with his bulge that she wasn't wrong. While the saleswoman lowered his zipper, Frank thought of Grace, the wife who, at that moment, didn't exist in his or in Mara's head. He thought of Audrey, of Simon. Each click of the zipper triggered another image of a happy family life. Click. Simon humming the melody Gizmo sang in *Gremlins*, which gave him his nickname. Click. Audrey applauding her ferrets when they obeyed her order to roll over on the rug. Click. The smell of cream on Grace's hands. Click. Him buying popcorn for the four of them at the movie theater. Click. Click. Click. The zipper was open, and all his thoughts vanished in a novel wave of pleasure—the pleasure of unknown lips doing something to him that Grace no longer did. He managed to banish his family from his mind during several of the acts that came after that. Until the saleswoman, her dress at her ankles, positioned herself in front of the window, inviting him to take her from behind. From there, through the venetian blinds and the grating on the outside, Frank saw the motor home he was about to buy. Its kitchen window brought to mind a family breakfast scene which, against his will, gradually took shape with each thrust with which he penetrated the woman in his hands: Grace's delicious omelets, Simon picking out the blue Froot Loops to eat them first, Audrey staring at her cell phone but laughing with the others when they remembered the jokes in the movie they'd seen the ni—

Frank let out a final grunt to force his family from his mind as he pulled out of the saleswoman to spill himself between her legs.

He didn't run off, ashamed of himself, as he would have expected he would. While they dressed, Frank was surprised at how calm he felt. He found it very easy to rationalize what had happened as something meaningless. Because it really meant nothing. The scent Grace left on her pillow when she got up first aroused more feelings in him than a stupid five-second orgasm with a saleswoman who, at any rate, didn't seem quite so attractive now.

"What document do I have to sign?"

He asked it as if he'd just walked into the hut. The saleswoman ran the zipper on the front of her dress up to the top, making the neckline round again. She also put on her shoes before sitting at the desk and taking a folder containing the papers out of a drawer. She checked one of them and put on a surprised face.

"Oh, it seems it was already signed."

She embellished the announcement with a triumphant smile.

At first Frank was annoyed he'd been tricked, but then it excited him to imagine her hatching her plan to get what she wanted. To get him. He left the hut certain that what had happened wouldn't be repeated, that he'd just slipped up. The saleswoman had made it too easy for him, and all he had done was satisfy a physical need, one his wife no longer satisfied as she had before. He didn't blame Grace at all—he knew he no longer satisfied her, either. It was a mutual thing, a deterioration for which they were both responsible. Their bodies were too familiar to each other. For ten years, they had enjoyed a passionate sex life together. If they'd been statues, they would have eroded to nothing from the number of times their bodies had rubbed together, they would've been reduced to two heaps of dust on the floor. But they were of flesh and bone, and their bodies didn't wear down. They remained intact, pressed together, year after year, seeing their desire disappear and unable to do anything to prevent it. They didn't want to attach too much importance to it. They even avoided talking about the subject, so that it wasn't real—it didn't seem right that something as trivial as their physical relationship should put other, much more important, connections between them at risk, connections that hadn't deteriorated over time, not even slightly.

Frank wanted to forget the incident. He denied to himself that it had happened or that it was worth remembering. Until the day came when they had to collect the RV. He showed up at the dealership on another Saturday morning, one when, this time, the sun wasn't shining. He walked anxiously, squeezing his umbrella handle so hard his thumbnail turned white. He had no desire to see Mara and remember his mistake. Or to talk about what had happened. As he approached the dealership's central building, he decided to act as if nothing had happened. As if he were just another customer coming to get his vehicle. The door opened before he reached it. Frank squared his shoulders. Someone was coming out, and it must be Mara Miller. Frank puffed out his chest. He had to remain impassive.

"Your motor home's ready for you." A salesman with a jacketed uniform held out his hand. "So you can take it somewhere with better weather than here."

While he accompanied Frank to his vehicle, the salesman apologized on behalf of his colleague. He said she had wanted to hand the keys to him herself, but she was attending to other customers at that moment. First Frank felt relieved, but his relief soon turned into another unexpected feeling, of wounded pride. Were those other customers more important than him? Did she sleep with every buyer who turned up there?

The fact that she didn't seem to care whether she saw him or not, even though it would be the last chance they would have, was a sharp stab to his ego. He had prayed inwardly that they wouldn't encounter her, but now that she really wasn't there, he missed the injection of adrenaline that having her close would have given him. He looked at the hut in the distance, searching for sparks of excitement to light up his gray morning. He thought he saw movement inside, as if someone had let the corner of the blind drop. Mara. Maybe she was spying on him from there, licking her lips while she watched him through the gap she had opened between two slats with her fingers. Perhaps she was—

"—I can help you with?" the salesman was asking.

"What did you say?" answered Frank, who hadn't heard a thing.

"Is there anything else I can help you with?"

Audrey, Simon, and Grace were outside the house to welcome him. They celebrated his arrival with their arms in the air, as if he'd crossed the finish line to win an Olympic gold. At last the RV was theirs, and it was time to plan their first big trip.

It would be a few months before the children finished school, so they had more than enough time to decide whether they wanted to go north, or south, to the coast, or to the mountains. "Let's go everywhere," said Simon, summarizing in a few words the philosophy that Frank had been trying to instill in Grace for the last year.

That night, Frank received a text message on his cell phone: Yes, I was watching you from the hut. It was true I had other customers. You looked great in those pants, although I prefer you without. MM. Frank had to lock himself in the guest bathroom, overcome with the excitement of knowing that a woman desired him this much, something that hadn't happened since the early years of his relationship with Grace. Rereading the message, he masturbated in the lavatory. Before he'd finished, another one arrived: Do you want my address? MM. When Frank ejaculated, he knew he would answer yes to that question. Because he wanted her address. Because he wanted to enter her again. Because he wanted to continue sampling a new body. Because he was a man. Because as much as he loved his wife, he also desired other women. Other breasts. Other waists. Other ankles. And this was a fact, even if he'd spent years containing it, masturbating every morning in the shower, trying at the start of each day to satisfy the suppressed desire that ate away at him from the inside.

He turned the tap handle to wash the sink, to wash away the sticky discharge that couldn't be so important. What difference did it make if he spilled it in secret into the sink at his house, or in secret into the shower drain, or in secret onto the floor of a sales hut? What did it matter if he spilled it onto another woman's sheets, between her breasts? All he had to do was wash it away as he was doing now, and nothing about his feelings for his wife would change. He would be no less certain he wanted to spend the rest of his life with her. To love her until they were old.

In the end it was several—many—times that he spilled himself on Mara Miller's bed. And in other parts of her apartment. A modern property, high up in one of the towering buildings built when home automation was coming into its own, decked out from top to bottom with voice recognition technology, including the elevator. "I didn't know you motor-home salespeople earned such good money," Frank said the first time he went in.

"Only the best ones," she replied before throwing him against a glass panel to fuck right there, in the living room. They also did it against shiny white walls, against others of bare concrete, in the hot tub on the balcony, or on top of the state-of-the-art appliances integrated into the apartment's design. With Mara, Frank did everything he no longer did with Grace, frolicking for hours like a youngster, or rather, as if he were her age again, not yet thirty. Mara undressed him as soon as he walked through the door because she really lusted after him, unlike Grace, who always asked him to take a shower first. It excited Mara to do it in the kitchen, and even to add an ingredient or two from the cupboard or refrigerator. She sucked him in places he didn't know could be sucked, and her finger went in places previously untouched. On the first afternoon they spent together in the apartment, submerged in the hot tub on a glass-enclosed balcony Frank would have loved to have himself, Mara emerged from the bubbling water with a mischievous look on her face.

"Do you want to make some amateur porn?"

She pointed at the camera in a corner of the ceiling.

"Wow, what you said about your security system was true."

"Good saleswomen never lie. We have a reputation for being the least honest profession in existence, but I know you can go further with the truth than with lies. Always. Though I admit I was economical with the truth when I said I'd installed them because they're cheap—that was a sales ploy to introduce the word *cheap*."

"I knew it."

"These actually come with the apartment. You've seen how modern the building is. We even have hot tubs on the balconies."

"You don't say." He stroked her back under the hot water. "Well, I didn't believe a word you said. Does anyone really install surveillance systems in a motor home?"

"A lot of people do, and what I offered you at the dealership was a bargain. Now, do you want to keep talking about security or shall we make that movie?"

Holding on to Frank to stop herself from slipping, Mara stood up in the hot tub. She rested a foot on the edge, on the side that wouldn't obstruct the shot. She offered him what was between her legs and he savored it like a fruit from which he was extracting all the juice. Afterward, with towels around their waists, they watched the recording on a monitor integrated into the wall at the entrance to the apartment. Frank had never seen himself having sex. In a high-angle shot, he saw himself with his face between her legs. In the grayscale image he saw himself stand up, and he was surprised at how big his erection looked from the side. Seeing the muscles in his legs contract excited him, and the expressions of pleasure on his own face excited him even more. Watching the recording beside him, Mara noticed how his towel was lifting. They knelt right there and started again, on the floor, reaching their second orgasm at the same time they reached their first on the screen.

Once the excitement was over, however, the video's existence didn't seem such a good idea to Frank.

"How do you delete it?" he asked, still naked.

He tried to interact with the touchscreen but, each time he tapped it, a red padlock flashed. His fingers began to tremble—he suddenly couldn't understand how he had allowed himself to be recorded, had provided a stranger with a file that was so dangerous for a married man.

"Relax, I'll do it."

"I'm awful with technology," he said, feigning calm.

"You won't let me keep the video so I can watch it by myself whenever I want?"

"I'd rather not," replied Frank, forcing a smile and an excuse. "I wouldn't want you to get bored of me."

Mara pressed her thumb against a fingerprint reader to unblock the system. Tapping the screen several times, she accessed the saved files, selected them, and deleted them in front of him.

"They delete automatically at midnight, in any case," she explained. "So we'll have to record some more."

Frank, suddenly overcome with regret again, didn't bother to think of a witty response to the suggestion. He left there that first afternoon convinced that he wouldn't reoffend. Just as he did on many future occasions—during the eight months the affair lasted—as he went down in the elevator lit with blue LEDs, repeating to himself that it would be the last time. That he'd satisfied his appetite for a new body. That the fantasies he'd fulfilled with Mara formed a bank of memories he could access during many future masturbations. He would cross the building's entrance hall to the exit certain that what he had with this girl could barely be described as an affair. He wasn't the kind of unfaithful husband he'd criticized so many times, because Mara wasn't his lover. She couldn't be his lover if he didn't have feelings for her. If anything, what he felt when he climbed into his car was a strong desire not to see her ever again. Driving home, he would promise himself he would never again give in to the temptation and would go back to being the old Frank, the one who didn't sleep with another woman in secret. The one who only needed his family to be happy.

Then time passed, the promise lost power, and the feeling that he'd done something bad became diluted, while his desire to see Mara recrystallized. With the same firmness with which he'd persuaded himself he wouldn't succumb again, he now persuaded himself that surrendering to desire was his best option, even for his marriage. It was clear: controlling himself too much could lead to him making the decision to leave Grace once and for all and pursue the dissolute sex life that some part of him longed for. And then the breakup would affect the children. And they would all suffer. As things stood, neither Audrey nor Simon nor Grace would suffer due to the unimportant fact that from time to time he gave himself relief with another woman.

The time he spent with Mara did not take a single second away from his family life—all the time was taken from his work schedule. He treated Grace with the same devotion as ever, with the same affection. He still took the peas one by one from her plate and put them on his, because she liked the combination of the rest of the ingredients in the ready-made rice she always bought. He still slept with his neck twisted every night so that she could stretch her arm out under the pillow. Compared to those gestures devoid of passion but full of love, surrendering to his sexual urges once in a while with some girl meant nothing. There may be a moral rule that says it's not right to cheat on your partner, on your children, but another more important rule was that you shouldn't hurt the people you love. If he kept quiet, Frank wasn't hurting anyone. Telling Grace the truth would have been like opening up a wound in her soul through which all her goodness would spill out. It would also discredit all the advice she had given her YouTube subscribers in years of videos, as an expert in marital happiness. And it would set a terrible example for the children. Each time Frank's reasoning reached this point, he called Mara again. He told her it was work that prevented him from seeing her more often—he didn't want her to know of Grace's existence. That way, his deceit of his wife seemed less significant, and it prevented any future complications. Not that it seemed as if things would become complicated with Mara, who didn't appear to be developing feelings for him. They were just two adults enjoying sex when the opportunity arose. And although the opportunity kept arising, whenever Frank dialed her number, he promised himself it would be the last time, that he had to stop calling her.

But he had stopped calling her and it had not worked. Because Mara was still there, present in his life, ruining his summer, and now sleeping outside, a few feet from his family and the motor home she'd sold them. Things had become much more complicated than he had foreseen. Everything always proves to be more complicated than it first seems.

The affair Frank thought he had ended had followed him. And with her presence she was forcing him to confess his darkest secret. As much as he tried to escape to the other side of the country, he wasn't going to be able to distance himself from the terrible past in which he was the worst husband in the world, the most despicable man ever to have existed.

Frank shifted under the sheets, restless, with Grace's arm stretched out under the pillow. He felt disgusted at himself for sharing a bed with his wife while remembering his sexual encounters with Mara. Everything he'd done with Mara. He separated his body from Grace, his back from her stomach, as if he might soil her with his corrupt skin. Poison her with his perverse morality.

Lulled by the crickets' chirping, Frank had a revelation. He would confess. Tell Grace everything. As he should have done from the beginning. If only he had. He still could. Right now. He could wake her and explain to her who the girl they almost ran over was. Confess what happened. And between the two of them, they could make a decision that would minimize the impact, especially on the children.

"And ruin my entire life . . ."

The words, barely audible, escaped in a sleepy outbreath. Drowsy, Frank cursed his situation. He cursed the plan to use this road, the moment when the RV ran into Mara. He also cursed his skill in swerving away from her, because everything would be much simpler had he not done so. Killing her would have been much more convenient.

Intermittent currents of air whistled as they found their way in through the cracks in the motor home. On the verge of falling asleep, Frank stopped censuring his thoughts.

If only he had killed her.

If only she were dead.

19.

Grace opened her eyes the moment dawn broke. The little light that filtered into the motor home was enough to wake her. She got out of bed before her first blink.

"Frank." She knotted the belt on her robe while putting on slippers. "Wake up, Frank, it's light."

With a knee on the mattress, she kissed him on the temple, where she kissed him in the mornings to avoid his breath.

"I know, I've barely slept."

Her husband didn't have the dry lips or puffy eyes he typically had when he woke. The smoothness of his face suggested he'd only been asleep a short while, but his grimace revealed exhaustion.

"I'm not surprised you didn't sleep, with all this going on." Grace smoothed down his eyebrows. "But the problems will be over today. As soon as we find the cell phones."

"Yeah, the cell phones . . ."

"Come on, get searching." She slapped the bed. "Who's going to check how our guest slept?"

She used the word on purpose, to make light of the situation, as if it were a visiting friend sleeping in the tent.

"I'll go," he said.

"And then I'll make a delicious breakfast for everyone."

Grace wanted to cheer Frank up—he seemed worried. He was only half up, sitting on the edge of the bed, his elbows resting on his knees. He looked at her over his shoulder.

"That's great, honey."

She heard him sigh as she left the bedroom. She woke the children on the sofa by rubbing their legs under the bedspread, apologizing that it was so early. She reminded Simon to change into his day patch as soon as he'd washed his face. One of Audrey's hands searched for something on the arm of the sofa, the place where she would have left her cell phone during the night if she'd had it. Even lying down, her shoulders slumped at the disappointment of not finding it there.

"That's why I've woken you up, sweetie," said Grace, "so we can all go look for the phones now that there's some light."

She caught Simon's foot and shook it until she heard him laugh.

Then she opened the door and descended the retractable steps.

With the branches and needles damp with the dawn, she could almost feel the dense pine aroma on her skin like a cool, fragrant lotion that revives the spirit. Grace breathed it in several times, allowing herself to be purified. With each breath, the situation they found themselves in seemed a little less serious. In a world that offered such a pure smell, nothing could be all bad in the end. That was why the sun, peeking over the horizon, was turning dewdrops into sparkling pale-yellow diamonds encrusted on the immense jewel that was the forest at sunrise.

Stretching, Grace felt as optimistic as the promise of a new summer's day. A refreshing current of air crept under her robe, between the buttons on her pajamas. She interrupted her stretching when she saw a plastic zip tie attached to the zipper on the tent. Connected to the structure's upper rod, it secured the opening.

"Frank?"

Her suspicion escaped from her mouth as a whisper. But her husband wouldn't do anything like this. Why would he imprison the girl? It was one thing wanting to protect his family by not allowing a stranger to sleep in the same room, it was quite another to cage her like a wild animal. It had to be an optical illusion. Grace walked toward the tent, her footsteps muffled by the soles of her slippers. When she reached it, she was no longer in any doubt. It was a zip tie. She considered whether Mara had put it on herself, to lock herself away from any dangers outside. Bears, perhaps. But bears neither know how to open zippers nor would bother to do so if they wanted to eat a camper—they would just rip the tent open with their claws. And she would have attached the zip tie to the zipper pull inside, not on the outside.

"Grace?"

She gave a start when she heard her name. Frank poked his head out the door.

"I told you I'd go see her. You come here."

Grace pressed her lips together. The rubber on her soles didn't muffle the anger in her footsteps now as she returned to the RV.

"How could you do that to her?"

"Do what?" Franks eyes opened too wide. "What happened?"

The specter of a suppressed smile visited his face for an instant.

"We have to take it off."

"What're you talking about, honey? Has something happened to her?"

"It's almost like you want something to happen to her, asking like that."

Grace elbowed her way past her husband in the doorway.

"We have to take it off before the poor girl wakes up and tries to get out." Climbing onto the sofa where the kids were still lying, she opened the first kitchen drawer. "Before she realizes you've penned her in like a wild animal. That's if she didn't try to get out in the night to take a pee . . . Oh, how embarrassing, Frank."

"I . . . I don't know what you're talking about, seriously."

She decided to attribute the tremble in her husband's voice to his sleepiness.

From outside, Mara's voice reached them. "Hello? Can you hear me? I can't get out."

In the kitchen, Grace gestured at the tent through the window. The structure shook with each frustrated tug on the zipper.

"I'm talking about that. You locked her in."

"Me?"

His surprise seemed genuine. She showed him the scissors she'd taken from the drawer and told him to go with her. They walked back to the tent together.

"Morning, Mara," Grace said. "It appears the zipper's stuck. Give us a minute."

She passed the scissors to Frank, ordering him in sign language to cut the zip tie. As soon as he'd done it, she snatched everything from him and hid it in the pocket of her pajama shirt, covered by the robe. The zipper lowered with a buzz. Mara emerged with tangled hair.

"It was stuck," Grace apologized. "The tent's new, looks like the zipper pull doesn't run very smoothly yet. How did you sleep?"

Mara looked first at Frank, with her eyelids half-closed, and Grace knew she hadn't believed the lie about the zipper. After Frank's excessively cautious behavior the night before, Mara must have guessed why the tent wouldn't open and who would've been responsible for taking such a precaution.

"I slept well," she told Grace, smiling. "There's nothing like a night in the wild to ease the pain of a broken heart. This peace is just what I came here looking for."

Grace touched the butterfly bandages over her eyebrow.

"This looks very good." She pressed on the ends to make sure they were stuck down. "Does anything hurt on your body?"

"No, not on my body."

Grace understood that she was afflicted by other pains, that they just weren't physical.

"Right, well, I'll take those pains away now with some breakfast," she said.

From inside the RV, the children asked for help to fold up the sofa bed.

"You go," she said to Frank. His frown revealed a reluctance to leave her alone with Mara—her husband really was harboring the ridiculous suspicion that the girl was dangerous. "Go on, they need your help."

This time he obeyed, but before going into the vehicle, from the steps, he gave Mara a threatening look.

"I'm sorry, really," whispered Grace. "You shouldn't have to put up with this kind of suspicion. I don't know why he's so worried about this situation."

"And the zipper wasn't stuck, right?" Mara asked. "He secured it."

Grace confirmed it by lowering her head. "Honestly, I'm so embarrassed." She felt her cheeks flush hot. "I'm so sorry."

"It doesn't matter, seriously. I can understand a man taking certain measures to protect his family." Mara touched Grace's elbow. "What gives me the shivers is thinking I spent the night in there locked up in the tent with a plastic zip tie, like one of those bags they put dead bodies in."

"Oh, don't say that."

The image gave Grace the shivers, too, and she shook her shoulders to get rid of them.

20.

Frank left the motor home with the children as soon as he'd finished folding up the sofa. He didn't want Grace alone with Mara.

"Where should we start looking for the cell phones?" asked Simon. Dressed in a T-shirt and jogger shorts, he'd put on the patch printed with monarch butterflies. "Because I've only got one eye and I have to choose the right place to look."

"You're going to look everywhere," Audrey replied, tying the laces on her sneakers with enthusiasm, eager to start the search. She was wearing gray leggings and a vest with a smiling emoji on the chest. "We have to find them."

"I hit the brakes over there, so they could be anywhere in that area." Frank glanced at Mara, as furtive a look as the first ones they exchanged at the dealership. They both knew that, as hard as the kids tried to find the phones, they would never appear. He gestured toward a long stretch of the road while announcing the inevitable: "At any rate, I don't think it's going to be easy to find them. They could have flown a long way— they might be in the bushes, or broken from the impact."

"Don't dishearten your kids. Those cell phones are here somewhere," Grace cut in.

"I'm sure they'll find them," Mara added.

Fury gripped Frank's stomach.

"And if need be, I'll go rooting through those weeds—no problem," said Audrey. "Come on, Si, you go right and I'll go left."

"It's the dampness that's the problem. Even if they turn up, they're not going to work if they've spent the night on the ground or among the plants. I don't know if there's much point in wasting time." Frank hated having to lie to his children. "Look how much dew there is everywhere."

Audrey gave him a proud smile. "Mine's waterproof, so that's not a problem."

"And mine has fingerprint recognition," Simon said to her.

"Oooh, how revolutionary! Dude, even coffeemakers have that nowadays."

They both laughed.

"At least your dad thought to put them in a ziplock, so they're protected. They'll work, for sure." Grace reproached Frank with her eyes for dispiriting the children in such a way. "I'm going to make breakfast while you search. Let's see if I have time to get it ready before you find them. And you can go look for your car key, Mara—that'll definitely work. It can't have gone far if you had it in your hand when . . ."

She cleared her throat to omit the first words that came to mind, words Frank knew would be *we hit you.*

". . . when you appeared on the road," she ended up saying.

While Mara joined the kids on an expedition that would come to nothing, Grace took Frank by the wrist and pulled him into the kitchen.

From the refrigerator she took eggs, milk. From the cupboards, cereals, a frying pan, cups. She turned the knob on a burner and held her ear close to make sure the gas was coming out.

"There're two new cylinders," Frank reminded her.

"Why did you shut her in?"

"It wasn't me, honey. Honestly, it wasn't."

"So why was she so surprised from not knowing what was happening? Why would she shut herself in with something that kept her from getting out?" Grace was cracking eggs against the edge of a bowl,

139

the shells breaking up between her fingers from too much force. "After an accident like hers, the poor girl told me she felt as if she'd spent the night in a body bag, as if she hadn't survived the accident, locked in with that zip tie you put on there."

Mara couldn't have known it was a zip tie that had secured the zipper unless she'd put it on there herself. He and Grace had cut it and hidden it before she came out of the tent. But Frank already knew that. Of course it had been her—he didn't even have zip ties in the motor home. And he also knew what Mara's intention was: precisely to create this disagreement between Grace and him. To make him look like the liar only his lover knew he was. The zip tie, the imprisonment, was to fuel suspicion of a lack of honesty between Frank and Grace. Which was exactly what Mara had come here to do. That piece of plastic was a symbol, a reminder that Frank had to accept the implications of his actions. Though furious that Mara's lesson had worked so perfectly, that she had sent him her message in such a subtle but devastating way, Frank knew it would be easier to admit his false guilt.

"All right, well, forgive *me* for wanting to protect my family."

Grace stopped the fork she was beating the eggs with.

"I knew it." She blew out with her disappointment at being deceived. She diverted her eyes to the chopping board, unable to look at the husband she never expected to lie. "I don't like you lying to me, Frank. I don't like it at all. What will we become if we can't trust each other implicitly?"

They would become something horrible. And that was why Grace couldn't know the truth—or all the lies—about him. She wasn't ready. It would hurt her too much, and she didn't deserve to suffer.

"I'm sorry, honey."

He tried to kiss her on the cheek but she bent down to pick something up.

"Go on, go find those cell phones."

Frank apologized again and went out. Audrey and Simon were bent over, combing the road, the light from the sun growing ever brighter. He crouched down like his children, rekindling an old pain in his lower back. Only by suffering like his kids could he ease the sinking feeling it gave him to see them working so hard at something that would never end in success.

"My car key!" yelled Mara.

The children turned their heads, the loud voice alerting them, but they returned their attention to the road as soon as they heard that she hadn't found a cell phone. Frank did approach Mara, relieved. Having the key could change the situation. Maybe he could persuade her to leave his family in peace, that they could resolve the problems between them without harming anyone else. When he was within a pace of her, Mara showed him what she had in her hand.

"Oh no, it's just a stone," she said.

She gave him a look similar to the one she'd given him the day she'd pretended to be surprised to find that the document she'd used as an excuse to draw him to the dealership had, in fact, been signed. In the smirk she gave as she threw away the little rock that looked nothing like a key, Frank could see how much she was enjoying toying with him, whether with a zip tie or a stone. He had to clench his jaw to prevent himself from opening his mouth and separate himself from her to avoid giving in to any other instincts.

He fled to where Simon was and helped him search while Audrey despaired a few paces in front of them. They continued their fruitless search until Grace announced that breakfast was ready.

They served it outside, by the door, on their folding camp table. They didn't bother to extend the awning. Mara ate one of Grace's omelets with relish, barely breathing between mouthfuls. It turned Frank's stomach to see her sitting at the table as an unwanted guest at one of the family breakfasts he cherished as some of the best and most intimate occasions he shared with his wife and kids. Grace, Simon, and Audrey, his most precious gifts, couldn't share a table with the woman who represented his worst vices. It was such an indecent scene, so wrong, that Frank lost his appetite. He had to sip coffee to help down the food, which fought its way with difficulty through his tight esophagus while Mara chewed merrily, cutting pieces of omelet with her fork and feeding them into her mouth before she'd swallowed the previous mouthful. Sickened by the churn of her mouth as she ate, all Frank wanted to do was get rid of her.

"Feeling better now, huh?" he asked her when she'd finished. "You and I could walk to the main road, now that you have all this energy from breakfast. We'd reach the phone at the restaurant in about four hours."

"Seriously, Frank?" Grace moved a bowl of Froot Loops closer to Simon so the drops of milk he spilled with each spoonful didn't go on the table. "How's she going to walk for four hours?"

"No chance," Mara added. "So I'm not going to be able to go yet. How annoying. Unless you can think of anything else we could do."

The slanted smile that wrapped up the sentence reminded him there was the option to confess.

"There's no need to do anything crazy—the keys will show up as soon as we start searching again," said Grace.

"Or even better, the cell phones will." Audrey was picking at pieces of bell pepper in her omelet. "I haven't been able to post photos of anything that's happened."

"More coffee, Mara?"

While Grace filled their cups, Frank thought about walking to the main road by himself. Leaving the family alone with Mara for four hours certainly wasn't an appealing option. He sipped his hot coffee while he weighed whether his wife could go with him. No, that would mean leaving their children with a stranger. Perhaps it could be Grace who went by herself, while he would stay to look after the children and watch over the intruder. A stupid idea—no husband would make

142

his wife walk for hours like that. He swallowed with difficulty as he pondered whether Simon was old enough to walk such a distance. He was too young, without a doubt, but perhaps Audrey wasn't. But what kind of father would send his teenage daughter off alone down a road in search of help? Having exhausted every possibility, Frank set his cup on the tablecloth with such force that he splashed his arm.

"Goddamn!" He slapped the table as he stood. Turning away from his family, he looked down the road as far as he could see. "Doesn't anybody ever come this way?"

The trees, the earth, and the mountain muffled his furious yelling, silencing it like an unwanted interruption in the harmonic melody of the birdsong and the whisper of the trees.

"You said yourself it was Idaho's best kept secret," he heard Simon say.

21.

Sitting on a chair by the side of the road, now dressed in his polo shirt and chinos from the day before, Frank unfolded the road map he'd found in the motor home's document folder. It was a plastic folder decorated with the same logo that was embroidered into Mara's uniform, the one that ended up down at their ankles that day in the hut. Frank opened his legs and extended his arms to spread the paper out. Looking over the edge, he was able to keep watch on Mara, who was sweeping around the tent with a broom as if it were her home, as if she intended to install herself there for some time. Frank grew anxious when he imagined the lengths to which Mara could go to have her revenge. He searched the map for the nearest towns, trying to imagine from which one it was most likely somebody would come.

"Is that what maps used to be like?" asked Audrey.

She'd penetrated the thicketed ditch at the roadside, the vegetation reaching her waist.

"Yes, sweetie, it is," he replied, struggling to keep the enormous sheet of paper taut. "This is what they were like."

"And how do you find the places? Where do you enter the address?"

"They don't work like Google Maps. You have to search for the right square using the rows and columns that—"

"Shut up, shut up, I don't want to know." Audrey wiped the sweat from her forehead with her wrist. Her hands were full of torn stems. "I was born in the era of cell phones. And that's why I want my cell phone."

She threw away the handfuls of vegetation and continued the search, making her way through the undergrowth like a farmer harvesting crops. Simon had accepted his father's pessimistic prediction as a certainty, giving up on the phones when they finished combing the road surface as far as it would have been feasible for the handsets to fly. At any rate, the boy only wanted his cell phone to keep leveling up in his video game, and now he'd discovered that the road offered other entertainment options that were just as fun. After collecting stones, branches, and pine cones, he was erecting a castle next to the RV. Having lain the foundations, he went off looking for new construction materials around the area. When he went up to Mara, Frank lowered his map.

"Do you want this?" She offered him a peg from the tent. "You could use it as a flagpole."

"Thanks, but I want to build it just with things from the forest."

Simon tried to push away the tool Mara was holding out to him but miscalculated, his hand cutting through the air.

"It's my three-D vision," he explained. "I'm still getting used to it."

"What happened?"

The map's paper crackled when Frank's fists squeezed shut.

"A medical thing," Simon replied.

It was the answer his parents had taught him to give. With that, the boy walked away and collected dry pine cones scattered around the road. On the opposite side, Audrey groaned.

"I pricked myself on something!" She put a finger in her mouth. "And I'm getting filthy with these plants! Some kind of milk comes out of them when I cut them!"

She showed Frank her dirty, sticky hands. Blades of grass were stuck to her skin, which seemed glazed with glue. Petals from yellow, white, and purple flowers decorated her forearms. Audrey sneezed. Then she cried out, angry at nature in general.

"Quit searching, honey. It's not worth it."

Grace came out of the motor home, alerted by their voices. Discovering that the racket was just Audrey having a tantrum, she positioned herself next to Frank's chair. She stroked the back of his neck, closing the book on her anger over the zip tie.

"Sooner or later someone'll have to come by here." The way the sentence trembled in her throat betrayed a certain amount of doubt as to whether it would really happen. "And if no one does, luckily we have a house right here and enough food for a week if needed."

"I'll die," Audrey said from amid the bushes. "If we're going to be here for a week, I'll die. I'm not Mabel Pines from *Gravity Falls*. Look how my first day in the wild's going."

She showed them her dirty arms.

"We're not going to be here seven days," said Frank.

Grace considered Mara, as well. Raising her voice, she suggested to Frank that he help Mara sweep, that she shouldn't be exerting herself unnecessarily.

"It's fine. It'll keep me busy and make the time pass more quickly." Mara rested her gaze on Frank. "Until your husband decides when we're leaving this place."

"If only it was up to him," said Grace, unaware of the hidden dialogue between them. "But on this occasion, we're in fate's hands. Are you OK? Really?"

"Seriously," Mara assured her. "A bit weak, nothing else."

"Is there something I can . . . we can do to help you feel better? Anything."

Mara's expression darkened, as it had each time she made a malicious remark.

"Do these RVs have a bathtub?" she asked. "I could really use a hot bath, get rid of all the dirt from last night."

There was the venom. The provocation, the lie. She knew full well what there was or wasn't in a motor home—she'd been selling them for years.

"I guess we all like hot baths—that's why we were on our way to the hot springs, right?" Grace noted. "But all I can offer you in there is a shower. I don't think there are RVs with a bathtub. Did you see any that had one on the internet?" she asked Frank. "Or when you went to buy it at the dealership?"

His offense at the way Mara was mocking him, mocking his wife, prevented him from articulating a single word. He just shook his head.

"But hey, the Idaho guide said there're still a lot of unknown hot springs in these forests," Grace went on. "So who knows, we might have a huge natural bathtub right there and we don't even know about it. If you want to go take a look . . ."

"I'll make do with a shower," Mara concluded.

Grace invited her to go into the motor home, but Frank went in before them. He earned an admonishing look from his wife for his paranoia about the stranger being dangerous. He justified his presence by turning on the water pump so the shower would have pressure, but Grace reminded him that everything was ready, and the boiler was also on—she'd just washed the dishes.

"It looks even bigger and nicer in the daytime." Mara contemplated the living room with her mouth open, exaggerating a false amazement that irritated Frank. "It must be lovely traveling with your family in a remote place like this," she said to Grace. "You and your loved ones, lost amid nature, without needing anything else. How lovely. If only I had the chance. You're a beautiful family and you have a wonderful life."

Frank wished he could tell her to shut up.

"Well, we have our bad patches, too, you know," said Grace, opening up to this stranger who was laughing at her. "I told you a little last night. And the most recent thing was . . . an accident involving the boy." She finished in a whisper, as if lowering her voice would make what happened less serious.

"The eye?"

"Yeah, a terrible thing," murmured Grace.

Frank could sense his wife trying hard not to look at him, so her eyes wouldn't betray her and reveal that she still blamed her husband, as much as she insisted to him that it had been an unfortunate accident.

"But there he is, running around." Mara gestured at Simon through the kitchen window. "He seems happy, healthy."

"He's a very brave boy," Frank broke in.

He took a towel from a cupboard, remembering they were there to use the bathroom, not chat about his family life and his son. Mara accepted it with a slanted smile.

"And you can't complain about your husband, either," she said to Grace. "Finding a good man isn't easy these days."

"That I have no doubts about—I've been very lucky in love. I even make a living from telling people how good we have it." Grace kissed him on a shoulder, rubbed his chest as if bragging about what a good husband he was. "And you? Have you been unlucky with guys? If we're going to spend this much time together we may as well get to know each other."

"Very unlucky," answered Mara, keeping her eyes on Frank's.

"You'll find the right man," Grace said, with the ease with which one wishes somebody else something one has achieved. "And we'll go out so you can make yourself at home. The bathroom's the door on the right. It's a normal shower, there's no trick to it. If you need help, just yell."

"It's my first time in a motor-home bathroom. I hope I don't slip."

Frank's saliva soured.

"Don't worry, it's so tight in there you can't fall," Grace said before going out.

Outside, Frank struggled to breathe. The effort of remaining passive in the face of so much provocation, so many veiled insults aimed at him and his wife, was turning into a knot of anxiety that compressed his chest.

"Are you all right?" asked Grace. "You don't look too good."

"Do you think it's safe to leave her alone in there?" he asked, blaming his unease on his concern for their safety. "With all our belongings?"

Grace held her hands to her cheeks as if she were Munch's *The Scream*.

"Oh no! She's going to steal the iPad!" she joked.

She burst out laughing, but the pressure in Frank's chest only increased.

22.

Mara looked at herself in the mirror. She didn't like the face she saw, her dark expression. It didn't belong to her. The pearl gray of her eyes that had always defined her unusual beauty was now a concrete gray. A sewer gray. She gripped the sink, fearing the onset of another panic attack. The kind that had besieged her since she found herself unable to cope with Frank abandoning her, since the bastard changed her forever. With his selfishness. His lies. With his lack of humanity. With the way he left her, as if she were disposable, just a girl he'd fucked a few times and now wanted to disappear. A secret to be ashamed of, to hide like a cat buries its excrement. An embarrassment to run far away from, taking his perfect family with him. His two children. His wife. The same wife he never remembered when they rolled around naked on the floor of her apartment. The same wife Frank did not have the decency to mention until Mara discovered the truth herself. He had always maintained the lie he told at the dealership, that he was divorced, but one Sunday afternoon Mara was spending on the sofa browsing YouTube, out of curiosity she clicked on a channel about marital happiness. The channel was called *Gracefully* and, judging by the titles of the videos and thumbnail images, she guessed it would be one of those channels where a satisfied wife recorded, edited, and shared her exemplary life with thousands of subscribers. This woman, for good measure, was called Grace, guided toward perfection from the day she was born. This kind of channel was the very opposite of what Mara would normally consume. After what had happened with her parents, she'd never believed in partnership or love—sex, yes, she believed in that, as an absolute and indisputable pleasure that always worked, provided it wasn't complicated by feelings or false promises. But she wasn't above taking pleasure in spying on the lives of people who repulsed her, so she played some of *Gracefully's* videos. The first recounted the youngest son's visit to the dentist. In the next one, Grace was making her own Christmas decorations. *Amazing.*

In the third video, Mara saw Grace's husband bringing her breakfast in bed on her birthday while the children jumped on the sheets to wake her up. When she saw the face of the man carrying the tray of toast, eggs, orange juice, and a flower, the laptop slid off Mara's knees.

Now she turned the faucet in the RV's bathroom. She splashed water on the back of her neck. Remembering Frank's first lie triggered a torrent of thoughts that usually ended in a panic attack.

The crisis the day before in the rest stop bathroom had been major, and she didn't want it to happen again. Or to throw up again. She regretted the way she'd responded to that lady, how unpleasant she'd been to the daughter, who wasn't to blame for anything. Brit and Bree. We all deserve a clean restroom. She looked at herself in the motor home's mirror in the same way she'd looked at herself the day before: disgusted. Struggling to recognize herself in the reflection, searching those eyes for the self she'd started losing as a result of Frank's deception. The deception that turned her into something she had never wanted to be. Into the other woman. The lover. The other women. The lovers.

The fling she thought she had been having with a divorced man was, in reality, a prolonged affair behind the back of a wife who loved him, perhaps as much as her mother had loved her father until she discovered the truth about him. With his lie, Frank had turned Mara into one of the women who had ended her mother's life, women she detested even though they were not really to blame for anything.

Only her father was to blame. It was he who sneaked out in search of other kisses, other embraces, other bodies, while her mother merely loved him blindly through more than thirty years of infidelities. Three decades of lies that stripped their marriage, their family, and their entire past of any meaning when the truth finally came to light. Because truth never dies. Even if you kill it. Truth always emerges. Even if you drown it.

One of those lovers had revealed the truth about Dad, who in thirty full years had never mustered the integrity to be honest with the woman who most deserved it. The disclosure of that affair was followed by others, so many that Mom was unable to find a single year of their marriage, not even the first, when she had not shared her husband with other women. And the life she had lived then seemed so false to her that she no longer wanted to live it. She said goodbye to Mara with an apology, asking her to make sure that no man ever made her feel as miserable as her father had made her mother feel. She wrote it in a note she left on the bedside table under two empty brown bottles. Mom died faceup on her side of the bed, the other half as empty as it had always been, even when Dad slept beside her.

From the moment Mara discovered that Frank was married, all she could think about was her mother. And then also Grace, the woman who sang her husband's praises in the videos on her channel, both in the glimpses of their everyday life she recorded with him and in the profound confessions she made in some private part of the house, speaking directly to the camera, to her subscribers. Disgusted with Frank, with herself, with men, with the entire world, Mara thought that fate had perhaps given her the opportunity to rewrite Mom's story through Grace. For this to happen, Grace had to receive the confession from Frank that mom never received from her husband. It had to be Frank who confessed—Mara wouldn't tell his wife. That afternoon, she had called Frank. When she mentioned *Gracefully* and what she'd discovered, he told her not to contact him again. He hung up without saying goodbye. Mara kept calling that Sunday, that entire week. She sent dozens of messages demanding that he confess. One day her call no longer got through, her messages bounced back. Frank had blocked her number. That was when she visited him at the hotel where he worked, until security asked her to leave. She also started walking past his house, looking at him from outside, from his yard, leaning against the motor home she had sold him, as he ate dinner with his family and got up from the table to close the curtains so he could no longer see her. Silent, rational pressure got her nowhere, so Mara had to change tack. Pressure him in some other way. And then the situation turned ugly. So ugly it brought her to this remote road with a knife in her purse so she could once and for all make Frank face up to the consequences of his actions.

Mara touched the butterfly bandages over her eyebrow. The wound was clean, it didn't hurt. Her stomach bothered her more. Swallowing the car key had been an extreme measure, but she'd thought of no other way out. Frank had started being a jerk with the idea of going to find her car, and his next movement would've been to search her. She'd seen it in his eyes. He wanted her out of the RV, any way possible. And if he'd searched her purse, he would've found the knife. The emergency weapon she'd brought with her in case things got complicated, though she never thought she'd end up using it. But she did end up using it. It was useful for puncturing the tires, preventing them from leaving.

The accident was an unforeseen event that altered the nature of the encounter and forced her to improvise. Everything could have been much simpler. Her initial plan had been to ask for help, for the family to come across a woman needing assistance in a peaceful place like this. It would have gained her access to the RV to watch Frank stew—with her in front of him—in his own simmering conscience, like a human body cooking in boiling, sulfur-infused thermal waters. But instead they almost ran her over. The blow to the head when she hit the ground hurt, and the blood filling her eyes frightened her. Then the plan became more difficult to execute, to the point that she had to swallow her own car key. Lucky it wasn't one of the bigger ones.

Had he searched her, had he found the knife in her purse, it would have been easy for Frank to prove she'd cut the tires. That they hadn't burst by themselves, as he'd told his family—a lie that surprised Mara but that she quickly understood. Frank didn't want to make her angry. Or for the situation to get out of hand. Just as he had closed his living-room curtains so many times to stop seeing her in the yard outside, instead of going out to send her away and arousing his family's suspicion. Frank wanted to buy time—he knew she could reveal the truth at any moment, that one false move could make her talk.

Mara herself sometimes wondered why she didn't just come out with it. Why she didn't stop messing around and reveal everything in front of the wife. She wanted to spare the children the experience—they shouldn't have to suffer because of their father. Or maybe they should. The truth is always worth knowing. But this truth was dirty work Frank had to do. He was the one who had to be honest. That responsibility couldn't fall on her, too. Or maybe it should. Maybe she should tell. Mara hadn't been thinking straight lately—she'd lost her sense of justice, of punishment. Mom had repeated to her several times that if only it had been Dad who had confessed, the truth would have hurt less.

But Mara, after being denied time after time, was like a bomb with a lit fuse. A fuse of an unknown length that was already smelling of gunpowder. Little detonations were warning signals of the imminent final explosion. One of those warnings had been when she'd stuck her fingers in the food-truck power socket. She must be pretty crazy to do something like that. Or badly hurt. The truth was, she hadn't thought the electric shock would hurt so much. Just as she didn't know, when the boy behind the counter had helped her, that taking his hand would transmit the electricity to him. Poor guy. He'd been so kind, giving her a free burger, worrying about her well-being. And she'd thanked him with a short circuit that left him shaking on the floor. When the boy regained his senses, his overweight coworker at the grill had berated her, called her crazy, a drunk, a junkie, while she fled home, crying in the rain, trembling from shock and cursing the fact that a man, Frank, had managed to make her feel so miserable. Exactly what Mom had asked her never to allow.

Still gripping the sink, she felt a stomach cramp shift the key in her intestines. Mara imagined it scrambled up with the wife's omelet, still only half digested. Egg. Tomato. Peppers. Ham. And chia seeds. It worried her to think how she would evacuate it, whether it would hurt as much as the time she and Frank had tried doing it differently. As well-endowed as he was, the experience had frightened her as much as it thrilled her. At first it hurt quite a lot, but then they both enjoyed it until orgasm. When they'd finished, from behind her on the bed Frank admitted it was one of the things he had never been able to do with his earlier lovers. And she asked him never to blame women for his own sexual dissatisfaction. And to please never blame a woman for any other defect or deficiency of his own—it was a terrible habit men had. In spite of everything, remembering that experience triggered an inappropriate flash of excitement in her belly. She squeezed her eyes shut, as if it would stop images of that encounter from entering her mind. And stop other images. Her apartment. The hot tub. The amateur porn. The honey. She pulled on her hair as punishment for feeling even a tiny trace of attraction to Frank. For desiring an undesirable man. A pathetic excuse for a man in whose eyes, last night, she had recognized, for an instant, the same flash of desire. So brief, so powerful. Mara tugged hard on her hair. Once. Twice. Until her burning scalp finally distracted her from the pain that thinking about Frank inflicted on her.

She removed the pajama top, avoiding the butterfly bandages on her eyebrow. She appreciated the warm aroma that came off the clothes and imagined Grace giving off this innocent smell in the double bed she shared with Frank, filling the entire bedroom with it. How unexciting such a smell would be for him. The smell of baby. Of cuddly toy. Of home life and nights of boredom in the suburbs. She let the pajama pants drop to her ankles, and she also dropped her panties, her bra. The bright red of the scrape near her navel had turned dark. In the bathroom she recognized elements from another bathroom, the one at Frank's house, which she had visited on a few occasions. The towels with embroidered initials. The perfumed toilet paper with flower-shaped perforations. The mesh sponge hanging from the shower faucet. On the floor, the gigantic pink bottle of the wife's shampoo: Pure Seduction, a kitsch Victoria's Secret product with a gold lid and extracts of red plum and freesia. When she saw it in the bathroom at the house, it struck her as an extravagance—in the limited space of the motor home it seemed grotesque.

In the shower she discovered something worse, even tackier than the gold lid on the plum shampoo. In two corners of the enclosure, there were units separating bathroom products into *His* and *Hers*. It was written in adhesive letters on each of the shelves. Grace's contained more bottles of hair treatment, as well as tubs of face mask made from exotic ingredients—pineapple, coconut, papaya—a pumice stone, another mesh sponge, a large lilac bar of soap, and a multipurpose gel labeled *For Kids* that must have been for the little boy. On Frank's shelf, as if it were a bad comic strip on the difference between men's and women's personal care, there was just a razor and a somber bar of dark-brown soap. Pine tar, no doubt. She held her nose to it and identified its characteristic smell of burned wood. So masculine. So stale. So old-man-ish. Seeing the razor and the bar of soap together gave Mara an idea. She searched in the cupboard behind the mirror. In the side compartments. In the drawers under the sink. Until she found a box of replacement blades.

She buried one of the blades in Frank's soap.

She remolded the soap to hide it inside the bar, though the edge would poke out again as soon as it was used. She imagined where he would rub the soap when he showered. Some basic, malevolent instinct hoped he'd be applying it to his crotch when the razor emerged. Castration as an exemplary punishment for the unfaithful male. That he'd cut off his testicles. His penis. That he'd find blood on his fingers, between his legs, like a first period. That this would make him understand some of the suffering involved in simply being a woman.

She returned the soap with the razor hidden in it to the corner caddy.

She smiled as she read the adhesive letters: *His*.

"Yours," she whispered.

Two blows on the wall outside shook the room.

"You taking a shower or what?" yelled Frank.

"Don't worry, Mara, take as long as you want," Grace added.

She heard them argue in whispers on the other side of the translucent window. And she smiled. She opened the shower door. She turned the faucet full to the left and got under the water, which was so hot it turned the enclosure into a cloud of steam. She clenched her teeth, enjoying the pain on her skin. The back of her neck burned, her fingernails burned. When she began to get dizzy, she turned the faucet as far as it would go the other way. The freezing water left her breathless.

23.

Frank walked away from Grace. He had no desire to continue arguing, much less due to Mara—that was what she wanted. He wandered around the RV, taking deep breaths. Passing the tent, he saw Mara's purse inside. He stopped. Inside that purse would be the knife, and he didn't want it near his children. And the car key, if she hadn't swallowed it as he suspected she had. But her cell phone would also be in there, and he could use it to call 911 right now. She had used it as a flashlight the night before—it was the only one she didn't end up throwing into the forest. Frank swept his gaze around him, locating his family: Audrey was still looking for the phones in the undergrowth, Simon was failing in his attempt to fold the map and restore it to its original form, and Grace was out of sight behind the vehicle, where the bathroom window he'd just banged on was. None of them were paying any attention to him. Frank walked around the tent as if checking its structure. He stretched the fabric out, pushed the pegs in. He knelt at the door, pretending to examine the zipper mechanism. He stretched out his arm, the only part of his body that penetrated the tent. With two fingers, he reached the purse strap and pulled on it, dragging it out. It was heavy. With sweaty hands, as if he were a pickpocket, he lifted one corner of the flap. Then the other.

"Frank!"

His wife's whispered cry sounded like the cry of a police officer arresting that pickpocket he felt like. Grace knelt and snatched the purse from him.

"I wanted . . . I wanted to make sure we're not in danger, check she's not hiding anything in there."

"This is unbelievable."

"Come on, open it, let's see."

"No, Frank, this isn't how we do things." She closed the fasteners on the flap. "Do you know how private the contents of a woman's purse are?"

"Mom, please, stop saying those things." Audrey had moved her search to this side of the road. "Stop promoting stereotypes about women, their femininity, and their purses."

"And you stop listening in on your parents' conversations. Get back to where you were, go on," Grace said. "And stop pulling weeds up, look at the state you're in."

Audrey crossed the road, ruffling Simon's map as she passed him. Grace put the purse back inside the tent, rearranging the strap into a casual shape on the ground. She instructed Frank to get up and return with her to the other side of the RV. They could hear the shower through the bathroom window. It was still running with the same intensity.

"She's going to use up all the hot water," said Audrey.

"Our boiler's tankless," Frank clarified.

"But what can be used up is the water," noted Grace. "And if we're going to end up spending a few days here, we should ration it."

"Shut up, Mom, we're not going to spend a few days here."

"Doesn't bother me!" said Simon.

"What if she fainted?" Grace scraped her fingertip against the end of her eyebrow. "From the bruise she got yesterday or something, a drop in blood pressure from the hot water. The first twenty-four hours after an accident are very dangerous, I'm telling you."

Frank shook his head. There was nothing wrong with Mara. If anything, she'd be emptying the tank on purpose. Leaving the family without water would be another way to create chaos, to put their lives at risk and force him to confess. He imagined her standing in the bathroom, watching the water run with a half-smile on her face.

"Just watch how quickly she gets out when I turn off the boiler."

He went around the back of the motor home to the right-hand side. He opened the exterior compartment where the controls were. When they were planning their first trip—the period that dragged out for such a long time—Frank himself had exchanged the tank system for a boiler like the one in their house. He pressed the red button. On the little screen, the flashing flame and shower icons went off. The water instantly stopped running, as if Mara had turned it off at the same time.

"What did I say?" Frank asked as he returned to his wife and daughter.

"Thank goodness." Grace withdrew her finger from her eyebrow. "She's all right."

The motor home rocked with Mara's movement as she walked from the bathroom to the door. Frank went to receive her first. The moment he turned the corner, his feet stuck to the ground.

Mara had come out naked.

Her breasts, her elbows, her hands were dripping water onto the road. The liquid that ran down her pelvis formed a stream that flowed toward Frank, as if the water wanted to bring them together again. Her soaked hair formed a grotesque mask over her face. When she smiled, her teeth showed through the wet locks.

"Help me," she whispered.

The knot of anxiety tightened in Frank's chest. She offered him the towel she was holding in her hand, still unused.

"I said help me."

Grace's voice came from the other side of the motor home. "Everything OK?"

"Help me." Mara shook the towel. "Please."

Frank heard Grace's footsteps coming around the vehicle, walking toward them. Simon joined her.

"No, honey, no, don't come, stay—"

But it was too late. Grace snorted when she discovered the scene. Simon's jaw dropped, leaving him openmouthed. His uncovered eye widened. Grace covered it, forming a second patch with her hand. Frank launched himself onto Mara, embracing her to cover her nudity. He quickly regretted his instinctive reaction, the improper familiarity he demonstrated by approaching the naked body of a stranger in such a presumptuous way. A body he knew all too well. His forwardness could arouse Grace's suspicions. But Grace was gone, she'd fled with the boy. Alone, Mara twisted in his arms like a water snake, making his clothes wet.

"I'm soaked," she whispered, "just as you like it."

Frank separated himself from her as if she burned. On the other side of the vehicle, Grace was telling Simon not to move, while Audrey argued there was nothing wrong or shameful about a woman's naked body, that all human beings come from the same place. Frank thought his wife would return angry at the liberties he'd taken with the stranger, but she didn't. The values that shaped her benign view of life could not coexist with the possibility—however remote—of her husband, the person in whom she placed all of her trust, being able to cheat on her with another woman, so when Grace reappeared, she was concerned only about Mara.

"Are you all right?" She encouraged her to use the towel. "Maybe that blow to the head was worse than we all thought, huh?"

"Why?" Mara combed her hair with her fingers and spread the strands out behind her head. "I'm fine, better than before. The hot water did me a world of good. I never imagined being able to shower so comfortably in an RV."

She rubbed her towel-wrapped hair. Her bare breasts bounced with each movement. Frank clenched his fists, containing the rage that this new provocation ignited in him.

"If you don't think there's anything strange about what just happened, then I certainly am worried about the blow to the head," said Grace.

Mara stopped rubbing and frowned.

"Strange?" She fell silent for a few seconds, as if she really didn't know what Grace was referring to. "Oh, because of this?" She opened her arms. "Because I'm naked? It bothers you?"

"What do you think?" Grace snatched the towel from her and wrapped it around her body, under her armpits, hiding her breasts, her pelvis. "There's a nine-year-old boy with us. And he's just seen a naked woman for the first time in his life."

"Oh, I'm sorry. Really, I'm sorry. I'm so sorry. Forgive me, really." The impudence had turned to remorse, and Frank admired Mara's variety of theatrical registers as she stretched the bottom of the towel to cover herself. "A lot of these hot springs are pretty much clothing optional, so I thought you would be, too. Or at least that it wouldn't bother you. It's pretty normal to see people bathing naked here. I'm not going to be the last person you see, I warn you."

"Clothing optional?" Grace put the question to Frank.

"Carl said something like that," he recalled. "I thought it was a joke."

"Well, the thing is, we're not nudists, so you need to get dressed."

"I left your pajamas in the bathroom. I don't have any other clothes."

"You don't have anything? Of course, you have it in the car. For which you don't have the key."

Mara held a hand to her belly.

"It doesn't matter," Grace went on. "I'll lend you something."

"She does have clothes," Frank intervened. "She can put the ones she was wearing yesterday back on."

"All torn and covered in blood and dirt?" Mara asked.

The two women looked at him. Grace, berating him for his tactlessness with the supposed victim. Mara, enjoying the chance he had given her to remind them of the accident.

"I'll bring you something comfortable, jeans and a T-shirt," Grace concluded. "Get in the tent, go on. I'll be right back with the clothes."

It enraged Frank to see Mara taking advantage of his wife's kindness. She didn't deserve to be lied to. Or deceived. Or for . . . or for her husband to sleep with another woman. When Mara walked off toward the tent, the air was filled with the smell of shampoo. The motor home rocked again under Grace's footsteps, but it was a gentler sway, less wild than the one Mara had caused. Frank fought not to draw parallels with the way each of them moved in bed.

Turning around, he found Simon standing at the back of the vehicle. He was looking at the tent with his mouth open. Frank remembered the not entirely sexual curiosity that a woman's body arouses in a nine-year-old boy. He had experienced it himself at his son's age. The poor kid would be wanting to see more flesh but, unfortunately for him, Mara had taken refuge in the tent. Then Frank looked in that direction. The door was wide open, so that the inside was visible. Mara was moving around in there without the towel on, showing herself.

"Simon!" he yelled. "Turn around, go with your sister!"

The boy obeyed, running the way he did through the hall at home when they sent him to bed because Santa Claus was about to arrive. Frank strode over to the tent and found the zipper pull without allowing his gaze to come to rest on Mara's uncovered skin. Just before he finished closing it, their eyes met.

"Do you like seeing my naked body again?"

Mara pushed her breasts together with her hands, offering them to him.

Frank pulled on the zipper, which was stuck.

"Confess," said Mara. "Tell her everything."

His tugging shook the tent.

"You're going to have to tell her."

The zipper pull wouldn't budge.

"Confess."

The zipper buzzed shut. Frank turned around just as Grace was coming out of the motor home.

"You don't have to stand guard over her, Frank."

He took a step to one side with his hands raised, as if he needed to prove some kind of innocence. Among the folded clothes his wife was carrying, he recognized plain jeans with a flower embroidered on one pocket and a white-and-blue striped T-shirt. These basic combinations were Frank's favorites, because they set off Grace's simple beauty. She didn't need to impress with complicated styling or elaborate makeup, all she had to do was exploit the radiance of her natural manner, a quality more valuable than any physical feature because naturalness is impossible to simulate.

"I'm a mess, huh?" she asked, feeling observed.

"No, honey, quite the opposite."

Inside the tent, Mara feigned a coughing fit. Grace opened a section of the zipper, just enough to hand the folded clothes through it.

"I give up!"

It was Audrey yelling. Frank and Grace turned around.

"I'm done with this!" Amid the undergrowth, she separated sweaty hair from her shiny face. "They're not here. The phones aren't here. Period. Bye-bye Instagram, and bye-bye life. I'll just have to deal with it." Her fists clenched. "It's not fair. Look at the mess I'm in!"

She had stalks tangled in her hair. Assorted plant remains—flowers, pine resin, spikes—were stuck to the skin on her arms and covered in milky sap.

"Clean yourself up and get in the shade, go on," said Grace. "The sun's beating down now."

It was bright above their heads with noon approaching.

"It's not fair!" Audrey repeated.

She jumped over bushes and ran to the motor home, brushing off her hair, her clothes.

"They'll show up," Grace told her.

She responded with a slam of the door.

"And then she tells us she's a young adult," her mother observed. "She's being as maddening as she was with the ferrets."

Frank blamed himself for the conflict between them. If only he could tell Audrey the truth, that the cell phones weren't going to turn up because the woman he'd hit had thrown them into the forest in the night. The woman who sold them the motor home and who he'd been sleeping with for months. The same woman who was getting dressed right now in his wife's clothes inside the tent he had bought with her, the two of them dreaming together about the family adventures of a perfect marriage. Frank took a deep breath to ease the knot that was tight in his chest.

"Relax." Grace kissed him on the lips, the same lips that had sampled every part of Mara's body, even the most hidden ones. "Everything's fine. Someone who can help us will come."

24.

A blanket of moist heat enveloped Audrey when she walked into the bathroom. The heel of her sneaker skidded on a little puddle on the floor. The mirror, the toilet—they were all splashed with water. Mara hadn't bothered to dry them after her shower. Audrey opened the window, hoping a current of air would thin the atmosphere and ease the unpleasant feeling of heat from someone else's shower. The condensation from another person's filth.

Standing at the sink, she turned on the faucet, leaving a milky residue on the handle. She rubbed her hands together under the water, without managing to dissolve the paste of sap, grass, and pollen. She searched for soap in the sink unit but didn't find any. She turned toward the shower. Toward the sexist segregation of the bathroom products her mother had established. *His. Hers.* Reducing everything to last century's binary conception of gender. A classmate during the school year had identified as nonbinary and had informed Audrey about the sliding scale between man and woman. The classmate even taught her the neutral pronoun that their community preferred to use: *they.* Purely out of solidarity for *them,* Audrey opted for her father's dark-brown bar of soap. She would use his masculine product on her female skin to demonstrate that all skins are the same, regardless of sex, color, or age. She held her hand near that corner caddy, but then she remembered the powerful campfire smell Dad gave off after showering.

"Just this once," she whispered as an apology as she picked up the lilac soap.

She wet it and rubbed it against her arms. The plant remains clung to the soap bar, which barely produced a lather. It smelled good, sure, but it was ineffective at dissolving the dirt. And the third time she wet it, a corner crumbled off as if it were a sponge cake.

Audrey returned the lilac soap to the female shelf and picked up the brown bar.

The aroma of pine tar, a burned-wood smell, came off the soap as soon as she wet it. She knew right away that this soap, made from more natural ingredients than the ones that formed the forced, perfumed delicacy of her mother's soap, would get the filth off her skin in no time.

She slid the bar over her forearms, pressing the soap against the dust stuck down with sap. A blob of pine resin resisted the friction. She rubbed harder.

Looking at herself in the mirror, she discovered that her cheeks were sticky, too, her lips dirty from her wiping the sweat from under her nose so much.

She held the soap to her face.

She scrubbed her features with the black bar, her eyes closed, enjoying the relief she felt from washing away the sweat, the heat, the effort. She rubbed her forehead, her cheeks. And her lips, pressing them together to keep the lather out of her mouth.

The fresh feeling was so pleasant that she moved to her neck, not caring when drops rolled down her chest, under her vest. She was even grateful for the shivers they gave her.

She scrubbed under her jaw.

First one side.

Then the other.

And she left the bar of soap beside the faucet.

She rinsed the lather from her face. The bonfire smell was energizing. In the mirror she saw her face rosy, clean.

But her arms still felt sticky.

She wet them from above the elbow before rubbing them with the soap again. She scrubbed the dirt with intense bursts of friction, as she'd seen her mother do on grass stains on the knees of Simon's pants. Her shoulders ached from the effort.

The pine resin wouldn't come off.

So she scrubbed again, harder, with the soap.

A sharp, unexpected pain ran down her left arm, from her thumb to her elbow.

Audrey stifled a scream.

Her face paled in the mirror.

She dropped the bar of soap in the sink, the impact flattening one of the corners.

With her other hand she covered the source of the throbbing on her arm, afraid to peek at whatever had caused the flash of pain. As if by not looking at the wound, she could keep it from existing. When she dared to take her hand away, she discovered a red spot near the wrist. A thorn was sticking out from the center of the throb. It must have been stuck to her skin and driven in with all the scrubbing. She pinched the protruding part and pulled it out with a tug. It was a prickle from a thistle, the length of a fingernail. No wonder it had hurt so much. She threw it in the toilet.

She would have to keep scrubbing.

She picked up the soap.

She was about to wet it under the faucet when Simon yelled.

"Dad!" Excitement crackled in his throat. "Dad! Dad!"

Audrey poked her head out the window to see what was happening, but her brother was shouting from somewhere outside her field of vision. She couldn't see her parents, either.

"Dad!" Simon shrieked. "Someone's coming!"

Audrey turned off the water. She set aside the soap. She didn't even bother to dry herself.

"Finally," she murmured before running out of the bathroom.

25.

A pickup was descending the elevation that was visible in the distance. It was moving in the opposite direction from the one they had been traveling in, as if returning from the hot springs. The relief Frank felt when he heard Simon's announcement quickly turned to worry.

"Someone's coming!" Audrey leapt down from the RV.

Her arms were wet, her vest dotted with water. She formed a visor with her hands, as Grace and Simon had. They all watched the dust cloud the truck kicked up among the trees on its way toward them. They could already hear the engine's rattle, the metallic clanging of beat-up bodywork. Frank saw Mara come out of the tent, doing up the zipper on Grace's jeans, the laces on her Converse shoes still untied. The outfit looked much better on his wife—his wife was much better in every way.

"Someone's coming?" Mara's voice conveyed disappointment.

Frank gave her the smile of someone deciding the battle was his, but he had to fight to hide his fear that she could yet win the war.

"Thank goodness, Mara." Grace took her hand. "Thank goodness. Help's coming at last."

"Problem's over," added Frank. "All of them are."

"Well, let's see if it stops," said Mara.

Frank rejected the comment with a snort. He gestured at their surroundings with open arms, highlighting how absurd it would be for someone not to stop and help a family with children and a motor home with flat tires on a road like this. Then he walked toward the pickup, which was about to reach them. He waved with his hand held high at whoever was driving, the patches of sun and shade on the windshield still obscuring the figure behind the wheel. Melodic eighties music was emerging from the cab. When the truck stopped in front of them, Frank recognized an REO Speedwagon chorus. A man was driving, senior enough to have a face covered in the brown marks of old age. His chest and arms, too, bare under overalls. As thin as he was, the shoulder straps almost covered his shoulders.

"Problems?" he asked, with a pointed elbow resting on the open window.

"And then some," Frank answered.

"The good thing about problems is, there's always a solution. If there isn't one, it's called death," the man said, with such conviction that it was impossible not to believe him. "What solution do we need here?"

His friendly manner seemed to turn the most complex difficulties into a triviality. His use of the inclusive plural "we" underlined his willingness to help.

"Most of all, help this young woman, take her somewhere," said Frank. "Her car broke down last night and, trying to get help, she suddenly appeared in front of us."

He finished by explaining how they'd almost run her over, the cut on her eyebrow, the motor home's flat tires, and their lost cell phones.

"A red car?" asked the man. "I saw it back there, by the side of the road, like a dead squirrel. I thought someone must be taking a bath in a hot spring somewhere around there."

"That's mine, it's dead," Mara confirmed. "No way to fix it or get it to start."

"Some serious problems you've had, yessir. You can thank God I came along. You could grow potatoes on his road in the time between one car passing and the next."

"Idaho's best-kept secret," said Grace. "Don't we know it."

"And that's why we'll thank God and whoever else we need to thank that you're here," said Frank. "Can we use your cell phone?"

He looked at Mara to see her reaction now that everything was about to be over. Now that a call would put an end to the prison in which she'd confined them.

Then the man showed his arms. They ended in two stumps a few inches below the elbow.

"Hard to press such tiny buttons with these hooves." He made a movement equivalent to waving two hands, though there were no hands or fingers to wave. "Not to mention those new screens you have to go about tapping."

"New?" Audrey whispered into Simon's ear.

Frank was shocked by the revelation, by the irregular form of the mutilated flesh, but Grace responded with her usual natural manner.

"Veteran?" She held out a hand. "Thank you for your service, sir. I'm Grace."

She shook the stump he offered her with confidence.

"Earl," he replied as an introduction. "Yes, ma'am, I'm a veteran, but I came home from Vietnam in one piece. This was from an accident in one of those darned holes full of hot water and rotten eggs. My dog jumped in one—one of the bad ones—and this old fool was stupid enough to try to save him. Thirteen years he spent with me, that flea-ridden mutt. But if you look at my hands—or if you can't look at them, I should say—you can just imagine how Chuck wound up."

With a finger on her lips, Grace asked him not to provide any more details in front of the children.

"Been a long time since I complained. I can do just about everything now, thank God. I can drive this truck better than a sixteen-year-old boy, I can kill every fly my wife asks me to kill in the kitchen. And when Halloween comes around, I can dress up as a pirate for a dime."

The joke earned a guffaw from Simon.

"So what if I can't use one of those ungodly telephones? I wouldn't want one even if I had three hands and fifteen fingers. Who the hell would I call from my car? This isn't Manhattan, it's just Idaho. If I need to speak to someone, I drive the two hundred miles to the next house and start bellowing like a moose."

Simon's laughter grew louder. Emboldened, he went up to the truck and showed the man his eyepatch.

"I've got things missing, too. I've got an eye missing, look." He lifted the material, uncovering his scarred skin. "And I can do everything, too."

"Sure you can, kid, that's the spirit. Who the hell wants a whole body, anyway? That's what everyone has, you get it when you're born—even a goat gets one. I'd rather be different." He showed his incomplete arms. "I lost my hands to a sulfuric acid soup. Who stole your eye?"

"A gun."

Frank thought he'd misheard.

"Psst," Grace quickly went.

Relaxed from laughing so much, or perhaps because of the instant connection he'd made with the old man, Simon had said the truth.

"Simon, don't tell—"

"It wasn't a gun, no—"

"Not a real gun—"

"And it wasn't anyone's fault—"

"It's all really complicated—"

"But it was an unfortunate acci—"

"—dent."

Grace and Frank spoke over each other, stumbling, treading on one another's sentences.

"That patch looks great on you, kid. What pretty butterflies," Earl said to Simon. "We'd make a good team dressing up as pirates next Halloween. What do you think?"

With a nod, Frank thanked him for changing the subject.

"Yeah!" replied Simon.

"So, I may not have a phone, but I'd certainly like to give you a hand." Earl arched his eyebrows to call attention to the joke. "What shall we do? I can change tires with these stumps. We can get that RV purring in half an hour."

"Turns out these vehicles don't carry spares," said Grace, as if she still hadn't fully accepted Frank's explanation.

"Seriously? I can believe it—that thing's a beast," Earl concluded. "With what it must weigh, it'd be dangerous to start fiddling with its belly, and I'd rather not lose any more limbs. Shall we take the young lady to her car? Let's see if we can fix it."

"I don't have the key," said Mara. "I lost it when they hit me."

"I actually swerved out of the way. My wife's hand was all she hit," Frank corrected her. "You could take her to the junction on the main road, where the restaurant is."

"Did you eat at Danielle's?" asked Earl. "Incredible cheesecake."

Frank explained that the girl didn't have insurance or AAA, but that she could call someone from the restaurant or the nearby motel. It was a situation she had to resolve by herself. Neither he nor his family wanted to waste any more time on the matter.

"Can you take her there?" persisted Frank.

"Sure can, I was heading there myself. But what will we do with you and the beast?" He gestured at the motor home.

"Frank, you go with them," said Grace. "Call AAA as soon as you arrive, and I'll wait here with the kids. We'll be fine."

"I don't like the sound of that, Mom," said Audrey.

Simon confirmed that it frightened him, too.

"Would you mind making the call for me when you arrive?" Frank shook Earl's right-hand stump. "My name's Frank. These are my children, Audrey and Simon. You already know my beautiful wife's name. If you get in touch with the breakdown service, we'll wait here for someone to come help us. We're in no hurry."

"And this is Mara," Grace added, giving Frank a harsh look for not introducing her.

"Could you make the call?" Frank asked again.

"Sure, as soon as I've finished my cheesecake at Danielle's." Earl stuck his tongue out at Simon. "All right, I'll call first. Even though I'm hungrier than seven wolves."

"Thanks a lot, Earl. My family and I are very grateful."

"So I'll just take the pretty young lady?"

Frank fixed his eyes on Mara.

"Yes," he said, narrowing his eyes. "Just her."

Despite his defiant look, Frank could feel his heartbeat in his neck. If Mara felt cornered, if she sensed she'd lost the chance to force him to confess, she might let the truth out herself. The saliva turned bitter in his throat when he thought of Mara as a scorpion surrounded by fire, but he resisted the urge to swallow to avoid showing even a hint of weakness. She bit her thumbnail. The changing furrows on her forehead suggested internal scheming. She looked at him, at Grace, and at Earl. Her visual trajectory ended at the children. Simon had his arms around Audrey's waist. Mara centered her attention on them for most of the duration of her analysis.

"Grace," she said after deliberating.

Frank stopped breathing.

"Can we talk, you and me alone? Inside the RV?"

"Inside?" Grace frowned. "Now?"

"There's no need to go anywhere," Frank intervened. "You can talk to all of us."

"It's about . . ." Mara stuck her hands in the back pockets of her jeans. "It's a girl thing. I'd rather we talked alone."

"Oh, please," Audrey blurted out. "There aren't girl or boy things—all human beings understand the feelings of other human beings. Honestly, you older people have to start getting over these prejudices, open your minds a little. It's almost 2020."

"You heard Audrey." Frank had never been so happy to hear one of his daughter's lectures. "You can talk right here."

"Grace . . ."

Mara looked at Frank, straightening her back like a soldier presenting arms. Her temples pulsed from the pressure with which she was clenching her jaw. She wet her lips, preparing to say something important.

Then, spontaneously, Simon separated himself from Audrey and went to hold Frank's hand, in silence. He stood next to his father, waiting for the stranger to speak. Mara's shoulders relaxed.

"I'd rather not go with the gentleman by myself," she finally improvised. "Why don't you go, Frank? You're a man, like him. You won't be in any danger. You won't—"

"What're you implying, miss?" Earl interrupted. "Don't you go there, because I haven't insulted you. I wouldn't harm a fly. And I've been unlucky enough to have been a victim of that thing you're referring to—yup, it happens to us men, too—and it's no laughing matter."

Grace held a finger to her lips again, asking him to be careful with the subjects he spoke about in front of the children.

"So, miss, decide if you want to climb on my horse, because this rider has a long way to travel but no desire to be insulted."

Earl opened the door on the passenger side.

He waited for Mara to get in.

"Miss?"

Nine eyes focused on her, waiting for her decision.

Mara took a deep breath.

And a step back.

Earl snorted and closed the door.

"You can count on that call," he said to Frank.

"Frank, come on, you go with him, go with the gentleman," said Grace, trying to find a compromise to ease the tension. "Mara can stay here with us. We'll wait for you here, it's fine."

"No, Grace, no." Frank was surprised at the gravity in his voice. "Enough now. We've already done everything we can for her, and now she has a chance to fix her problems with her car, her insurance, or whatever. Our friend Earl here is offering the exact same help she needed when she tried to stop the RV. Why doesn't she want it now? We've been waiting since yesterday for someone to come by and help us. And here he is. His name's Earl. A great man who served the country, who we have no reason to distrust. She's going with him. We'll stay and wait for the help they're going to request for us. Problems over. Everything taken care of."

He knew the real problem wouldn't disappear just because Mara traveled a few miles west, but it would buy him some time.

"Should I go?" asked Audrey. "You haven't considered me, but I'm a young adult perfectly capable of contributing in a situation like this."

"I want to go, too! I like the man, and between the two of us we'll make a whole body. We can be pirates in the forest."

Simon's enthusiasm made Earl laugh, but Frank snorted at the stupidity of the idea. Imbued with a mixture of desperation and bravado, he went to the tent and took out the bag containing Mara's dirty clothes. He also picked up her purse. He thought about asking her to open it—to show everyone the knife, the cell phone, to get her to explain why she had them. But he was afraid she must have foreseen the move and hidden them somewhere else, the way she'd hidden her purse last night before Frank visited her in the tent. It would be a masterstroke in making him look paranoid. He handed her the belongings, shoving them against her chest.

"I . . . I have to get changed. These clothes are your wife's."

"It doesn't matter, take them. You're not going to wear your torn clothes all covered in dirt and blood." With ulterior motives, he appropriated the words Mara had used earlier. "For the inconvenience caused. And take this hundred dollars"—he took the bills from his back pocket—"in case something comes up. It's our way to say sorry, us to you, for appearing in front of you on the road in the middle of the night."

Frank could almost feel the heat from the rage that turned Mara's cheeks red, how much the money offended her with the obvious double meaning it encompassed.

"No . . . really . . . I should . . ."

She was left without excuses for refusing Earl's help. The dark intentions of some deep scheming returned to her eyes. Her tongue would be fizzing with the desire to blurt everything out. Frank remembered that it had been Simon who'd disarmed Mara before, so he went over to the boy. And to Audrey. He hugged them from behind, forming a perfect family photograph in front of her, a dad with his daughter and son. He challenged her to be cruel enough to destroy their relationship right there, malevolent enough to hurt two innocent children, to throw the terrible truth about their father in their faces—a truth that would be like an acid that would disfigure them for life.

Audrey wriggled away from Frank's hand.

"What're you doing, Dad?"

"It's for the best, Mara," Grace concluded. "The sooner you start dealing with your stuff, the better. And please, get a doctor to take a look at you. With the shower and sweat, those butterfly bandages on your eyebrow are coming loose. A blow that doesn't hurt on the outside can be very dangerous inside. I don't care about the jeans. I have moving boxes full of clothes traveling to Boston right now."

It annoyed Frank that she'd revealed their final destination.

"It's the best option," Grace added.

"It is," Frank said. He rested a hand on Mara's shoulder, pressing her to move, to get in the truck once and for all. "And please, Earl, don't forget to make that call for us."

Mara turned around.

"It won't be necessary. If I go with him, I'll call for you, don't worry. Let him eat his cheesecake as soon as he arrives. We've put him through enough trouble already. And anyway, I owe you, for giving me somewhere to sleep, for the clothes, so I'll take care of the call. It's the least I can do."

She gave Frank her characteristic half-smile.

Frank approached Earl and whispered in his ear. "You call." He squeezed his shoulder as if congratulating him for some romantic conquest while they drank a few beers together, trying to strike up a classic male connection. A connection through which he communicated that he didn't trust the girl, just as he knew Earl didn't after she offended him by implying that simply because he was a man, he might want to have his way with her in his truck. "You call."

Earl agreed with a slight nod.

"Jump in, miss."

He opened the passenger-side door for the second time.

Mara walked with short paces. She turned her neck from side to side, searching for an excuse to cling to.

"Great, Mara," said Grace. "It's about time you saw a doctor."

She climbed into the truck. Hugging her purse and dirty clothes, she sat on the seat's edge, as if still trying to find a reason to get out. To stay. To make him confess. Frank closed the door with a force equal to his desire for her to disappear.

"Watch it, cowboy," Earl complained. "This old mule doesn't take kindly to beatings. What it needs is love and affection."

He stroked the steering wheel with what remained of his forearms. Then he stuck one out the window.

"High five," he said to Simon.

The words and the nonexistent hand made the boy laugh. He lifted up his patch before slapping the stump.

"We can do everything!"

"Sure we can, kid."

The rest of the family said goodbye to Earl and wished Mara luck. Close together, their arms over one another's shoulders, they waved to the truck. Frank felt the knot loosen in his chest. He began visualizing it as a harmless piece of cord that would end up dropping to the ground at his feet.

Then Mara turned her head in the cab.

Through the mottled skin that was the rear window, between the changing patches of sun and shade, she fixed her gaze on Frank's.

This isn't over, her eyes said.

This is far from over.

The dust the wheels raised hid the truck. When the cloud of dirt cleared, the vehicle was gone. The sound of the engine gradually moved away, fading until it dissolved into the birdsong.

26.

"So, you were all on your way to the hot springs?"

Mara didn't bother to respond—she barely noticed the old man's voice. She reduced it to some annoying interference among her tangled thoughts. She touched her cheeks with the back of a hand. They felt hot. Rage was burning her inside. She shuffled closer to the window in her seat, hoping the air would cool her, soothe her. She bit her thumbnail, ignoring the pain, angry with herself. Unable to comprehend why her courage had failed her. Why she hadn't confronted Frank. Once again, he'd gotten rid of her. His words had confused her and dragged her into this rust bucket driven by a mutilated old man intent on striking up a conversation. *Idiot*. What an idiot she'd been. She hadn't come all this way so Frank could just get rid of her again, at the first opportunity. A fool, that's what she was. A fool. Only a fool would keep quiet like she had. She should have spoken, she should have revealed everything before climbing in this damn truck with no suspension that was wrecking her spine.

The children. It was because of the children. She couldn't say anything in front of them. What kind of person would she have become? Simon had gone to his father, held his hand, as if he was his oracle and sanctuary. That feeling—the young child's love for the father he sees as an infallible hero—is unique, precious, and, sadly, fleeting. The child no longer feels it when he's older. But while it lasts, it's one of the miracles that gives life meaning. Mara couldn't destroy that with her words. She couldn't be the one to take away a father's superpowers in front of the boy who loved him most. It had to be Frank who took off his disguise in front of Grace. And the two of them together, as a married couple and parents, would explain to the children that Dad's costume was always a sham, that he was never the superhero, but the villain. But now Mara's rage was threatening to consume her, to make her lose any principles she had. What had just happened couldn't happen again. She wouldn't pass up the next opportunity. The truth would defeat any indecision. And that woman would know what her husband did when she wasn't looking. She needed to think. She needed silence to think.

With his stump, the old man turned up the music.

He tapped the steering wheel to the rhythm of something by Air Supply. Orchestral arrangements and hyperbolic lyrics about love were the opposite of what Mara needed. Restless, she shuffled in her seat. She looked out the window. She turned around. The road wound off behind them, farther and farther away from Frank.

"A beautiful family, huh?"

"Beautiful?" Just what she needed to hear. "You don't know what you're talking about."

"I can't recognize a beautiful family when I see one?"

Mara shot the old man a look. Behind him, the speed they were traveling at turned Idaho's wooded landscape into a flurry of green and brown sprinkled with golden flashes of sun. A flurry that, with every second, increased the distance between her and Frank. Between Frank and the truth. She couldn't allow it. She had to do something.

"Stop," she said.

"What?"

"Stop the truck. Hit the brakes."

"What the hell are you saying, miss? It's still a long way to the junction from here. I can't even smell the cheesecake yet. You young people, you're always so impatient. Can't you just enjoy the scenery and the music?"

He turned the volume on the car stereo up even louder. The music occupied space in Mara's head that she didn't have right now.

"I'm asking you to stop." She was trying hard not to shout. "I have some things I need to take care of back there. Things that're none of your business. Let me out here. You drive on and we're done."

"But I agreed to take you, miss. To call someone to help that family and help you with the situation you're in—no insurance, no AAA. You young people—"

"I have insurance," she cut in. The old man stuttered without ultimately saying anything. The perplexed look he gave her amused Mara so much that she decided to keep it there with a string of confessions. "I've got everything. I've even got my phone." She undid the twist locks on her purse and showed it to him. "And I also have the car key. It's here." She stroked her belly, causing even more confusion. "As you can see, you don't know anything. You don't understand anything about what you've seen or who you stumbled across."

"How can I let you go back? What will that family think of me?"

"What do you care what some people you don't even know think? I'll just tell them you kicked me out of the car, that you turned out to be less friendly than you seemed."

"I do care, miss. I don't know where you're from, but around here we value a good potato and a little thing called dignity. And we try to help each other. I'm not going to allow you to get out here alone on this God-forgotten road where not even the ants come. It'd be irresponsible for me to do that."

"Stop! The! Truck!"

The screaming and the strange cadence in her words set off the first alarm on the old man's face. The blemishes of old age curled around his eyes when he frowned. He was beginning to realize Mara was serious. A Vietnam veteran was perhaps struggling to understand how a woman he only knew to refer to as *miss* could be threatening him. That she might be dangerous. His reaction was to step on the gas.

"What're you doing?" she asked. "I'm telling you to stop."

The old man maintained the pressure on the pedal.

"If you prefer, I can tell them another version. That you were the sexual predator I feared you were. I'm sorry, honestly, I couldn't think of another excuse not to go with you. But if you keep accelerating, I won't be sorry anymore, I'll enjoy telling them I wasn't wrong. That you attacked me and I managed to escape. I'll ask for help again and they'll give it, with better reason than before."

"Why would I do that? What the hell are you saying?"

The old man accelerated.

The engine rebelled.

And Mara had no option but to pull out the knife.

"Hey, hey, hey, easy, easy."

"Stop," she ordered.

She brandished the weapon in the old man's direction, toward the tangle of white chest hair that poked out from the overalls. He swerved in the opposite direction, as if he could escape the blade. Mara had to grab hold of the dashboard so she wouldn't lose her balance.

"What's your problem?"

"I told you, you don't know anything. And it's not your concern. Let me out."

The old man swallowed, gestured at the knife with his chin. "What're you going to do with that?"

"Let me out."

"For God's sake, there were kids back there."

When he held a stump up in her direction, Mara was able to imagine the open hand that wasn't there. The condescending open hand of a man trying to pacify a woman he considers hysterical. She grabbed the stump and pushed it away from her face.

"Stop," she said through gritted teeth. "Now."

Fear seized the old man's face, but in his eyes Mara saw the spark of courage of someone putting his firm determination before his own safety. As he no doubt would have in Vietnam if necessary, the old man was going to carry the bomb as far away as possible, even if it blew him up. He took possession of the steering wheel with both arms and stepped hard on the gas, taking Mara away from the family, away from the children he was so concerned about.

She grabbed the hand brake and threatened to use it. She didn't know what would happen if she pulled it with the vehicle in motion, but it was too late to expect rational behavior from herself. She was out of control with rage, and the only thing she knew was that she wouldn't allow Frank to get away with what he'd done. She wrapped her fingers around the brake, ready to pull. The old man turned the wheel from one side to the other in a sudden burst of movement that unbalanced her. Mara fell into the footwell, her back against the door. The tip of the knife brushed against her own cheek. The butterfly bandages on her eyebrow came open, and she felt blood roll down her cheek as if she were crying.

With a smile, the old man continued to swing the truck from side to side, varying the speed, snaking along the road, making the cab shudder. They were soon surrounded by dust. Grit hit the bodywork from all angles. Mara coughed on it.

She used her elbows to get back onto her seat. The tremor threatened to unseat her again. Brandishing the knife in one hand, she grabbed the brake lever in the other.

And she pulled.

In an instant, down was up and left was right.

Mara hit the truck's roof with her tailbone, the steering wheel with her elbow. Her face smacked against the old man's. She felt his skin's pitted texture on her forehead, the moisture of his lips on her ear, the warmth of his breath. A black Converse floated in front of her eyes as if there were no gravity, just before her bare foot hit the rearview mirror. The sound of machinery fracturing accompanied each jolt. There was the smell of hot scrap metal. Mara managed to grip on to something, and it turned out to be the strap on the old man's overalls. The two of them rolled around inside the cab like astronauts, like dice in a fist. He grunted and she screamed until, at the very same instant, they both fell silent. Because both knew that the knife had pierced flesh.

The windshield had cracked on the first roll. On the second, it shattered and fell out. Then the movement stopped.

Mara's groans intermingled with the screech of crushed metal and the whistles of liquids and steam. When she tried to sit up, her head hit the steering wheel, which somehow was now part of the roof. The old man was underneath her, motionless. His white chest hair was now red with splashes of blood. Among the many pains wracking Mara's body, she couldn't discern whether one of them was due to a blade stuck into her groin, armpit, or belly. When she rolled off the old man, she saw the knife plunged into his thigh up to the handle, which marked the center of a bloodstain expanding on the denim fabric. Mara held her hands to her mouth. She took them away when she tasted organic fluids that might not have been hers.

"Oh my God," she jabbered. "Oh my God, oh my God."

She slapped the unconscious old man.

"Oh my God, wake up, I didn't want this."

She grabbed the knife handle the way she'd grabbed the hand brake that caused this disaster.

"Sir! Earl! Sir!"

She pulled. The blade came out, making the sound of a letter opener. Blood spurted from the wound. Mara took hold of the overalls' straps, shook the old man's flaccid body. There was no response.

"No, no, no . . ."

Mara recovered her purse from a seat she couldn't situate, unable to perceive whether it was up or down, whether it was hers or the driver's. Tears rolled down her cheeks, mingling with the blood that came from her eyebrow. Or from some new injury.

With trembling hands, she took out her cell phone to call an ambulance.

She tapped *9* on the screen.

But she couldn't call anyone.

She had caused the accident.

She had stuck the knife in.

The knife was hers.

It was her fault.

It was Frank's fault.

Everything was Frank's fault.

Mara got out of the truck through the front window. She heard clothes and skin tear, she knew she was cutting herself on the ragged metal of the frame, but she no longer cared about pain or death. She crawled along the road, knife in hand, scraping her knees. The blood on the blade turned into a brown paste when it mixed with the grit. Standing, she hung the strap of her purse over her shoulder. She looked at the upturned truck, the old man's body lying along the cab's roof that was now the floor. Shoeless on one foot, she went over to retrieve her sneaker, which was hanging by laces tangled with the turn-signal lever.

Mara put the shoe on and set off in the direction of the motor home.

She stopped when she heard a detonation in the engine.

Without giving herself time to regret her decision, before her mind persuaded her that an explosion would make it harder to detect the knife wound in the old man's body, Mara returned to the truck. She opened the door closest to the old man's head. She took hold of him by the stumps, gritting her teeth against her distaste. Mara pulled the body out of the compartment. Lucky the old man was pure bone. She dragged him along the road, away from the vehicle-bomb. She left him amid the undergrowth on the opposite side.

Now.

Now she could go back for Frank.

She cleaned the brown paste from the knife on Grace's jeans.

27.

Grace spread a tablecloth over the camp table they'd had breakfast on. She was going to prepare sandwiches for lunch, and she wanted to keep the kitchen clean so they would be ready when AAA came.

"Alone at last," Frank said.

With a deep sigh of relief, he put the last tent pole away in its bag. He'd begun dismantling it as soon as the truck left. Grace pegged the tablecloth down at each corner.

"Don't blow it out of proportion. She was a good girl."

"It was a hassle I'm very happy we've gotten rid of."

Frank threw the tent on top of the suitcases and slammed the compartment door shut. Then he brushed his palms together as if he really had rid himself of a serious problem, whether it was Mara or stuffing all of the tent into its bag. Simon handed him the map, perfectly folded up—he'd managed it at last. It touched Grace to see Frank congratulate him for his efforts with a few slaps on the back, making the boy's face light up with pride at having helped his dad.

"Si," she said. "What did we agree about telling people about the gun?"

"I know, Mom . . ." Simon lowered his head, guilty. "But I liked that man. He had body parts missing, too, and he was real nice. I felt like being honest."

"Then you felt right." Frank ruffled his hair. "Being honest is a very good thing to want to be."

Grace felt her chest fill with warm tenderness at seeing the two of them smile, as proud as ever to share her life with a man who taught their children such important values. She went over to them and stroked the back of Frank's neck. She knew her husband appreciated affection whenever the gun was mentioned—he still hadn't gotten over the episode or managed to stop blaming himself. Simon must have sensed his father's remorse, too, because he hugged him around the waist and squeezed until Frank complained, though he was also laughing, asking his son not to love him quite so much. The boy promised to let him go but only if he came with him to visit the castle he was building.

Holding hands, they walked down the road toward Simon's fortress. The child's fingers hooked around his father's made the warmth in Grace's chest spread to the rest of her body. She blinked to dry her eyes. A far-off echo, like thunder, disrupted her bright thoughts, suddenly clouding them, threatening her with a torrent of memories. It was the echo from the gunshot in the bedroom upstairs. The flurry of recollections brought with it a smell of smoke, of gunpowder. The image of Simon's disfigured face, so scared he'd forgotten how to cry. He had stood there with his mouth open, not knowing what else to do. That night was the culmination of some bad times—a time to forget—that had begun a while before . . .

It wasn't easy for Grace to identify the moment when everything had taken a turn for the worse, or when they'd begun to refer to what happened before the gun as *bad times*. Without the gunshot, without that final episode that threatened to destroy their life as they knew it, they hadn't even thought of the preceding events as a part of some *bad times*—they would have just suffered them and overcome them as the setbacks that happen in anyone's life. Everyone goes through difficult periods. What Grace did remember was the last truly good weekend they spent together as a family. It was the Saturday when Frank picked up the RV, in the spring of last year. After insisting for months, Frank had persuaded her it was a luxury the family should allow itself. He insisted that taking the children away whenever they could would be one of the best investments they would make in their upbringing and future. And to him, it didn't make much sense to travel to Europe or South America when they didn't even know their own country. Neither of the children had ever left the state. Well, Audrey had visited the nation's capital on a short school trip—she returned exhausted from the long flights, without having taken much in—but even counting that visit, she had never set foot on a piece of land that wasn't called Washington.

They spent the entire spring afternoon Frank came home with the RV daydreaming about the trips they would go on as soon as he could take at least a week's vacation. Though he'd assumed he'd be able to take one in the summer, the hotel company was so busy they couldn't give him leave until several months later, in winter. So they made plans to escape to the south, to flee the cold and wet winter months. Excited, Audrey showed the rest of the family photos on her phone of the place she most wanted to go: Salvation Mountain in the California desert, a hillside turned into a colorful work of art. But as Frank's eagerly awaited week of winter leave approached, when they could have set off on the motor home's maiden voyage, Audrey had lost interest in going any-where. Her ferrets had disappeared, first one and then the other, and she had no intention of leaving the house until they returned. So the trip in the RV was postponed again.

Grace discovered the first ferret's disappearance one afternoon when she returned from the gym. She left her keys and sports bag on the long sideboard in the hallway, next to Audrey's and Simon's backpacks. They had arrived at the house a little while before her after one of the last days of class before the Christmas break. Normally, the three of them met on the way home.

"Jeez, Mom," Audrey yelled from the living room.

Walking in, Grace found her daughter on her knees, her arm under the sofa.

"What is it?" She dried the sweat from the back of her neck with a towel. "What're you doing?"

"I've told you a thousand times to never go out without shutting the back door."

"I did shut it. With this cold, how could I not?"

"No, Mom, you didn't." Audrey gestured at the sliding glass door that led to the rear porch and the backyard. "It's closed now because I just closed it, but when we got here it was open. Ask Si if you don't believe me."

The boy nodded with his eyes as open as his expression was sincere.

"And? What does it matter if I forgot to close it?"

Audrey stood up.

"What matters is that Joy's disappeared." She swallowed before she could go on. "She escaped because you left the door open."

"No, honey, no."

Grace went to the corner of the living room where the ferrets' cage was. Sure enough, just one, the gray one, was scampering up and down the ramps between the levels in a futile search for its companion, or perhaps enjoying the extra space it suddenly had.

"Wait a minute—and you left the cage door open?" she asked her daughter.

"Of course not."

"So?"

"So what, Mom?"

"So how could your ferret have escaped?"

"I don't know, Mom, but Joy isn't in the cage, and I've looked all over the house. What a coincidence that you just happened to leave the door open. She must've gone that way, and now I don't know where she is or how . . ."

Her voice faltered when she pointed at the backyard, which stretched off in front of her until it reached the forest that surrounded their house. Confronted with the green expanse on the other side of the glass, she let a tear slide down her nose. Then she threw herself on the sofa, covered her face with a cushion, and cried like the child she still was, however much she tried to be mature for her age.

Grace sat down at her daughter's hip. She apologized, certain that being happy is always better than being right.

"I'm sorry, OK? I could've sworn I closed it before leaving, but maybe I didn't." She withdrew the cushion from Audrey's face, dried her tears with her fingers. "I am sorry. Anyhow, I'm sure she'll be back. I don't think she's going to walk out on Hope just like that, do you? That's not what friends do. Or are they a couple?"

Audrey sniffed.

"I don't know . . ." She dried her nose, giving a faint smile. "I guess she wouldn't leave her behind, no."

From the entrance came the sound of Frank's keys dropping into the bowl on the sideboard. He appeared in the living-room doorway.

"What's the teenage crisis today?"

After the warning look Grace gave him, he quickly said he was sorry, switching tone to that of a concerned father.

"Actually, I am a teenager and this is a crisis," said Audrey, "so you used the correct words, Dad, don't worry." She got up from the sofa. "And thank you for apologizing, Mom."

She took a handful of food and a ball with holes in it from the cage, taking the opportunity to scold the remaining ferret for allowing the other one to leave. Then she went out onto the rear patio through the sliding door and, crouching, called Joy's name, tempting her with food and the toy.

"A ferret's gone missing," Grace explained when she approached Frank to give him the welcome-home kiss she gave him every afternoon.

"What?"

"A ferret, it's escaped."

"Oh, the teenage crisis."

"And it looks like it was my fault." Grace shrugged.

"Uh-oh, I wouldn't like to be in your shoes," Frank whispered. "Teenagers are vindictive."

But Audrey didn't seek revenge. All she did was become sad. As sad as if it were her best friend who'd abandoned her, sad enough to want to cancel all their travel plans and refuse to embark on the RV's maiden voyage until her ferret came home. She wanted to be there to welcome her. But Joy never came home, and then the second ferret also disappeared. One morning the following week, while the rest of the family was eating breakfast in the kitchen, she yelled from the living room. Grace ran out, still holding a box of Froot Loops.

"What is it, honey?"

"Hope's not here."

Audrey's whole arm was inside the cage, rummaging in every nook and cranny—under the ramps, in the hammocks—in the absurd hope of finding the clearly absent animal. It broke Grace's heart to see her inspect even the feeding trough, digging about in the food.

"Don't look at me, the back door's closed." She indicated it with the cereal box. "It wasn't me this time."

Without responding, Audrey ran upstairs. Her footsteps traveled to every part of the second floor while Grace served breakfast to Frank and Simon. Audrey came down and scoured the living room. She went into the kitchen and searched under the table, asking them to move their legs. She opened every cupboard, stuck her hand in the trash bag.

"How could she have gotten out?" she asked, wiping the dirt from her hands with a cloth. "Everything's closed. The stairs down to the garage, too."

"Have you searched everywhere?" Frank asked.

Grace detected a new gravity in her husband's voice. He'd treated the first ferret's disappearance as a joke, but the second one seemed to really worry him. It moved her to see her husband taking the girl's feelings so seriously, even if all that had happened was a pet going missing.

"She's gone," Audrey concluded.

"Are you sure?" Frank had even stopped buttering his bagel.

"The cage was closed, too, Dad, that's the thing."

"See? It's like I said the other day," Grace broke in. "How could Joy have escaped when the cage was closed? I think those ferrets are smarter than you and know how to open their hatch."

"OK, but in that case, where's Hope? The other day you'd left the back door open, but last night everything was closed, right?"

Grace nodded.

"So someone came in and stole my ferret."

A knife fell onto the floor. Frank's chair screeched when he moved to pick it up.

"A ferret thief?" Grace sipped her coffee. "I don't think that's a thing."

"There . . . there're people who steal dogs," said Frank, clearing his throat. "They even ask for a ransom, sometimes."

He used the knife from the floor without cleaning it.

"But a dog's a dog. Yours are ferrets, honey, it's not the same."

Audrey crossed her arms. Her chin trembled.

"I honestly think they have some way of opening the cage," Grace went on, "and Hope might've gone looking for Joy. Or better still, Joy might've come back for her, and they might have escaped together— two fugitives, like Thelma and Louise, driving off into the sunset in a convertible for ferrets."

"It's not funny, Mom." Audrey left the kitchen and opened the door to the garage stairs.

When they resumed breakfast, Grace noticed Frank spreading butter on his bagel with an absent look, moving the knife but concentrating on something else.

Audrey's trembling voice came from below.

"M . . . Mom?"

Frank was first to react. He stood so quickly he knocked over his chair. When Simon and Grace reached them in the garage, Audrey was pointing at a broken square of glass in the side door's frame. The glass fragments were scattered across the floor. The door keys were in the lock inside.

"Oh God, Frank, my studio."

Grace ran up to the office where she recorded her videos. She found it intact. The new Canon, the old one, the iMac, the two laptops, the iPad—it was all there. In the kitchen, with Frank's help, she moved the refrigerator. She removed the tile that concealed the space behind the wall where she kept her jewelry. That was also all there. Frank opened drawers in the living room, in the master bedroom. He returned saying their money, their cards, everything was still in its place.

"What a fright." Grace released her tension in a sigh so deep she had to sit down—her legs had gone weak. "It wasn't a burglary."

"They stole my ferret, Mom," said Audrey. "Don't you care?"

"Are we sure the glass wasn't broken before? We never use that small door—we go in and out of the garage in the car," Grace said. "Your ferrets love climbing, and Hope could easily have gotten out through that hole. No one steals a ferret and leaves a Canon 80D like I have upstairs. The camera's worth much more." She regretted her words as soon as she'd said them. "Sorry, honey, you know what I mean."

But Audrey didn't know. Without saying another word, she left the kitchen and went up to her bedroom. Breakfast remained on her plate until lunchtime, and then lunch remained on the table until dinnertime. For two weeks, Audrey answered Grace's questions with monosyllables, looking away from her when they crossed paths in the hall or when her mother asked her for the soy sauce at the table. Accepting that there's a teenage logic there's no point in trying to reason with, Grace apologized to her every day for leaving the back door open. One night, on the sofa, the girl burst out laughing at a scene in *Unbreakable Kimmy Schmidt* and then got up to hug Grace, saying she was sorry for giving her such a hard time. They watched the rest of the episode holding hands, sharing the reclining armchair.

When this difficult period was over and Audrey had accepted that her pets were lost forever, the plans to break in the motor home resumed—perhaps they could go during the spring break. But that was when the marks appeared on Grace's scalp and she began to lose hair. The bad times were taking shape, and the trip was postponed again.

The outbreak happened overnight, scabs and blemishes on the scalp that soon translated into hair loss. One morning, as she checked whether her skin had improved after she'd applied an overnight lotion, an entire lock of hair came off as if it were a strip of Velcro. She barely slept, gripped by a sense of foreboding and fixated with finding suspicious lumps on her body that would confirm the inevitable, until tests and a dermatologist's diagnosis ruled out any serious conditions. At his clinic, the dermatologist confirmed that the attack on the scalp had come from external agents. "It's as if you picked up the wrong bottle in the shower and used hair removal cream," the specialist speculated, "or used the most aggressive solvent in your house as a conditioner. Just to be sure: You don't keep household cleaning products in the bathroom, do you?"

Grace shook her head, a little offended by the doctor's ludicrous assumption. She kept the cleaning products under the kitchen sink like everyone else, and there wasn't even any hair removal cream in the bathroom. In any case, her Victoria's Secret shampoo, Pure Seduction, with its lovely red plum and freesia scent, came in such a distinctive container that it would be impossible to confuse it with a bottle of turpentine. That was when a terrible thought germinated in Grace's mind. She took Frank's hand. He was sitting next to her in the consulting room.

"Could she be that angry with me?" she asked.

Her husband's face twisted out of shape. His gaze was lost somewhere outside the room. Seeing his disturbed expression, Grace felt like a horrible person. *He* couldn't even entertain the awful thing she was implying.

"Because of the ferrets," she explained. "She didn't speak to me for two weeks."

Frank's shoulders relaxed.

"Oh. Audrey," he said, as his face smoothed out. "Of course, of course."

"Do you think she'd be capable? She's convinced it was my fault the ferrets escaped. She might've wanted to play a joke on me or, I don't know . . . take revenge by putting something in my shampoo."

She asked the doctor if that would explain what had happened with her hair, and he confirmed that it would make sense. Grace looked her husband in the eye, searching for the sensitivity she needed at times like this.

"Frank, do you think Audrey would be capable of putting something bad in my shampoo?"

Her husband's blinking stopped in an unnatural way. Grace could sense the effort he was making not to divert his gaze. His silence felt eternal—long enough for her to accept that if he got up from his chair right now and left her forever, she would deserve it. The suspicion she'd just raised about her own daughter made her the worst mother in the world, a woman who didn't deserve such good children and such a good husband. Any other mother would blame herself and admit that, without realizing it, perhaps, she'd gone to the kitchen sink and washed her hair in bleach.

"Au . . . Audrey?" Frank swallowed. He fell silent again for a few seconds. He looked down at the floor, at his hands, at Grace. His jaw muscles pulsated with the accelerated rhythm of his thoughts. "Maybe."

"She saw me scratching and crying all this time and said nothing?"

Saying nothing, Frank nodded.

The doctor intervened, judging that the girl wouldn't have gauged the effect of the toxic substance she'd used. That she might just have wanted to punish her mother with an itchy head and that, now that the matter had gotten out of hand, she was afraid and didn't know how to admit what she'd done.

But Audrey didn't admit anything when they told her that afternoon what the dermatologist had suggested. Bigger tears than the ones she'd shed for the ferrets appeared on her lower eyelids.

"That hurts, Mom." She dried her eyes with her pajama sleeve, sitting on the sofa with her laptop on her crossed legs. "Even more than what happened with Hope and Joy. Do you really think I'd do that to you? And that I'd sit here acting dumb while you turned into Eleven? Dad, how could you both think that? What kind of person watches someone suffering, knowing the cause, and says nothing?"

Frank looked down to avoid eye contact, and Grace felt guilty for making him feel such shame.

"I'm not even angry with you, Mom," Audrey went on. "It wasn't your fault the ferrets got out, all right? I get it. I'm not a child anymore, I'm a young adult, and adults accept things and move on. We don't go around taking revenge or lying."

Frank left the living room.

"So?" asked Grace. "Why am I like this?"

She gestured at the bald patches on her head, the marks that made her look like a mangy cat.

"Some makeup turned Emma in my biology class red for a month. When you stop using cosmetics tested on animals, you won't have these problems anymore," said Audrey, taking up another cause. "Or, I don't know . . . maybe the ferret thief put something in your shampoo."

Grace snorted. "That makes no sense, honey."

"It makes more sense than accusing me of putting stuff in there."

Without closing the computer, Audrey uncrossed her legs and left, leaving the blanket, which had gotten caught on her ankles, lying in the middle of the room. Grace followed her daughter to the stairs without knowing what to say. She found Frank there, and he shrugged when Audrey slammed her bedroom door shut. He was on his way down with an armful of bathroom products. In the kitchen, he emptied their contents into the sink.

"You just threw hundreds of dollars down the drain."

"Your skin's worth a lot more than that."

"We could've complained to one of the brands for selling a defective product," Grace said, half joking. "Now we have no proof."

"I don't want lawsuits, or money, or free shampoo for a year." Frank finished squeezing out a green bottle. "I want your hair to be OK."

It was a while before her hair was OK, but as soon as the scabs disappeared and she was able to cover up the bald patches by styling it in a certain way, she began recording videos again. And as soon as she saw hair growing in the most affected areas, she knew it would all go down as a passing complaint.

Both she and Audrey soon found themselves eager to start organizing the trip again, but the plan was cut short once more when, one night, Grace woke up in the early hours with her stomach tight, alerted by a bang. She wondered whether she'd heard it in a dream, but another thud, like something falling onto the floor, confirmed that both sounds were real. When she whispered Frank's name, he was already going out through the bedroom door.

"You stay here," he said before leaving.

Grace covered herself in the sheet up to her eyes, too frightened to disobey the order. She tried to follow her husband's movements by listening to the floor creaks, to his slippers brushing against the steps. His hand squeaking on the banister was the last sound she identified. Then, complete silence. She stopped breathing. A nocturnal breeze ruffled the leaves on the trees in the yard—perhaps the fugitives Hope and Joy were now living in a burrow among the roots of one of them. She was sure Frank would return saying it was nothing. It was what always happened when there were bumps in the night. But he didn't return, nor did a new sound reveal his whereabouts. When her concern eclipsed her fear, Grace poked her head out the bedroom door. The children's doors were closed, and everything was calm. Simon was snoring, as he'd started doing a few months ago—little by little her boy was becoming a young man. Containing the urge to call out to her husband, Grace advanced to the stairs. And there, she heard—or believed she heard— Frank whispering.

Crouching on the top step, she hooked her hair behind her ears to improve her hearing. Was Frank talking? Who could Frank be talking to? The supposed conversation was little more than a rustle, so weak that Grace could have been fabricating it from the murmur of the leaves blowing in the breeze. She couldn't be sure what she was hearing. A possibility made her skin prickle: that her husband was calling for help, unable to yell because it would alert the burglar who had broken into their house.

Grace's feet moved by themselves, deaf to any sense of caution if Frank was in danger. She slowly descended the stairs, straining to decipher the whisper that might not be a whisper. When she reached the second-to-last step, a wooden creak resounded in the silence with the intensity of a thunderbolt in summer. Revealing her presence triggered more sounds. Agitation in the kitchen. The thief must have realized the game was up and wanted to escape through the side door. Grace ran into the kitchen, driven by unexpected courage. She found Frank there, standing in front of the open door, peering out at the porch.

"What is it?" All of Grace's contained shock burst out in a cry: "What is it!?"

He opened his eyes wide.

"It's nothing, honey." He brushed her depleted hair with his fingers. "Why are you here?"

"What was the noise? We heard a noise. That's why you came down here."

"Sure, there was a noise. We both heard it. I told you not to come down. But it was nothing, there's no one here. It's always nothing."

"And the open door?" she indicated the one leading to the side porch.

"I just opened it to check. You must've heard some other sounds— I've been opening all the cupboards. But everything's fine. There's no one here, and nobody's tried to get in or anything."

"So who were you talking to?"

Frank raised his eyebrows.

"Talking? Me?"

"I thought I heard you talking, sort of whispering."

"Oh, to the ferrets? I was talking to the ferrets, honey. I'm starting to think they haven't gone far and they're living in the walls. It must've been them making the noises. Just now, I was telling them to come out and give Audrey a nice surprise, but they don't seem to pay any attention."

Grace nestled into Frank's chest.

"How scary! I thought you might be trying to call for help or something."

"You've been watching too many movies."

Her husband comforted her with a hug that extinguished all her fear. Nothing truly bad could happen with him by her side.

"Best not tell your daughter about the ferrets in the walls," Grace said. "It could give her false hope."

Audrey appeared in the kitchen, yawning. "What're you doing making so much noise at this time of night?"

"We were . . . ," Grace stuttered. "We were keeping guard in case the Ferret Thief returned."

She made the joke without thinking, intoning the criminal's name as if it were a cartoon villain. For an instant, she thought she'd screwed up. She could almost hear her daughter slamming her door behind her after going back to her room in a temper. But Audrey opened her mouth in surprise at her mother's nerve, then burst out laughing as if she also wanted to make light of her pets' disappearance. She hugged Grace in what was the final act of forgiveness between them, if such a thing ever exists in a mother-daughter relationship.

"Get back to your room, go on," Grace said when they'd stopped laughing. As soon as Audrey had gone up to her bedroom, Grace announced that she was going to call the neighborhood watch coordinator anyway. "If it turns out it wasn't the ferrets and there really was someone prowling around here, it's best if we're all on the alert."

She had the phone at her ear when Frank took it from her.

"Leave it, honey. I'll speak to Bob tomorrow, face to face." He pressed the red button on the screen. "It's really late now and you're going to alarm people more than necessary. What're you going to say? That everyone should get out on the street because you heard some noises that in all likelihood were ferrets?" He put the telephone in her pajama pocket. "No one came in, I'm certain."

Frank confirmed the next day that Bob had promised that the neighbors would keep a closer eye on the area around their house for the next few nights. But on the next few nights, nothing happened— there were no more noises. And when the deafening noise came, when the real tragedy happened, not even a hundred police cars surrounding the house could have prevented it.

Because the danger was inside.

On the night of the gunshot, she and Frank were sitting on the living room sofa watching an episode from one of the HBO series they reserved for when the children were in bed. It may have been the show's sexual content, or because her hair had finally regained a good volume, which had made her reevaluate the importance of feeling beautiful and healthy . . . or even because it had been more than eight months since she and Frank had made love, and that's a long time even for a woman who lacks appetite and has been sleeping with the same husband for eighteen years. Whatever the reason, Grace suddenly felt more aroused than she had in a long time. Her pulse accelerated, the temperature in the living room went up, and Frank, at the other end of the sofa, seemed irresistible all of a sudden. Unshowered, unshaven since Friday, his hand resting on his abdomen in a pose as carefree as it was manly. Grace thought about stretching out her leg, trying to excite him with her bare foot—ankles were one of the body parts that most turned him on—but the idea suddenly made her feel embarrassed. It had been so long since they'd sought each other out that she didn't know how he would react. It saddened her that the idea of seducing her husband made her feel shy, as if they were strangers.

It was what happened when sex had become an exception, when for so many months she had preferred to give herself relief in the shower when Frank was at work rather than sleep with him. For a long time, solitary sex had seemed more appealing than any other option, and she guessed he felt the same. She imagined him masturbating in the shower they shared— both of them pleasuring themselves separately, in the same house. And again, she felt sad. She envied the two people they had been, the couple that made love under that shower until their ears were filled with water and their skin wrinkled. A couple they no longer were because they each pleasured themselves so they wouldn't have to suffer the awkwardness of pressing their bodies together, bodies they'd grown bored of, they'd had their fill of. Determined to rediscover her husband's body—the only body she'd promised to devote herself to until death parted them—Grace stretched out her leg. She rested the ankle on Frank's thigh, not in the tender way she did it to prompt him to stroke it while they watched a TV show, but in the provocative way, closer to the groin than the knee, which she hoped would excite him. She saw surprise in Frank's eyes, delight as he understood what she was hoping for—right before the explosion upstairs.

The glasses in the cocktail cabinet clinked together with the detonation.

Several dogs barked down the street, but not much more than when someone let off a firecracker or a garbage can fell over.

Grace landed face-first on the carpet when she tried to get up, her foot caught between Frank's legs.

"There's someone in the house," she said.

The expression on his face was of pure terror. They both ran. They blocked the living room door when they tried to go through it at the same time, and Grace pushed Frank through with trembling hands. They climbed the stairs, stumbling over each other, crawling up the steps. There was a moment when she just sat, looking down, without moving. Listening only to the whistle in her ears. Wondering why there was a smell of gunpowder. After that, she must have gripped the railing and gotten up, because she somehow reached their bedroom. And then she lost her voice, almost lost consciousness. She'd heard on many occasions that a mother could lift up a truck that had run over her child with her bare hands, but she was paralyzed. Frozen to the spot.

She saw Simon trembling near the bedside table on Frank's side. His face was wrinkled up like a giant crying baby. The most terrible scream imaginable should have come from that mouth, but Simon made no sound—he was surrounded by a horrifying bubble of silence. Grace didn't understand why the boy was holding a toy pistol in his hands. She dreamed up absurd theories for how he'd managed to make a gunshot sound with his mouth as realistic as the one that had echoed around the house, or for what he'd used to make the hole in the wall that looked just like it had been made by a bullet. Any absurd theory was better than accepting that what he was holding was a real weapon. Or that what was spattering the sheets, the lamp, and her tub of hand cream on the bedside table was her son's blood. And not a fine crimson film glazing a wound on his knee, or two drops emerging from his forearm after a nurse's pinprick for a test, but a wasteful jet of pure life that made Grace dizzy. All that blood at once smelled like the loss of a child.

Frank's reaction was very different. He didn't seem surprised by the vision of the gun.

"How did you find it?"

He scolded Simon before attending to him, taking the weapon from his hands and stuffing it into the drawer like someone hiding a secret. The boy later explained to them that he'd found it in Dad's bedside table while searching for Audrey's ferrets, that he'd been hearing noises in the house at night for weeks and he'd wanted to surprise his sister. But at that moment, Simon didn't respond to the question. He didn't react to any stimuli. Frank examined his disfigured face. With trembling fingers, he tried opening the eyelids from which blood was flowing. He snapped them back with a cry of pain, though he wasn't the one injured.

He told Grace to call 911.

She obeyed but remained absent, without fully reacting until, in the intensive care unit at the hospital, the doctor confirmed to them that Simon would lose an eye. The bullet hadn't touched the boy, but the weapon's recoil had split his eyebrow and hit his eyeball with enough force to rupture it. Though the doctor didn't use an analogy, Grace thought of an egg cracking. And of her boy's beautiful iris, his pupil, spilling like yolk as they cracked, the miracle of sight reduced to a useless blob. The doctor tried to ease their concerns, explaining that Simon was very young and would become accustomed to living with a single eye. Before leaving, he informed them that they could go in to see him in a few hours.

"Why was there a gun in the house?"

Grace asked the question to nobody in particular, her attention fixed on the green band painted onto the hospital floor, blurry through her tears. She was incapable of looking at her husband.

"For security, honey. In case someone was breaking in."

"*Now* you think someone was?" She wiped mucus from her top lip. "It was you who tried to tell me there wasn't. You said it was those damn ferrets. In the walls."

"I couldn't be sure. What if it was someone?"

"Why wouldn't you tell me you'd bought a gun?" Grace sniffed. "You're totally against guns, Frank. You always have been."

"I didn't want to worry you, I didn't . . . I don't know what to say, honey. I guess it was a mistake."

"A mistake?"

She repeated the word in a slobbery whisper, two syllables that couldn't begin to express the impact Frank's negligence would have—forever—on Simon's life.

"Your son." Grace summoned up the courage to look him in the face. "Your son has lost an eye because of you."

Frank walked off without saying anything. He left her there, standing on the green line. She thought he must have gone down to the cafeteria, or out into the hospital garden. But when she finally went to look for him, she couldn't find him anywhere. She called his cell phone repeatedly, letting it ring at least thirty times—the plucking in Jewel's song would be playing over and over on his handset—but there was no answer. Grace sent a text message to Audrey, asking if Dad had returned home. He wasn't there, why would he be, her daughter replied. And then she became worried. Maybe she'd been too harsh, her accusation too hurtful. Now Frank would feel too ashamed to return, too guilty to be near her, near Simon. She imagined him wandering the city's streets, unable to face the consequences of his misguided decision to obtain a weapon. A weapon that, at the end of the day, he had bought to protect them. His intention had been good. He had certainly never thought their son would blow his eye out.

Feeling increasingly bad, Grace dialed Frank's number again, resolved now to apologize for what she'd said. To promise him she would manage to forgive him for his carelessness. Listening to the endless ringing, Grace vowed to herself that she would never blame Frank for the incident again—anger never led to anything good. It was going to be tough, she knew, but it was what any woman would do for the husband she loved. And it was also what a devoted mother would do for her son. The two of them had to be more united than ever to support Simon, the real victim in all this. All her calls ended in disconnection signals, for the tenth time, the twentieth time.

Frank returned hours later without having answered his phone and with no wish to talk, ask for forgiveness, or accept apologies. He arrived just as the doctor came out to give them permission to go into the ICU and see Simon.

The smile the boy greeted them with, holding a hand up for a high five, instantly wiped away any negative feelings, any concern other than their son's well-being.

It was the next morning when Frank first proposed the idea of leaving Seattle. He argued that they'd have to move, that much was certain, because he couldn't continue to live in the house with the hole from the bullet that cost his son an eye. And that if they were going to move, they could turn the change into a new start for the family. Far away from all the bad things that were happening to them this year in Seattle. It was as if the city were telling them to leave, so the smart thing to do was listen. To go. He would request a transfer, and Grace, with her computers, could work anywhere. He asked the company to move him while Simon was still in the ICU. Ten days later, they informed him there was a vacancy in Boston, an opportunity that would also mean a promotion for him. The universe was usually good to Frank—it always seemed to conspire in his favor. They would still have to wait until Simon finished the first phase of his treatment, for his wounds to heal and so they could take the correct measurements for his artificial eye, but the process could be completed in Boston. The doctor asked for three weeks to finish his work with Simon before transferring the case to the new hospital.

That was how the RV's maiden voyage, the big trip they'd been postponing for over a year, ended up turning into the family's permanent move to the other side of the country. Sometimes, Grace laid the blame for everything that had happened to them on the motor home, claiming it was cursed, but she soon accepted that this was nothing but an absurd superstition. Perhaps there were enchanted houses, but who'd ever heard of a cursed motor home?

◆ ◆ ◆

Nonetheless, the superstition wouldn't go away, and, as if the motor home really did attract disaster, here the four of them were, stuck out on the most deserted road in Idaho after hitting a poor, innocent woman. Fortunately, if everything went well, Earl and Mara would reach the highway soon and call someone. Grace guessed they'd receive assistance before nightfall.

She finished setting the table for lunch while Frank and Simon planned construction of a second tower on the castle. The boy improved his new perception of distances with each day. A week after the gun went off, while he was still in the hospital, Simon asked them, and especially his father, not to feel guilty for what happened. That it was his fault for going in the drawer without permission and for wanting to see whether the pistol was real. At the age of nine, Simon had had the integrity to accept the consequences of his actions in order to ease his father's suffering. That was how brave he'd been. How generous. How honest. As Frank had just said, being honest is a very good thing to want to be. And the boy was learning these values from his father. Grace was proud of her husband, of their marriage, and of their great teamwork bringing up their children.

She looked up and breathed in the aroma of the pine trees, of the sun warming the earth, of the still-damp flowers in the shade. A feeling of well-being, of good fortune and hope for the future, ran through her. They were a beautiful family beginning a new chapter in their lives. Things had gone badly for so long, and now it was time for their luck to change.

From this moment on, everything would be better.

Grace knew it.

She could feel it.

28.

It hurt Mara to swallow.

Her panting had dried her throat until it felt as if it were full of sand.

Sticky sweat covered her skin.

The moisture under her armpits and on her back made her clothes exude the smell of Grace's fabric softener. She walked several miles before her sweat neutralized the nauseating aroma of whatever it was supposed to be—jasmine, sea breeze, or tropical sunset—that came from the material.

"Marital Betrayal," whispered Mara with a smile.

She imagined the label on a softener with that name, hundreds of bottles filling the shelves of a supermarket where thousands of deceived wives would buy it.

When she could no longer bear the length of Grace's jeans, she stuck the knifepoint in the denim, above the knee. Remnants of the knife's blood-and-grit paste had dried in the heat. They came off like scabs now. Mara cut around her leg, ignoring the pricking pains. She repeated the process on the other leg. After two paces in her new shorts, she heard an explosion in the distance. Black smoke rose toward the sky. She wondered whether it had been such a good idea to pull the old man out of the truck.

The pain from a sudden stitch stabbed at her side.

But she didn't slow down.

She wanted to reach the motor home as quickly as possible.

She wanted to put things right.

29.

Standing on the road with her eyes closed, Grace let the last rays of sun play across her face. Frank had been watching her for a while without her knowing, appreciating the beauty of her gold-lacquered features. He saw the exact moment the sunlight evaporated, when the shadows on her face disappeared. She opened her eyes as if waking from a dream. Finding Frank's eyes, she smiled. She held out a hand, inviting him to contemplate the surrounding landscape with her.

"How I love this time of day," she said, indicating the sky, the forest. "The sun hides, and it takes its shadows with it, but its light stays. It's at this moment the world shows us its loveliest color. Its true colors."

She rested her head on Frank's shoulder. He stroked her cheek; it was still warm.

"Every moment's lovely with you," he whispered to his wife.

They both took a deep breath.

"So, how long's this going to take?" Audrey yelled through the motor-home door. "You said they'd come before night and it's almost dark."

Grace checked her wristwatch. She showed it to Frank.

"They *are* taking a while," she whispered to him. Then she yelled to Audrey. "Honey, first they had to get there—it's a long way—then call, explain where we are, that we need replacement tires, then AAA has to get here . . . it all takes time."

From his fortress, Simon shouted that he didn't mind waiting. He liked it here and preferred not to leave the castle half built.

"That's the spirit, Gizmo," said Frank. "And it's just us at last, the four of us as a family. As it should've been. Now that we've gotten rid of her—I admit I didn't like that woman at all. The fewer strangers around my kids in an isolated place, the better."

"You guys are always afraid of everything." Audrey got down from the RV. "Your generation is too sexist, racist, homophobic, and easily scared. People are good, generally. And especially women."

"And saying that isn't sexist?" asked Frank.

"Of course not."

Frank looked at his wife for support, but she shook her head, advising him not to try to make sense of adolescent impertinence.

"You all know what we're going to do to make the wait more bearable?" With her promising tone, Grace caught the attention of the three of them. "Hot dogs!"

Simon ran toward them with his arms in the air. He ran around his parents, around Audrey, who stopped him by grabbing his head. She wasn't going to join the celebration until she'd made sure they would all enjoy the feast.

"Yes, honey, yes," Grace replied before her daughter had even asked the question. "I brought veggie dogs, too."

They had dinner at the same table where they'd had breakfast and lunch. The tablecloth was covered in crumbs when they finished, and it was almost night. A single frankfurter survived on one of the paper plates Grace had taken out, the other plates now dirty with ketchup, mustard, and crispy fried onions.

"I'm liking this, not having cell phones," said Frank. "Did you notice how much we talked during dinner?"

It surprised him to realize that their previous dinner, at Danielle's, had taken place just twenty-four hours earlier. It felt as if a lot more time had passed.

"Shut up, Dad, don't even joke about it." Audrey was still chewing her hot dog.

"Where's your sense of adventure?"

"My sense of adventure?" she repeated, incredulous.

"Frank, I wouldn't call running a woman over an adventure," Grace corrected him.

"Sorry, but being out in the middle of nowhere, eating delicious hot dogs with my wife and kids, that's what I call an adventure. I've already forgotten about the unwelcome guest," he said, as if he really believed it. "And with this dinner, I've confirmed my theory that ketchup tastes better outdoors."

He mopped the plate with a piece of bread, stuck it in his mouth, and groaned with pleasure.

"I liked the woman," said Simon, "and I liked Earl even more. See how I'm going to lead a normal life even though I'm missing an eye? He was driving with no hands—unbelievable!"

"By the way"—Audrey leaned forward with her elbows on the table and lowered her voice—"what do you think he was saying about being a victim of sexual abuse? What do you think they did to him?"

"Audrey," Grace complained. "Please."

"Mom, I'm a young adult who can understand conversations in code now. I just want to kno—"

"Audrey, be quiet. I'm serious."

"OK, OK . . ."

She bit into her hot dog. Simon took the opportunity to take a jab at his sister.

"Yeah, shut up, Audrey."

"You shut up. You didn't even get it."

When she pointed at her brother with the hot dog, she splashed his face with ketchup. It went on the patch as well. Simon felt the material, checking the severity of the disaster. Suddenly serious, he took it off, revealing the hole in his face. Frank looked away to avoid seeing the wound, and Grace squeezed his knee under the table. Then Simon sucked the blob of sauce from the patch and, with a mischievous smile, picked up the ketchup bottle. He squirted a jet onto his sister's hair.

"Now we're even."

"Even? More like you're dead."

She counterattacked with mustard, covering Simon's face in yellow spots. He stuck his hand in the bag of fried onions and threw a fistful at her as if it were grapeshot.

"Kids, stop!" yelled Frank.

They both halted, about to squeeze their respective bottles again. That was when Grace threw two slices of dill pickle at him.

"Tell me you didn't just do that."

"It wasn't her," Audrey lied. "It was me."

The blob of mustard she fired onto his nose sparked off the battle.

"Everyone get Dad!" urged Simon.

Spurts of both sauces, handfuls of crispy onions, and more pickles rained on Frank. He tried to offer resistance, but there were no weapons left on the table. He could only try to defend himself with an empty plate he used as a shield, though it was inadequate protection against the barrage of ingredients. Frank could hear his family laughing, and he ended up bellowing with laughter, too.

"All right, all right, that's enough, stop. Stop!"

He raised his hands, surrendering. A couple more splashes landed on his face before the attack ceased. Simon looked at him with a hand over his mouth, while Audrey and Grace contained laughter that escaped through their noses. Frank examined his hands, arms, T-shirt. He felt his forehead, cheeks, jaw. There wasn't an inch of clean material or skin.

"Just wait till we're stuck out here for days and you remember all the food you wasted throwing it at your own father."

He blinked to alleviate the mustard sting in his eye.

"Shut up, Dad, we're not going to be here for days."

"Of course we aren't," Grace assured Audrey. "They must be about to turn up."

She looked down the road as if AAA would arrive right then.

"Right now, I'm going to turn on the boiler, because what I really need is a shower." Frank got up with his hands held high, without touching anything. "And this polo shirt can go straight in the trash."

"You'd better not touch anything in that state," said Grace as she also got up. "Go straight to the bathroom. I'll turn on the boiler."

"Do you know where it is?"

He guessed from his wife's expression that she had no idea, but she had no intention of admitting it.

"Do you think she doesn't know because she's a woman?" Audrey cut in. "Because us girls don't know anything about motors, right? Dad, honestly . . ."

"OK, OK, I'll leave it to you." He turned around without saying anything else. "But I'd like to take a shower sometime in the next two minutes."

Before climbing into the RV, he heard Grace ask her daughter in a low voice whether she knew where the boiler was. Audrey replied that of course she didn't.

30.

Grace knew it was in one of the side compartments. She remembered Frank explaining it to her when he switched the original tank boiler for a tankless one, but now she realized that perhaps she hadn't paid enough attention. She took the bunch of keys from the door and started trying locks. The first compartment that opened, on the driver's side, was the water inlet.

"You really do have no idea," said Audrey.

Grace held a finger to her lips to stop her from speaking so loudly her father might hear her. She continued investigating that side while her daughter disappeared into the RV. Audrey returned with a plastic folder.

"Here, learn, and stop perpetuating the stereotype of women knowing nothing about mechanics."

It was a folder from the dealership where Frank bought the motor home, its logo adorning the cover. Grace opened it. Something flew out, and she caught it at her thigh. It was a business card, probably belonging to the agent who made the sale. Without looking at it, she inserted it behind all the documents and took out the vehicle's thick manual. When she tried to turn the pages while holding the folder, she dropped the bunch of keys.

Beside the rear wheels.

She bent down to pick them up, and for the first time she saw the damage to the flat tires. Crouching, she touched the burst area on one of the wheels. She ran her finger along a split that seemed too uniform, too straight. An alarm bell she would have preferred to ignore went off somewhere in her head. When she was about to stand up, she noticed that the other wheel had an almost identical incision. Just as uniform, just as straight. The alarm rang loud when she understood they had been slashed. Deliberately. She dropped the keys again with the shock. They jingled in her trembling fingers as she rounded the rear of the motor home. Passing the table—where Audrey and Simon were gathering up food debris from the battle—she threw the manual onto it.

"Did you find the boiler?"

Grace didn't answer her daughter—she didn't even know whether she had the voice to do so. She felt herself going dizzy as she skirted around the sofa. She opened the bathroom door without bothering to knock.

She found Frank naked, with a foot in the shower.

"It's on?" he asked, smiling. "I didn't think you'd find it."

He turned on the water and tested the temperature.

Grace closed the door behind her, not wanting the kids to hear her. She crossed her arms, positioned very close to Frank. It was all the bathroom's dimensions allowed.

"Why didn't you tell me?"

He opened and closed his mouth as if unable to produce words.

"T . . . tell you?"

"Tell me why you didn't want that woman here."

Frank swiveled around to turn off the faucet, but Grace knew he was only doing it to escape her gaze.

"Frank."

"What?" His face formed several different expressions within an instant. "I don't know . . . I don't know what . . ."

Grace noticed that his penis had shrunk, how withdrawn his testicles were. It might have been the jet of freezing water that had hit his hand, but she knew it was really because neither he nor his body knew how to lie. She always got the truth out of him.

"You don't need to lie to me, Frank. I know."

His back tensed, making him seem taller. He breathed in so loudly it was audible.

"Honey . . ."

"The wheels." She revealed the truth. "I've seen the wheels. They're not punctured. They've been slashed."

Frank let out the inhaled air, regained his usual posture.

"The wheels?"

"Stop it, stop playing dumb. Yes, the wheels. They've been slashed deliberately."

"You think so?"

"Please, Frank. Come with me."

"Now?" he asked, gesturing at his nudity. Grace handed him a towel.

"Let's go."

She left the vehicle and waited outside for the time it took him to find some flip-flops. Frank came out with the towel around his waist, and they walked together to the wheels. Grace pointed at the slashes, but he seemed indifferent. He killed a mosquito on his shoulder.

"What are you reading into this, honey?"

"That's why you were acting so strangely," she said in a whisper—she didn't want to alarm the children, who for some reason were singing the Taylor Swift number they'd sung the night before. "It was Mara who slashed our tires."

"No, I don't think—"

"You noticed and you didn't want to scare us. That's why you behaved in such a weird way around her, why you wanted her gone." Grace set out her theory while Frank's face alternated between expressions again, without coming to rest on any of them. "Why would she do something like that, Frank? What could that woman have against us?"

The flurry of expressions stopped.

"I don't know, honey. But yes, that was why I was being like I was. I noticed the slashes last night."

"Oh, Frank, I knew it." The relief she felt at her husband admitting the truth soon turned to unease. "Why would she do it? How creepy." She sought refuge against his bare chest, the warmth soothing her goose bumps. "My God, was she really dangerous?"

"I don't think so, not really." Frank held her away from him to look her in the eyes. "It was probably just a kind of revenge, a moment of anger. We hit her, or so she believes, and then she realizes she won't get anything from us because the accident's her fault. So she punctured our tires like an angry little girl, that's all."

"Sure, but that means she had a knife. Oh my God, a stranger with a knife near my children."

"Now do you see my point?" Frank raised his eyebrows. "In any case, it could just be a penknife. No one comes camping in a forest like this without a penknife. She might've had some cans that needed opening. Let's not assume the worst."

"I hope you're right. That she wasn't looking for anything else. It's scary to think about it, so alone out here . . . And then I lent her my pajamas and clothes." A shiver ran down her back. "And we treated her so well. We were good to her, Frank, and this is how she repays us?" Grace gestured at the wheels. "Leaving us stuck out here?"

"The important thing is, she's gone now. And I managed to keep the little secret so neither you nor the kids got scared. I wanted to get her out of here before you realized." He gave a broad smile with a hand on his chest, caricaturing a champion's pose. "A feat that practically makes me a hero."

Though she knew he was joking, Grace caught her husband's face between her hands.

"You are, Frank, you really are." She kissed him on the lips with her eyes closed. "You're my hero. Our hero."

"Well, I'm going to take that shower. Do you want to keep searching for the boiler?"

Grace shook her head with a smile, admitting her ignorance. Frank took her by the hand to the other side and showed her where it was. He turned it on in front of her so she could learn how to do it. Then he climbed back into the RV, and Grace went around closing the other compartments she'd opened during her fruitless search. When she went back past the flat tires, she turned around, looking at the road. The impending onset of night—or the new information about Mara—made it seem more solitary, more dangerous. She thought she could see a column of black smoke in the distance, but it could have been anything. In the dying light, the trees' foliage merged with the sky, turning everything into a single darkness that stalked them. Grace turned the motor home's exterior light on and sat at the table with her children, the same table she'd thrown the folder from the dealership on. She sat between the two of them—she needed to feel them close. She channeled her nerves into a shaking foot.

"Dad found out you had no idea where the boiler was, huh?" asked Audrey. "And you looked like the typical wife who can't solve a problem without help from her husband. Some future you older women are leaving for us young women, with an attitude like that."

"This young woman didn't know where the boiler was, either," she replied, tilting her head toward her daughter.

"This young woman still has time to learn."

Grace put an end to the discussion with a forced smile—she didn't have the energy to argue with her daughter. She scraped her thumb against the corner of the motor-home manual, flicking through the pages, again and again, making a sound like cards being shuffled. She watched the road, wishing AAA would finally arrive. She was afraid it would be the stranger with a knife who reappeared.

31.

Frank went into the bathroom holding his breath. When he closed the door, he let it out with a loud sigh that turned into a pant, almost a sob. It pained him to lie to Grace so much, it truly pained him. But there was nothing else he could do now. Except there was. Right now. He could walk out there naked and confess everything. As he should have done last night in the bedroom when he saw Mara throw away the family's cell phones. As he should have done last year, the first time he had sex with her in the hut at the dealership. If only he had done it then. If only he hadn't allowed the problem to grow. Frank touched his lips, the ones Grace had just kissed as she told him he was her hero, the kids' hero, too. A kiss he'd accepted as if he really was that hero—he'd even joked that he was, when in reality he was a despicable creature, a fraud, a barefaced liar. Once again, he'd managed to make Grace believe what he had wanted her to believe, that Mara had no motive to slash their tires other than simple revenge for their near-accident. It had prevented Grace from beginning to pull on the cord of Mara's real motive—a cord that, if she followed it, would guide her through the maze of lies her husband had built to the terrible truth.

Frank shook his head. There was no point in punishing himself like this. He was only protecting his wife's and his family's happiness. They would gain nothing from knowing about some mistakes he regretted, mistakes he would erase from his past without hesitation. His only objective was to prevent his family from having to erase them, to ensure they would never be part of their present or their future. And for now, he was managing to do it. He knew the problem hadn't disappeared just because he'd put two hours of road between them and Mara—he was certain she was already planning another ploy to make sure Grace discovered the truth—but he'd bought some time. He had come out of the mire, momentarily, and could plan his next step. The next lie.

"Oof . . ."

The sound that came from his chest relaxed his taut stomach in an instant. Then he looked in the mirror. He still had ketchup and mustard spattered on his forehead, his hair, his neck. Those marks—and his family's laughter while they squirted the sauces at him—gave him a feeling of peace that revived his conviction that everything would be all right. That he'd continue to get his way and hide the damaging truth. That his wife and children would never know, because they didn't need to know, and they would enjoy lunches, dinners, and food fights together for many more years to come.

Frank took off his towel and left it on the sink. The reflection of his nudity discomforted him. It was just another body, naked like any other, and he couldn't understand why he'd felt such an urgent need to show it to someone, to surrender it to any woman other than his own wife. He looked down. Had that part of his body—the one hanging between his legs, the one that was just another appendage, just another finger, another piece of flesh and skin—really been so important that he would risk his home, his family, everything that made him happy? He got in the shower, slid the door across to stop seeing himself, to stop thinking.

He turned the faucet but avoided the jet of water until it came out hot. When his whole body was wet, he turned it off so he wouldn't waste any more of their fifty-gallon supply. Mara had used plenty that morning. He searched for the bar of soap in his corner caddy, but only found his razor. He rummaged through the collection of products on Grace's caddy, but it wasn't there, either, only the pink one she used. Frank opened the shower door to look on the sink, and there it was. His pine tar soap. Audrey must have used it when she came in to wash the plant debris off her arms, angry about the lost cell phones. Frank stretched for the soap from inside the shower. He rubbed it on his hands, forming a white lather despite the product's dark color. As always, he started on his chest, his armpits, his arms. He pressed down on the skin to remove the encrusted mustard. He moved down to his legs, his feet.

And then up to his face.

He closed his eyes, rubbing hard.

His hair, as well.

He continued to scrub his face without realizing the lather was turning red.

The drops of blood that fell on the shower base diluted in brief spirals.

Unaware, Frank held the soap to his genitals.

The first rub dealt him an unexpected stab of pain, but nothing suspicious—he thought he must have pressed too hard.

He rubbed again.

The soap got stuck, as if caught on the testicle skin.

Without giving himself time to assess why this had happened, he pulled.

This time the shot of pain was so intense his pulse accelerated. He suddenly felt unwell. He took his hands away from the painful spot, letting go of the soap, which fell onto one of his big toes. Unable to see, his eyes closed against the foam, Frank couldn't understand why his crotch was burning, why he could feel a new texture on his hands, thicker than water. He turned the faucet and rinsed his face.

He looked down.

He blinked, unable to believe what he saw.

A dark red, almost black liquid was flowing down his thighs, his calves, following the route of his leg hair. When it reached the white shower pan, it dissolved and disappeared down the drain. Frank quickly recognized the smell of blood. The liquid was blood. His stomach churned. He stopped breathing to counteract the nausea, to halt a menacing retch in his throat.

Before he had fully gotten over the shock, he felt between his legs. The lines on his hands became channels for the blood to run down, filling his palms until it spilled over the sides. Confused, he inspected his testicles, searching for the source of the blood, but it made no sense. Except it did, because he soon found two cuts on his scrotum, one deeper than the other.

"What the fuck?"

He searched for the first explanation in his fingernails. They weren't sharp; he'd cut them before they set off on the trip. Then he picked up the bar of soap. Examining it, he caught his thumb. The new cut betrayed the presence of something stuck in the bar, embedded in it.

It was a razor blade.

"The fucking bi . . ."

Frank trotted on the spot in the shower stall, his rage at Mara making it impossible to stay still, though he didn't know what to do. The blood dripping from between his legs, the shower pan turned red, was an image he never thought he'd see as a man. He felt an urge to strike the shower door with his elbow, to break it. Tear the entire bathroom to pieces.

Something hot, and thick, oozed under his eyelid, making the world turn crimson, the color of his fury. The drop of blood in his eye reminded him that he'd scrubbed the soap all over his body. He checked his chest, stomach, arms. They were unharmed.

Then he thought of his face.

He slid open the shower door and looked at himself in the mirror. He found a mask of foam and blood.

225

"Christ!"

The cry escaped his throat. He covered his mouth with his hands—the last thing he needed was to attract Grace's attention. He observed the damage in the reflection through a thin layer of condensation. The hot water must have taken the sting out of the pain when he made the three clean cuts across his cheek, his forehead. The image of his lacerated face brought back the nausea. His back hit the cubicle, and the soap slipped from his fingers again. When he crouched down to pick it up, the bathroom door opened.

"Why're you yelling?" asked Grace. "What is it?"

Frank remained squatting, keeping his head low. He pretended to be soaping his feet.

"Nothing, I almost fell."

He splashed water on the blood that was dripping from his groin, trying to dilute it so it wasn't visible.

"Are you all right?"

"I'm fine. You can go."

Blobs of red lather dislodged from his face and floated in the pool of water at his feet.

"You sure?"

"Yeah, honey, I'm sure. Go on."

His position opened up one of the cuts on his testicles.

"Frank, what's that?" Grace knelt in front of the cubicle, pointing at a mark on his shoulder. "Is it blood? Did you hurt yourself falling?"

She lifted his face by the chin. Her expression contorted in the same way his had when he saw himself in the mirror.

"Your face, Frank. You're bleeding. What've you done to yourself? How . . . ?"

She was left speechless when she discovered the bloody discharge on the shower base. Her eyes followed the trickle of blood in reverse, from the drain to his feet, from the feet to the bent knees, from the knees to what was between his thighs.

"Wh . . . what . . . ?"

When Frank tried to hide the soap behind his body, she snatched it from his hands. She looked at the razor embedded in it, confused, unable to explain it.

"I . . . I must've left the soap on top of one of my razor blades," he improvised. "It got stuck there and I didn't notice it."

"Frank, this isn't stuck on top. It's been pushed in, with force. As if someone wanted to . . . oh my God." Grace took a deep breath. "It was the girl."

"Her? You think?"

"She had a shower this morning, Frank. She was alone in this bathroom, she could've done anything. This is . . ." She dropped the soap. "This is insane. I'm scared, Frank. That woman's crazy. We hit a dangerous woman and now she wants revenge. Our kids could've used that soap."

"It would've been clear it was mine." Frank gestured at the letters on his corner caddy. "If she wants revenge on someone, it's me. For hitting her with the RV, must be."

"I don't know. I don't want to know. We have to get out of here, Frank. We have to go, right now. Clean yourself up. We'll walk if we have to."

Frank rinsed his injuries in cold water, thinking about what to do. Trying to find more excuses. Grace passed him the large towel so he could press it against the cuts on his testicles, and a smaller one for his face.

"Mom?" Simon's voice came from outside. "Dad?"

They fell silent, their muscles tense.

"Someone's coming," the boy added.

Grace looked at Frank with eyes wide open, afraid of the deranged woman who for no apparent reason had it in for her family. He looked at her with eyes just as wide, his fear caused by the real threat, the threat of the truth coming back to ensnare him after all. A final drop fell from the showerhead into the pool around the drain. Frank observed the circular waves it made on the water's surface, a subtle alteration that sent everything out of balance.

Audrey's untroubled yell confirmed his worst fears.

"It's Mara!"

Grace dropped the towel she was pressing against Frank's face. She left the bathroom.

"Grace!" he yelled. "Honey, wait!"

The whole motor home wobbled under her footsteps. Frank slipped as he got out of the shower.

32.

Grace climbed down the steps, hearing Frank slip in the bathroom and curse. She recognized Mara's silhouette in the distance, in the darkness, approaching the motor home's field of light. When she reached it, Grace could also see her ruined clothes, her purse, bloodstained. She heard her labored breathing.

"It . . . it was Earl," Mara said. "That old man tried . . . he wanted . . ."

She broke down in tears while she continued to limp on. She showed them bruises on her arms, marks on her pants.

"Oh no," whispered Audrey.

She got up from the table and ran to Mara before Grace could stop her. She received her with a delicate hug, separated the sweaty hair from her face.

"What did he do to you?" Audrey inspected her face, her body. "You're covered in cuts and bruises. Are you OK?"

Simon wrinkled his nose.

"Earl? It can't be."

He also got up with the intention of going over to them, but this time Grace reacted in time to catch him. She pulled on his T-shirt neck and they walked together. She protected the boy with an arm over his shoulders, keeping him close.

"He did that to you?" Simon asked as they approached.

Two paces before reaching her, Grace stopped. Keeping a certain distance would be safer and make it easier to hide her nerves. Her main concern was for Audrey to come away from Mara. Having accepted Mara's role as victim without hesitation, the teenager was continuing to show affection and devotion to her. From up close, Grace examined the damage to the clothes she'd lent her that morning. The blue-striped T-shirt she'd worn for the last time at a beach picnic with the kids was now covered in dried bloodstains. The jeans were now a pair of torn shorts. Grace preferred not to think about the implement she'd slit the garment with, or where she had it hidden right now. Forcing herself to hide her fear, Grace suppressed the screams that tickled her throat.

"What happened, Mara?" she asked, and she swallowed. She also held out a hand, inviting Audrey to come to her and Simon. "Come here with your brother, honey, let me take care of her."

But Mara closed her fingers around the girl's wrist, not with force but as a warning. She must have sensed Grace's unease after all. Grace looked her in the eyes, establishing a silent dialogue in which they each tried to decipher what the other woman knew. If Mara squeezed harder on Audrey's wrist, her guise as an innocent victim would be gone. If Grace leapt to her daughter's rescue, she would reveal that she knew Mara was lying.

"You were right not wanting to go with him, then," said Grace. "We'll take care of that, don't worry." Deciding to take the risk, she went close and, crouching, pretended to examine one of the cuts on Mara's legs. Perhaps surprised at her willingness to help, Mara let down her guard and released Audrey to point out the injury's course, winding up toward her groin. Grace took her chance. She grabbed her daughter and pulled her away.

"Leave us alone!" she yelled, retreating backward, dragging Simon with her as well.

"What're you doing, Mom?" Audrey pulled her arm away to free herself.

Grace fixed her eyes on Mara.

"Get out of here." She said it with all the fear she'd been containing, with all the force with which she intended to protect her children. "Leave us in peace."

"Mom, what is it? We have to help her."

"I knew it. Earl didn't do anything," concluded Simon.

"Why're you here?" Grace blinked to get the sweat out of her eyes. She had both hands busy with the children. "What the fuck do you want?"

Grace never cursed, which was why the word sounded so violent on her lips, so cutting on her tongue.

"Mom, why would you say that?" Audrey scolded her.

"Go inside," she ordered, whispering through her teeth. "Lock yourselves in the RV."

"No, I'm going to—"

"Get in!"

If Grace never swore, she was even less likely to shout at her children. Audrey sensed the seriousness of the situation, and her attitude changed. She cooperated, taking Simon with her. Holding hands, they ran back to the motor home, as if escaping a fire. Halfway there, they saw Frank, who had finally come out. Grace saw her husband limp—the fall in the bathroom must have been more dramatic than she'd imagined. He was wearing jogging pants and a sweater without a T-shirt. There were splashes of water on the clothes, and blood. His hair was still wet. The cuts on his face weren't bleeding, but they stood out in dark red.

"What happened to you?" Audrey asked.

"Dad, you've cut yourself."

"In!" yelled Frank. "And lock it from the inside. The windows, too."

Simon hid in his sister's chest, and they climbed into the vehicle together. Obeying her father, Audrey closed the door. Grace heard the locks being activated from inside. The turn signals blinked twice. Then the two open windows were closed and the children scurried around inside, no doubt looking for a place where they could see what was happening.

When she had him close, Grace held Frank around the waist. His body was giving off heat from the rushing and moisture from his recent shower. And there was also another strange vibration she was unable to identify. There was something in his face she didn't recognize, an unusual mutation she found disturbing. She attributed it to the cuts—it must have been that. After so many years, she knew all of Frank's expressions.

"Look what you've done to my husband." Grace held his chin. "Look at this face and tell me how you feel, look what you've managed to do with your soap."

Mara took the accusation without blinking.

"Maybe . . . maybe it wasn't her," said Frank. "The blade could've gotten stuck there somehow."

"And the tires?" Grace aimed the question at Mara with her chest puffed out. "What did you do to the tires?"

"It might not . . . ," Frank stuttered beside her.

"You slashed them, deliberately." Grace felt as if she were drowning in her own indignation. "The wheels didn't blow, you punctured them. To strand us out here. To punish us when you realized you wouldn't get anything from our insurance because it was your fault."

Mara's expression remained unchanged despite the barrage of accusations. She just listened with unsettling composure to everything Grace threw at her. Unmoved, she looked at Frank and crossed her arms, as if expecting something from him.

"They might've blown," he said, "when I hit the brakes, the wheels . . ."

232

Grace shook her head, unable to understand Frank's attitude. There was no reason to hide anything now, he didn't need to protect her from the truth, and now even the kids knew how dangerous the stranger in front of them was. It was time to hit back.

"Frank, it was her. The tires were slashed with a knife."

They had just discussed it, before his shower—they'd both agreed. It made no sense for him to deny it now. And yet, he made another argument in favor of the flat tires happening by chance.

Mara let out an exhausted sigh. She told Frank to be quiet.

"It was me, Grace," she confessed. "I cut them. I did it. With this."

She took a kitchen knife from her back pocket, one of the dangerous ones that were more like weapons. It came out of the same flower-embroidered pocket where Grace, at that picnic, had kept a Starburst for Simon. The waning moon shined its light on the metal, and the gleam ran down the knife as if showing off its blade.

Grace took a step back, hiding behind Frank.

"Stay calm," she whispered. "Please, stay calm. There're children here."

"I am calm," said Mara. "Really, I am, Grace. It's your husband who's the nervous one. He knows why I slashed the tires. He's done some things, too."

Frank's shoulders went up and down in time with his breathing, which accelerated all of a sudden.

"He hasn't done anything to you," Grace blurted out. "You showed up out of nowhere on the road. It was you who was careless."

"Trust me, Grace. You husband has done some things."

"He hasn't done anything. He wanted you to sleep outside to keep us safe. He tied the zipper to protect his family. And seeing what's happening"—she pointed at the knife Mara was brandishing at them—"he was right to do so. How naïve I was. Always believing everyone's good.

That's why I took you in, took care of you as well as we could. None of this would've happened if I'd paid more attention to my husband."

Mara smiled in a way that Grace couldn't interpret, an expression between pity and pleasure. It conveyed an insolence that offended her.

"What the fuck are you laughing about?" she said, the swear word once again strange and powerful in her mouth.

Mara looked at her husband.

"Come on, Frank. Are you really not going to say anything to your wife after all this? Look at you, look at us. What else needs to happen?"

The new register in her voice confounded Grace. It was as if she was speaking to a different person, as if a close bond of trust had just been established between them. It was also the first time she heard Mara address Frank by his name. And the familiarity with which she said it was inappropriate. Grace stepped out from behind his back and faced him with a questioning look.

"Frank?"

His eyes escaped to the ground. To the motor home. To Mara. When they returned to Grace they were bright, reddened. His forehead was as furrowed as it was when he cried.

"Honey . . ."

"Frank, what's happening? You're scaring me."

He bit his lip as if struggling not to retch, as if he knew that when he opened his mouth something dreadful would come out from inside him.

"Come on, say it," Mara weighed in. "Don't think about it. It's time, Frank. You've owed it to her for so long. The kids won't hear anything. They're in there with the windows closed."

Mara moved the knife so that the moonlight reflected on Frank's face. He covered it with his hands, hiding behind a mask of fingers. He took a deep breath, as deep as the regret that caused it must have been.

As final as a surrender. Frank opened his hands, revealing his face as if removing a disguise.

"I'm sorry, honey. I'm so sorry. I never wanted to hurt you."

Grace remained silent.

A deep silence.

The kind of silence that precedes the worst news.

"I slept with her, Grace." Frank lowered his head. "I was sleeping with Mara for a few months. But it's over, I promise, it won't . . ."

Grace saw that Frank was still moving his mouth, but she could no longer hear. Her ears must have become blocked, the way they had when they drove up into the mountains, because she could only hear her own breathing. Her heart beating. Sounds that confirmed her body was still functioning even if her soul had received a fatal wound. She read the word *love* on her husband's lips several times, but all of a sudden she didn't know what the term meant. She had thought she'd known for the last twenty years. She had proudly explained its properties to hundreds of thousands of subscribers, of people, in dozens of videos about marital happiness, but nothing she knew about love was remotely like what Frank had just confessed. Frank, the man who once recorded "You Were Meant for Me" on both sides of a cassette for her.

"What?"

Her devastation was reduced to a monosyllable. It was a while before she could say anything else. When her ears unblocked, the owls were still hooting and the pine cones still falling. The world hadn't stopped, but it could never be the same again. Because the question Grace asked next was consistent only with a distorted reality, a different universe to which she didn't want to belong.

"You slept with this woman?"

Frank lowered his head again to concede.

"So you know her?" Grace was gradually regaining her senses. "You've known who she was since yesterday and didn't say anything? How do you know her?"

He locked his hands together behind his neck and turned away without saying anything.

"Tell her, Frank," Mara intervened. "You've started, now tell her everything. Do you want me to say it? I'm not going to keep quiet any longer." She granted Frank a few seconds of silence that he opted not to use. "Grace, I was the one who sold you this RV. I'm the saleswoman from the dealership."

Grace blinked several times, trying to remember that spring Saturday when Frank went to collect the motor home.

"Is what she says true?"

In the twisted reality to which Grace now seemed condemned to belong, her husband, the father of her two children, nodded.

"Frank, please . . . Frank, what's happening?" Grace didn't recognize her own voice—she'd never heard herself speak like this, through her nose, through her eyes, through profound pain. "She's . . . what? A crazy lover of yours? I don't know what I'm saying, Frank."

And yet she was beginning to see things more clearly.

"She's here because of you? It was you who brought *this* here." She gestured disdainfully at Mara, her grotesque appearance, her knife. "Near your family? Your children?"

She breathed. Her thoughts were whirling around in her head, in her heart. She grew dizzier as she sensed another revelation on its way.

"It was no coincidence that you were on this road," she said to Mara. "You wanted to stop the motor home, you wanted to . . . and that's why she slashed the tires, that's why she stuck the razor blade in your soap." She was addressing Frank now. "It was your soap. She wanted you to cut yourself. Why? Out of spite? What is she, a fucking lunatic?" Her mouth was eager to let out all the curses she hadn't used in her life. "You slept with a crazy woman who wants to take revenge by harming the whole family? Oh no, Frank, please, no. No, no, no, no, no . . ." A realization had made her entire body turn cold, and she felt her blood rush to her feet. Her face must have paled badly because Frank's mouth opened when she faced him to ask, "Is it her? Is she the one who was coming in the house?"

Frank's tongue clicking was the most terrible confirmation. He looked at her unblinking, fighting back tears that finally overflowed. She also felt tears run warm down her pallid face. She turned to Mara.

"Was it you?"

Mara nodded. And then Grace remembered her superstition about the motor home. The idea that the vehicle was the source of all the bad things that had happened to the family since they'd bought it, an idea she had tried to dismiss as a senseless superstition but which now took on a whole new meaning. It wasn't that the motor home was cursed. It was that her husband had started sleeping with the unbalanced saleswoman who'd sold it to them.

"And you knew?" She faced Frank again, fearing the dark, heartrending place where her deductions were leading her. "You knew all the time? You knew she'd taken the ferrets but you let your daughter suffer? You watched her cry all those days without saying anything? You let her blame me for leaving the door open when you knew it was her . . ." She indicated Mara. "And you. You put something in my shampoo, like you did now with the razor in the soap. Oh my God, Frank, this can't be real . . . you watched me breaking out with marks all over my head, losing my hair . . . you watched me cry in front of the mirror with tufts of it in my hands and you held me to console me. You said yes when I asked you if it could've been Audrey." She held her hand to her mouth as she realized this. She dried her eyes with her forearm. "Frank, please, tell me you went to speak to Bob to get him to keep a closer watch on our street."

He didn't move.

"No, of course you didn't go. Why would you if you knew who was responsible for everything? All you would've achieved would be for them to catch your lover breaking into the house, and I'd find out about everything. You would've called her in secret to negotiate with her, right?

"To beg her to stop. You were bored of fucking her but she wanted more. Is that it? And you started getting scared because she kept coming in the house. She was threatening you by playing games with us, with your family. You were really scared. And that's why you went and bought a gun. Without telling me anything, because you couldn't explain it. According to you, no one was coming in the house—it was all the ferrets' fault. And as anti-gun as you've always been, you buying one made no sense. But you did, because only you knew there was a dangerous woman coming for us. And then Simon . . ."

Something inside Grace had warned her that her deductions were leading to a dismal discovery, but really facing up to it, having to construct it with words, was as painful as reliving the episode when the gun had gone off. As if the bullet had hit her. "My God, Frank. Your son lost an eye because you brought a gun into the home to protect yourself from a woman who wants you for herself. That's what happened. Our boy will be missing an eye for the rest of his life because of you. Because of . . . this."

She gestured at the two of them with contempt, moving her hand with a disdain that made them something appalling, something hard to look at. In this new distorted reality Grace had been transported to, everything was hollow, and awful. And if the person responsible for this distortion was the person she loved most, then everything she knew about the world was a lie. Love didn't exist. Goodness didn't, either. Frank nodded. He lowered his head, accepting the full weight of the guilt that Grace had tried to take off his shoulders since the incident but that now made so much sense.

Mara cleared her throat. "It isn't exactly like that."

Frank looked up with eyes full of hate.

"It's incredible how misogynist we women can be," Mara said to Grace. "How easily we blame one another before blaming the man. Crazy, unbalanced, in love with your husband. Is that the first explanation you arrive at? I'm the crazy one, right? The one responsible for everything. And this is all my doing." She stretched out her arms to illustrate how extreme the situation was. "Why? Out of spite? Out of love? Because your husband's such an incredible man that a woman like me will lose her mind after sleeping with him a few times, to the point that I'd threaten his wife with a knife? It's not that, Grace. I'm not threatening you. You're a wonderful woman who's had the misfortune of being another victim of your husband's staggering lack of honesty. He deceived me, too, denying your existence for months. Telling me he was divorced."

Another crack opened up on Grace's heart. She looked at Frank's ringless left hand. He'd never worn it—he said he was uncomfortable in it, just as he never wore a watch or a necklace. He didn't even wear sunglasses. When Grace commented on it in one of her videos, many of her subscribers remarked that it seemed like a lack of respect on her husband's part to refuse to wear the wedding ring, but to Grace that sounded like the antiquated argument of conservative women. A piece of metal didn't make their marriage any worthier.

"I would never have done anything with a married man," Mara went on. "If you knew the pain something like that caused in my fam—" A sob interrupted her words. She closed her eyes and shook her head as if fighting against a memory that tormented her. When she opened them again, full of malice, she aimed the knife at Frank. "That's why I'm here. Because he made me play a part in cheating on another innocent woman." Her fingers squeezed the hilt with rage. "And because of everything he did to me afterward. Because you haven't heard all of the truth yet, Grace. There's more. Much more."

Frank took a step toward Mara, who brandished the weapon firmly.

"Don't come near me."

"Please . . ." He held his hands together as if praying. "Don't do this."

Grace took his arm as though he was a stranger.

"Do what?" she asked. "Say what?"

Frank didn't respond, didn't even look at her. His eyes remained fixed on Mara's, half pleading, half intimidating.

"What?" Grace insisted.

It was Mara who spoke.

"The night your son . . ." She cleared her throat, preparing herself for what she was about to say. "The night your son lost his eye . . . I guess you missed your husband when you were at the hospital."

Grace nodded. Frank had disappeared for a few hours, roaming the building's surroundings, overcome with guilt because of what had happened to Simon, hurt by the accusation Grace had made.

"He was with me," said Mara. "He came to see me at my place."

"Shut up," Frank muttered. "Please, stop."

Grace felt her soul being pinched.

"You went to see your lover while your son was in the hospital?"

"But he didn't come for *that*, Grace." Mara swatted a mosquito on her arm. "Let me tell you why he did come, what your husband did that night."

Mara already had a foot in the water when the intercom bleeped. Since she'd moved to the apartment, every party night had ended in the tub on the balcony—there was no better way to sober up than to relax for a while in the hot water. She could turn on the bubbles or not, depending on how drunk she was and whether she wanted to make use of them in the other pleasant way she did from time to time. That night, for the time being, she wasn't going to turn them on—the tequila shots at the end of the night were still making her dizzy. To this day, she still didn't understand why she kept drinking those shots, knowing how unwell they made her feel. Well, she did know: it was Gabby's fault. Gabby always shrieked the idea at her, with her eyes popping out, at eleven o'clock at night. The hot tub would be the perfect way to subdue the last waves of drunkenness from those shots and everything else she'd drunk. But just as she dipped her foot in, the intercom began bleeping with an urgency as alarming as it was annoying. One of her guests must have forgotten something.

Mara covered her nakedness with a towel tied around her chest. She walked from the balcony to the intercom, dodging red plastic cups and knocking over a can of Rainier that spilled beer on the floor. She mopped it up with someone's sweatshirt she found on a stool, which might have been exactly what the person ringing the doorbell like a lunatic had returned for. She also trod in something sticky with her heel and hoped it was more spilled beer and not vomit like in another of her recent parties. If she didn't know why she always ended up drinking tequila shots, she found it even harder to understand why she kept organizing parties with more than thirty people in her apartment, given that when they were over and it was time to clean up, she always promised herself it had been the last. It must have been that, in the end, her vanity got the better of her and she wanted to show off her home, the newest and most sophisticated in her friend group. Many of those friends wondered how she had gotten her hands on such an apartment downtown. Only her closest ones knew the sad truth. After Mom's death, Dad got rid of the house where his wife had taken her own life. He sold the gigantic property on the outskirts and offered the money to Mara by way of a strange apology for cheating on her mother for thirty years. He persuaded her to accept it by assuring her that it was what her mother had wanted—apparently, for over a year, Mom had been suggesting the idea of selling the house that was now too big for them and using the money to help their only daughter. Mara accepted the money, but not the apology.

It wasn't a guest Mara now saw on the intercom screen, but Frank, who was staring straight at the camera as if wanting to look her in the eyes.

She buzzed open the street-level door and waited for him at the apartment entrance with the door open a crack. The elevator's blue lights announced his arrival on her floor. Frank ran out and pushed her apartment door open before Mara could react to his sudden appearance. Inside, seeing him pace around in circles with his hands on his head but unable to articulate a single word, Mara thought she understood what had happened.

"Did you tell her?" she asked. "You finally told your wife?"

Frank looked at her with contempt, the kind of contempt a woman does not allow in her own home and that filled Mara with the desire to kick him out. She was about to do so when the pain and desperation she saw in his eyes brought out her compassion. She asked him again if he'd told Grace about their affair, but he snorted, dismissing the possibility as if it were absurd. Then he bit his lip as his eyes welled up and his chin trembled.

"Stop," Frank said. "Please, stop now."

Mara tried to take his hand, but he moved away.

"What is it? I haven't done anything else. I haven't been back to your house."

Frank rested his back on the glass partition between the entrance hall and the living room and slid down it until he was sitting on the floor. Covering his eyes with his hands, he told her that his son, his youngest, had just blown an eye out with a gun he'd found in his bedside table. Right now the doctors were deciding whether they could save it or he'd be one-eyed for the rest of his life. At the age of nine.

"What're you doing here, then?" Mara asked. "Why aren't you at the hospital with him, with your wife?"

"I needed to ask you to please stop," said Frank, uncovering his reddened eyes. "Leave me in peace, stop tormenting me. I have money, I can give you money. Or give you back the RV, tomorrow, for nothing, so you can sell it again at the dealership. Anything, but please, stop doing this to me. Leave my family in peace. They don't deserve to suffer like this."

The mere mention of money offended her. Frank knew her objectives were different.

"You know the only thing I want, Frank. For you to put right what you've done. For you to tell your wife. It's not just that I want you to do it. It's the least your wife deserves. To know the truth. To know her husband."

Frank looked up at the ceiling and let out a sigh that contained a barely enunciated plea. A pitter-patter caught his attention, approaching along the microcement hall floor.

"What's all this?" he asked, indicating the debris from the party.

"I just had a little party. We under-thirties still have them, you know."

The pitter-patter snaked between the plastic cups, wet ice bags, and empty soda bottles, until two curious snouts emerged from the detritus. Audrey's ferrets chased each other on their way out of the living room.

"You still have them," said Frank.

"Sure. They'll go home to your daughter when you confess, you know that. None of this is Audrey's fault. You're the one who forced me to use your family. You can end this whenever you want. You decide."

"Please, stop." His shoulders slumped. "Look how far you've taken this. Look what you've done to my son."

"Me?" The accusation outraged her enough to almost sober her up, like a big fright. "That gun has nothing to do with me."

"I bought it because of you," Frank whispered, "after you started coming into my home like some crazy woman out of *Fatal Attraction*."

243

"And you didn't think that a crazy woman out of *Fatal Attraction* coming into your house might be because you've become the disgusting unfaithful husband in that movie? When're you going to take responsibility for your actions, Frank? If you're man enough to have an affair, you should also be man enough to tell your wife. To be frank. So she knows the life she believes she's leading isn't what she thinks it is."

Just as the life Mom lived had been a lie. Mara had not stopped thinking about Mom, about her pain, her unjust end, since she learned of Grace's existence. It was in this pain that Mom suffered, and in her determination to prevent it from happening to another woman, to other children, Mara found the justification for taking whatever measures were necessary to force Frank to confess. Silent pressure had not worked, so she had been obliged to adopt more extreme methods: to break into his home, steal his daughter's pets, tamper with his wife's shampoo. With the shampoo she had overplayed her hand, miscalculated the quantity. But some lost hair was a very small price for Grace to pay for her husband's honesty. For the truth.

"Please, leave me in peace," Frank pleaded.

Mara returned to the balcony to take the bath she needed. She wasn't going to allow Frank's crisis of conscience to ruin it. Not after he had dragged her, with his lies, into a situation she detested more than anyone. A conscience was precisely what a man who repeatedly sleeps with another woman before going home to sleep with his wife *doesn't* have.

"Besides, what were you intending to do with a gun?" she asked him near the hot tub, Frank behind her now. "Shoot me if I'd gone back in your house? God, Frank, all I did was steal some pets and mess with your wife's shampoo—I didn't kill anybody. And I repeat, you can end this whenever you want. It's not fair for you to get off scot-free after cheating on your wife, on the mother of your children. On your own children. It's not fair."

"Then tell her," said Frank, offering her a cell phone he pulled from his pocket. "Go on, call her and tell her, if that's what you want, but stop doing all the other stuff."

"No, Frank." Mara batted the phone away with a smile. "Telling the truth's up to you. You're the only one making the situation worse every day. If you'd been honest with your wife from the start, after the first time in the hut, I bet anything you would've had a chance to fix it. A lot of wives end up forgiving their husbands if it's just one time, a moment of madness. We're all human, women understand that. But you kept quiet. You're still keeping quiet, just like my father did. He was silent for thirty years. He stole thirty whole years from my mother." Mara clenched her jaw when she mentioned her father, spat the tragic consequence of that betrayal through her teeth. "He stole her whole life from her. And you've kept quiet to protect yourself even when your lover broke into your house to harass your family, your children. I promise you, that's much harder to forgive. The longer you take to tell her the truth, the more Grace is going to hate you. When my mother knew the last thirty years of her life had been a lie, that my father had shared his love with other women . . . it destroyed her, Frank. It's not right for a man to hurt a woman so much, and I'm not going to let you do it to your wife. I'm not going to give you that amount of time."

"So that's what this is? I'm revenge for something from your past? That's why you're enjoying this," he said, clenching his fists. "You're enjoying seeing me suffer, making me pay for something your father did that has nothing to do with me."

"I enjoy making a man be honest with his wife. I enjoy the truth."

"Please," Frank whimpered, holding his hands to his chest. "My son's lost an eye."

"And I'm very sorry. I'm sure he's a wonderful boy. But I didn't do it. You bought the weapon and the bullets. You kept them in a place where he could find them. You're the one who did that to your son, like you did this"—she removed her towel, showing him her naked body—"to your wife. When're you going to stop hurting your family?"

Mara gave Frank a lascivious look, sitting on the edge of the hot tub. Her taunt twisted Frank's face into a grimace of hatred that frightened her. Moments before, Mara had seen the urge to hit her pass over Frank's face like a thundercloud. Now he struck like lightning, fast and merciless. So fast that Mara only felt the impact on her face when he had already retracted his hand. She felt heat there, pain in her eye, fire in her chest, and tension in her teeth. But also shame in her stomach, a victim's unjust humiliation.

The slap left her disoriented for a moment. She didn't know whether to respond first to her indignation or her pain. Then her disorientation turned into a loss of balance, and she slipped into the tub. Her body fell into the water, her head hitting one of the acrylic corners. The sound of the blow to the back of her neck, the organic crunch of a watermelon hitting the ground, made her bite her lips and tense her fingers in horror. It felt like the electric shock from a blow to the funny bone, but all over her body. Then the pain blinded her, it emanated in waves from the corner behind her neck, synchronized with her accelerated pulse. She imagined an enormous heart beating in the back of her head, on the corner of the hot tub, sending not blood but boiling acid to the rest of her body, painfully dissolving her entire system, turning her into a strange electric jellyfish that feeds solely on pulses of pain. One sense remained unaltered during her agonizing delirium: taste, revealing to her that death is soap-flavored. Soap stuck to the roof of the mouth, as if the jellyfish she now was had a mouth. And if it did, it could speak. She tried.

"Eat all the needles, they're made of ice," she said.

Her own ravings—the meaningless words that came from her mouth when what she'd wanted to do was ask for help—alarmed her. She blinked, fighting against the bright light that was blinding her, which turned out to be just the balcony light. Her balcony. Little by little the french doors, the rest of the room, her motionless body under the water came into focus. And Frank, standing by the hot tub. From his contorted face she gauged the seriousness of the fall, and in his eyes she could see the distress of someone witnessing a terrible accident. She saw pity in them, but also the relief of someone who isn't in the victim's situation. The fear he exuded infected her, injecting her with adrenaline.

"Frank, help me." This time her lips said what she intended. "Frank, please. I can't move."

Her useless body didn't respond to any of her attempts, as if she really had mutated into a strange jellyfish specimen whose tentacles were unable to interpret the orders from a human brain. Her limbs remained underwater as if they were dead, and her back was slipping on the acrylic, sinking her slowly.

"Come on, Frank, get me out."

In his frightened expression she perceived his desire to help her, the human instinct to assist someone injured. But before he responded to that impulse, the light in his eyes changed.

"Frank!"

Mara's backside was descending the smooth surface, dragging the spine, the neck, the head with it. The corner of the hot tub had gone from her neck to her skull, her hair was floating around her eyes, her chin was underwater. Frank simply watched what was happening, the instinct to help now gone from his eyes, now glazed in an unsettling glow that scared her even more. Because she began to understand what it meant.

"I'm sinking, Frank. You pushed me. You did this to me. Frank! Help me!"

He kept looking at her without doing anything, the glow in his eyes darkening just as the decision he'd made darkened his soul. Mara yelled again, but her words were just bubbles, her mouth underwater now. The taste of soap, that bitter taste of absurd death, reached her stomach. All the fear she'd felt in her life until then was nothing compared to what shook her now, finding herself unable to breathe, to move. The feeling of comfort she'd had from persuading herself that nobody drowns in a hot tub—in such a stupid way— disappeared, because in reality she knew that these domestic accidents did happen—it was happening to her. Stupid deaths are only stupid when they happen to other people. And now that Mara knew she could die in a hot tub, she understood that there was nothing funny about it, as it may have seemed to whoever would read about it tomorrow in a news item shared on Facebook. Those people were unlikely to understand how someone could drown in two hundred gallons of water, but for Mara the hot tub was as big as the Pacific Ocean, and she was a wretched dying jellyfish sinking to the seabed in a goddamned hydromassage bath.

With the top of her head still above the water, Mara pleaded with her eyes for Frank to help her. She whined like a stray dog. She shook her head, making her hair go in her nose, her eyelids, forming a mask. She hit the acrylic in desperation, stoking the pain in the back of her neck. And though she knew she would swallow water and there was no point in calling for help, she couldn't stop herself from letting out one last cry.

"Barbarbraaaaaehb!"

That was the sound to which her words were reduced. When she was about to submerge completely, Mara saw Frank's grimace relax with his satisfaction at what was happening in front of him. It was easy to guess what he was thinking. She was a drunk woman, alone at home, with a serious blow to the head resulting from an unfortunate slip on her hot tub—an accident that paralyzed and ultimately killed her, like so many other similar incidents. The fact that Frank was responsible for her slipping, that he'd unbalanced her with a slap, the redness from which would soon disappear, would be a truth only the two of them would know—and in a few minutes, as soon as she'd finished drowning, only he would know it. The door hadn't been forced, and no one knew about her relationship with Frank. Even in the event that some sharp forensic scientists suspected they were looking at something other than an accident, they would name thirty suspects before him: all the guests who'd come to the party. The floor was covered in organic traces from dozens of people.

But no one would come to gather samples. A drunk woman drowning in a tub, with no abusive partner or known enemies, in a property neither broken into nor attacked, is an obvious domestic accident. Mara read all these thoughts in Frank's eyes. All he had to do was stand there and wait for his biggest problem to solve itself. Wait a little longer for the impertinent woman who wanted to teach him a lesson to drown in front of him, taking his darkest secrets with her, the very secrets she'd worked so hard to force him to reveal.

Mara accepted that the last thing she would see would be the undulating silhouette of the man who'd decided to let her die. She also accepted that her whole life was worth less than the secret of an infidelity. From under the water, she saw Frank take his first step toward the exit, deciding to leave and forget about her forever. That was when her big toe responded. Mara felt it move—just that toe, but she could control it. She managed to insert her toenail into one of the nozzles at the bottom of the tub, enough to stop her body from sinking and propel it upward. Forehead, eyes, and nose emerged first. A final push that threatened to break the toenail was enough to also bring out her mouth. Mara sucked in a desperate mouthful of air that hurt her chest, and the injection of oxygen made her dizzy.

Frank took a step back. He narrowed his eyes, frustrated to see his secret resisting being hidden under the water, being silenced.

The truth always emerges. Even if you drown it. Mara gave him the closest thing to a smile she was able to give.

"You're not going to get rid of me, Frank," she said, as if she'd won some kind of battle. Then desperation overcame her again. "Frank! For God's sake, help me."

The cry filled her mouth with water. She choked on it, coughed. Her convulsions ended up breaking her toenail. When she lost her support, Mara sank a few inches, but her ankle caught on the same nozzle, preventing her from going under.

"*Farbabrar.*"

Her plea was translated into bubbles, her mouth underwater again. Only her nostrils remained above the surface, and at least she could breathe through them. Her whole body tingled—recovering its mobility, perhaps. Or maybe it was losing sensation forever. Mara moved her head, trying to find a better position, but she inhaled water, and she choked again. She left her neck in the position that enabled her to breathe. One eye was submerged, the other was not. With this one eye she saw Frank watching her desperate maneuvers closely, without doing anything. He just rested his hands on his waist like someone who, after fixing an engine, wonders why the car still won't start. What he would be wondering was why this woman wouldn't drown.

His frustration filled Mara with satisfaction. Now that she could breathe again, the situation didn't seem so serious. Even if she could have spoken, if her mouth hadn't been underwater, she wouldn't have asked Frank for help. She would've yelled at him to go, to leave her. She felt capable of holding on as long as necessary, until a friend worried that she wasn't answering her phone and came to her apartment to save her. Mara would rather wait for all the water in the tub to evaporate than stoop to ask Frank for help again, so she could get out with the same desire to make him confess.

Despite the degrading and humiliating situation, Mara fixed her one eye on Frank, defying him. Making the coward know that he was very wrong if he thought he was going to be lucky enough to kill her with a harmless slap. If her big toe had come back to life, that meant the blow to the back of her head might not have been so serious. Soon she would start to move her foot, both her feet, her legs, her arms. She just had to hold on a little longer. And she could hold on for as long as it took, because she had the desire, the rage, and a beautiful hole in her nose through which to take in as much air as she needed until the coward was gone.

But then the coward took a step toward the hot tub.

And he did it with a thumb.

With just a thumb.

As if she were an insect on the table to be squashed, Frank rested his thumb on her temple and pushed down. The little force he applied was enough to sink her head, submerge her nose, take away her breathing. The ankle that served as a brake came off the nozzle, and her body slid down the tub's curved paneling again, submerging her. Mara tried to flail with her entire body, to flap as if she were drowning out at sea, but with her paralyzed anatomy her efforts translated only into a slight movement of her big toe. She shook her head to splash water out of the hot tub, to empty it, to make the water level descend to below her nose. It was no use. She bit the water in an absurd attempt to propel herself upward like a fish, like a tadpole. She even beat her eyelids, expecting some illogical kind of propulsion from them. That was when Mara felt her lungs expand until they were like enormous empty tanks in her chest. Then the instinct to breathe filled them with water, shrinking them, making them heavy. And hot. They burned. They burned until every uncomfortable feeling suddenly disappeared.

Mara drowned with her nose just a couple of inches from the air on her balcony, where the man who'd ended up killing her with a single finger, like a flea, stood watching. Her last thought, before feeling death and its soap flavor finally take her to a radiant and placid space beyond the water and beyond the world, was to hope that the security camera on the balcony ceiling had recorded everything.

Frank stood watching the bubbles that rose to the surface from Mara's face—her nose, her mouth—and disappeared in little explosions that carried off her being, transforming it into air. The last bubble that popped left the water calm, establishing a sharp boundary between life on the surface and death underneath.

As he did the first time he slept with Mara, Frank found it very easy to rationalize what had happened. And he was clear in his mind that he hadn't done anything. A slap doesn't kill anyone, and the slip had been Mara's fault—she was the one who hadn't been able to keep her balance. Nor could the fact that he'd pushed her head underwater, in a tub, with a finger, a single thumb, be considered a cause of death, unless that death was already about to happen. Whether he'd been in the apartment or not, the outcome for Mara would have been the same—she wouldn't have held on in the position she was in for much longer. Everyone knows how dangerous it is to fill a bath while drunk, when more prone to falling. Even the friends who'd been with her at the party would think it. And they'd blame themselves, they'd regret leaving their friend's house without tidying up afterward, without asking how she was. Or without staying to keep her company overnight and saving her life.

As Frank stood entranced by Mara's pale body, a light came on in his pocket: the screen on his cell phone. The plucked strings in "You Were Meant for Me" rang out on the balcony. In front of his lover's dead body, Frank listened to the song with which he'd persuaded his wife, twenty years ago, that they were made for each other. Listening to the ringtone without answering, he imagined Grace in the hospital, walking in circles in the corridor, wondering where her husband was. He had to get back to her before it became more difficult to explain his absence. When he turned around to begin his escape, a memory gripped his stomach. The afternoon Mara suggested making a homemade sex tape in the very same hot tub. He looked up at the ceiling, fearing what he was going to find. There it was, the apartment's security camera. And he was looking directly at the lens to offer a close-up portrait of his own clumsiness. Perfect for a wanted poster for the most inept criminal in history.

"Christ!"

Frank cursed his incompetence. He had known perfectly well that the camera was there—he'd let himself be recorded by it months ago, showing off his sexual prowess. But the idiot Frank hadn't remembered it when he slapped a woman, left her to drown, and with his thumb even helped her remain submerged. He could say goodbye to the theory of the domestic accident on which he'd based all his decisions in the last few minutes.

Frank ran to the surveillance system's control panel at the entrance. From which Mara had deleted that homemade porno. He tapped the touchscreen to activate it. The padlock symbol occupied the monitor while a fingerprint icon flashed blue. An arrow pointed from the icon to a sensor. Frank rested his thumb there. He received an error message. He tried with another finger. Error.

"Shit!"

But it was logical: only Mara's fingerprints would activate the system. Frank pinched his bottom lip, thinking about what to do. And he headed to the kitchen. He selected some large scissors from the utensil drawer. Kneeling beside the hot tub, he lifted Mara's left hand out of the water. He trapped the thumb between the implement's two blades. He applied pressure on the digit before realizing how stupid his idea was. A drowned woman's body with a finger cut off would look like anything but an accident. He only had one option.

He dipped his arms in the tub, getting his polo shirt and part of his pants wet. His heart was beating in his chest, his neck, his ears. He lifted Mara's lifeless body, slipping on the large quantity of water that overflowed when he did so. Her arms hung like the pincers on a gigantic lobster. Her hair dripped water all over the balcony and the living room, creating a river all the way to the entrance. Frank tripped on a beer can, slipped on an ice bag, and both times almost lost his balance. He touched the screen again to activate it, but now it was Mara's thumb he placed on the sensor. He'd read in some article that fingerprint readers don't work with dead people—he hoped it referred to people who'd been dead longer, not the still-warm body of a newly drowned woman. It didn't work at first, but after he dried the thumb and pressed harder with it on the sensor, the red background on the screen turned green. The padlock disappeared. A menu of options welcomed him to the system. Frank sighed, blowing out his cheeks.

Without letting go of the body, he returned it to the hot tub, leaving it in the water. The wave the immersion caused splashed onto his shoes. Crossing the living room, he saw the mess he'd made, water splashed everywhere, his footprint in some of the puddles. He decided to make even more of a mess, emptying plastic cups on the furniture, beer cans on the floor. Anyone seeing it would think the party had gotten out of hand.

In the system's welcome menu he searched, disoriented, through the various options. Battling with this electronic puzzle, in his mind he heard the repeated echo of the thousands of times Audrey had called him a digital dinosaur. He remembered the exasperation with which Grace tutted when she tried to tell him about her YouTube channel, her subscribers, her live or archived streams, and saw the bewildered look on his face. Now that he really needed to navigate these touchscreen menus to resolve the awful mess he was in, Frank regretted his pride at being the digital technophobe who drove his daughter crazy, resisting technological progress as if it was something to be proud of, when all he was achieving was arriving later to the same future everyone was heading toward whether they liked it or not.

Frank tapped icons, bars, and windows until he found the recordings folder. A mosaic of thumbnail images sorted them by time, starting from midnight the day before. There were miniatures of the empty apartment in the morning, of Mara lying on the sofa in the afternoon, of the living room full of people a while later. He remembered Mara explaining to him that the files were deleted automatically at the end of each day. Even if Frank left the apartment right now, the most likely possibility was that the incriminating evidence would be gone in a couple of hours, before anyone even began to worry about Mara. But he couldn't take the risk. He pressed the thumbnail for the time frame that corresponded to his visit and was presented with five horizontal bars labeled Living Room, Entrance, Kitchen, Bedroom and Balcony. One for each of the rooms that had a camera. He discovered that running his finger along the bars skipped through the recording. He relived his arrival, his argument with Mara at the door. He switched cameras to see what happened in the hot tub. He saw the slap he gave Mara, recorded as clearly as the time she'd stood to offer him what was between her legs.

Jewel's plucking emerged from Frank's pocket, the delicate melody that was so out of tune with the situation. Grace was calling again, unable to imagine that, at that very moment, her husband was watching his lover hit her head to be left paralyzed in the water. And watching himself fail in his duty to help her. While the country singer on his phone sang about breakfasts of pancakes and maple syrup, Frank saw himself pushing Mara's head under with his thumb. Taking away her breathing, her oxygen, her life. The video continued with Frank moving the body. It ended on the camera at the entrance, when Frank accessed the system.

He pressed and held the five bars on the screen to select them. A trash basket icon appeared in a corner. He tapped it with a sigh of relief, anticipating the files' disappearance. A notification sound made him jump, but it was just a window confirming the deletion. He tapped to confirm it. And he heard another annoying sound.

Is it really you? A smiling icon asked the question on the screen, and the fingerprint sensor flashed again. *Confirm your fingerprint to delete file(s).*

"Fuck!"

Frank felt like sitting on the floor, covering his ears, hiding his head between his knees, and giving up. But he resisted the urge and returned to the balcony. He pulled the body out of the water once more just as his cell phone rang again. That pest Jewel was waking up at 6:00 a.m. again to make smiley faces with egg yolks while Frank, for the second time, pressed a corpse's thumb against a fingerprint sensor.

His knees, flagging now under Mara's weight, threatened to give way with the relief he felt when the system's screen confirmed the files had been deleted. The thumbnail for the removed time frame disappeared from the folder of videos. In case it was suspicious that a single hour had been deleted, Frank selected the entire day and used Mara's thumb to send all the files to the trash. He also stopped the cameras' recording. He grinned at the black, empty screen as if the events in the hot tub had never taken place. From now on, only he would remember what happened, and he intended to forget about it as soon as he set foot outside the apartment. From that moment on, he would make sure that the place in his brain reserved for these memories would be as black and empty as the screen in front of him.

As he returned to the balcony, Audrey's ferrets played between his feet, unbalancing him. The animals sniffed Mara's hanging hair. One of them leapt up onto her belly, explored her wet breasts, investigated the corpse's mouth, the nose. Frank threw the body into the tub with the ferret on top, and it escaped the water in terror just as its companion fled the tsunami that formed on the balcony.

Frank stood hypnotized for a few moments at the final vision of Mara in the hot tub, but the cell phone that lit up in his pocket again required his attention. With a final check of the apartment, as chaotic and untidy as he wanted it to be, Frank ran to the door and left.

Grace squashed a mosquito on the back of her neck with a smack—the motor home's outside light was attracting them. In front of her, brandishing the knife, Mara killed another insect with her free hand, echoing the slap Frank had given her on the balcony.

"You left the hospital and didn't answer the phone for two hours," Grace said to Frank, beside him on the road. "You came back soaked in sweat saying you couldn't stand being in the hospital, that you felt too guilty. You told me you'd been wandering aimlessly around the streets." Grace repeated what Frank said had happened, to reinforce those events, to make them true, a truth much easier to come to terms with than the one Mara had just revealed. "You went to her apartment?"

"No, honey."

"Of course he did. And what he did was kill me and try to cover it up, Grace. I swear to you, I felt what death is. The first thing I thought of when I came around was the same thing I thought of before dying: the security camera. When I saw that all the recorded files had been deleted, I knew Frank would've had to pull me out of the hot tub to access the system with my thumbprint. So first he killed me, but then he may have saved my life, too. Apparently, apnea in an unconscious person can perform miracles like that. You should've made sure I was underwater when you left, Frank. You should've made sure I couldn't come back to life." She drew quotation marks in the air as she said the final words, like it was an inappropriate joke.

Grace blinked several times to dry her eyes.

"Is what she's saying true, Frank?"

"No, honey, of course it isn't." Her husband gave her a sidelong smile, like on the bench outside Starbucks where it all began. "She's unhinged, she's a psychopath."

"Stop lying to your wife, Frank. Stop it now," Mara ordered. Then she looked at Grace. "Do you want to see what he did?"

She took a cell phone from her purse.

"What're you doing?" asked Frank.

Mara browsed the device with her thumb until she found what she was looking for. She threw the handset to Grace, who caught it in midair. Mara told her to play the selected video, apologizing for how much it was going to hurt her. Frank stuttered, trying to say something he never managed to say.

When Grace tapped the screen and started watching the recording—the horrible reality of what Frank had done—the strange world she seemed to have been exiled to since her husband admitted his infidelity now continued to mutate until it became uninhabitable. She wanted the vacuum in her chest, created when so many good things were suddenly absent, to suck her up completely. To make her disappear, taking with it the pain of the deceit, the shame, the deep sadness. Beside her, Frank didn't even bother to peek at the cell phone's screen. He just lashed out at Mara, accusing her of trying to trick his wife with some material she must have fabricated as part of her sinister plot. But his yelling stopped when the plucking from Jewel's song came from the telephone's speaker. Grace thought she would faint at the horrifying scene on the device.

"It can't be," Frank murmured to himself. Then he yelled at Mara. "It's not possible! I deleted all the files. All the day's recordings."

"Come on, Frank, you're smarter than that," said Mara. "You deleted it locally. Before midnight I was able to access a backup copy of all the videos on the cloud, from my own cell phone. You didn't delete anything."

Grace recognized her husband's characteristic ineptitude with technology in Mara's words. Her hands began to tremble.

"Honey," he said, "please, honey, I didn't . . ."

Frank must have seen in Grace's eyes the vacuum that was destroying her from the inside. Faced with the sudden but total absence of love in the gaze that had adored him for twenty years without cracking, he finally collapsed. He sat on the road, hiding his head between his legs. He begged her to forgive him, weeping in a way that almost moved her.

"I am so sorry, Grace. I really am," said Mara. "For everything that's happened. For your hair. For that video. At first, I just wanted your husband to admit his cheating, so you wouldn't suffer like my mother did when it was already too late, but now I need him to confess something much more serious. I need Frank to give himself up to the police."

Frank stood, filled with rage.

"Come on, you're a psycho who's enjoying all this." He waved his arms and spat as he spoke. Then he turned to Grace. "Honey, I don't deserve this. You and the kids don't deserve it. She came into our house, she took Audrey's ferrets, she burned your hair. Who knows what she's done now to poor Earl." He indicated the blood on Mara's clothes. "I deserve you leaving me, I deserve to have to give up my home, my children, to regret for the rest of my days that I lost the love of my life because of a stupid impulse. But I don't deserve this madness. Whatever her father did isn't my fault. And if she had that video, why didn't she go to the police the next day? Why aren't they coming to arrest me? That was the logical thing to do, not all this nonsense."

Grace saw some logic in what Frank said, so she asked Mara the same question.

"It took me a few days to come around. I don't know if I completely have yet," she replied. "What Frank did to me changed me forever, Grace. I'd never felt my life was so worthless. His admitting what he did to me would be the first step to regaining my self-worth. I don't want statements, arrest warrants, investigations, or to be questioned, like women always are. I want Frank to confess what so many men deny doing to so many women. I want him to do it for all the victims who never made it out of the bathtub, the kitchen, the bed, who never had the chance to seek justice. I have been given that chance, and I demand that my executioner confesses."

Frank snorted. "Please! Can you hear yourself? Speaking as if you're a martyr?" he said. "You love this."

"I loved the face you made when you saw me on the road again, when you hit me—I won't deny it. Raised from the dead for you. It was a moment I'd been waiting for. I gave a lot of thought to how I'd show up, like a ghost, but you decided to escape before I had the chance. You deceived your family again to drag them to the other side of the country with the ridiculous excuse of building a new future. And I had to improvise, show up here, stop you from getting away. Just moving to another state in itself makes any legal action more complicated, more drawn out, without your confession. Do you see why I need you to turn yourself in?"

Frank feigned a grotesque laugh.

"You really are crazy if you think I'm going to hand myself over. Take that video to the police, tell them your version, and we'll see if they come looking for me."

"It's up to you, Frank," she said with a smile. "I'll take the video to the police, then . . . and I'll publish it on the internet, as well."

Grace stifled a scream.

"It was what I first thought of doing," Mara explained. "Upload the video to the web so everyone can see how some men treat their darkest secrets, which unfortunately tend to be related to women. I'm sure it'd go viral—your thousands of subscribers would make sure of it, Grace. And the video would end up on the news, you know that. The court of public opinion will be way harsher than any judge. But that would affect you"—she gestured at Grace with affection—"and the children. And I don't want that. None of this is their fault. I don't particularly want to be known forever as the woman killed in a tub, either, but I'll do it if you leave me no choice, Frank."

Grace looked at her husband, who was motionless, his mouth open as if he was going to say something, but silent. Even his blinking had stopped.

"Frank?"

She could hear his breath scratching his throat. A pungent smell of sweat emanated from his body. His fists clenched.

Frank leapt at Mara with a roar that frightened Grace, but she wielded the knife firmly, without losing her nerve, forcing him to stop. His face was an inch from the blade.

"Don't you dare," Mara said through gritted teeth. "You will not touch me again."

Frank raised his hands, showing his palms.

"All right, relax. I'm sorry, I lost control." He took a couple of steps back. "None of this is necessary. I'll go with you. But put that knife down, please. Don't hurt my family. We'll go right now if you want. It wasn't the law that scared me—all I cared about was my wife, my kids, that the people I love most wouldn't know the terrible things I've done . . . and now Grace knows. I'll go with you, but put the knife away, and let's all calm down. The children are in there. They shouldn't have to see something like this."

Mara interrogated Grace with her eyes. She accepted the proposal. If Frank was prepared to do the right thing, as he was saying he would now, there was no reason to keep threatening him with a weapon. But as soon as Mara lowered the knife, Frank broke his promise and charged her. He grabbed her wrist and twisted it toward her back, immobilizing her with an arm around her neck.

"Frank!" cried Grace, feeling as deceived as Mara.

Even she was offended that her husband had taken advantage of his size and strength—such basic and unjust weapons, the eternal natural disparity that justified men's superiority over women. Mara squirmed and managed to free her wrist. With the knife, she attacked the arm that was strangling her. Frank screamed with each cut from the blade. He ended up letting go of the armed animal that was wounding him.

"Oh, Frank." Mara's voice was trembling with rage, the knife shaking in the air. "Oh, Frank, I promise you that was the last time you'll try to trick me. Oh, Frank, now you're going to come with me back to Seattle. Whether you like it or not." She fell silent for a few seconds, plotting something, her posture restless. Then she turned to Grace. "Get out of here," she told her. "Take the children. Go, far away."

Frank asked her what she was suggesting, but she ignored him, keeping her eyes on Grace's, trying to make a connection between two women disowning the man who'd made them both suffer.

"Go," she repeated.

Mara recovered the cell phone Grace was holding and ran off up the road in the direction of the hot springs they never reached. Her frantic footsteps on the earth could be heard even after she disappeared into the night's darkness.

"Honey . . ."

Frank tried to touch her, but Grace dodged him and fled to the motor home. She had to get the children away from there.

33.

Mara pressed fingers against the stitch in her side. She kept running even though each stride hurt. Her cell phone flashlight lit the way, guided by the tree trunks lining both sides of the road. The pine needles were shining in the faint light from the sliver of moon. The sweat that soaked her clothes gave off the smell of Grace's fabric softener once again—it refused to die despite the dust, the perspiration, the blood. As if the home the cozy smell belonged to itself also refused to die in the face of betrayal and deceit. When she reached an upward slope, Mara's body wanted to give up, warn her she couldn't go on. But she accelerated, screaming to give herself the strength she needed to make Frank go with her. She reached the top with fire in her legs, in her chest. She regained her breath on the way down, leaning backward. The pain from the stitch subsided, or maybe she got used to it, as she'd gotten used to so much pain lately. She dried tears of exertion, of rage, of her desire to make Frank pay.

At last the flashlight illuminated the rear of the car, the curious combination of letters on the license plate: SKY. Mara thought of Molly, or Polly, the nervous girl at the rental office. Just like the boy at the food truck, or the waitress at Danielle's, Mara hadn't treated her well. She could have been more understanding of the girl's inexperience instead of making her first transaction more difficult. But the fact was, she had asked too many questions that Mara had no idea how to answer. When is a woman supposed to return a car when she's going after the man who killed her?

With both hands on the hood, Mara took deep breaths that eased her pulse. Thirst had thickened her saliva, and using her T-shirt she wiped a string of drool like glue from her face. Regaining some composure, she pulled on the car's door handle. She burst out laughing when she found it was locked, because she suddenly remembered where the key was. She hadn't thought about it once on the way here, fixated with her fantastic plan of returning with the car to get Frank—run him over if necessary—to take him herself to the police along with the video of the hot tub. But the car wouldn't start without a key, and the key was inside her body. Her laughter overcame her, a crazed fit of cackling.

She was still laughing when she stuck two fingers in her mouth, down to the base of her tongue. The first retch twisted her stomach, hurt as if her sides were cramping, but it was unproductive. The taste of her fingers—of dust, earth, and blood—made her feel worse. The next retch grated her throat, flooded her eyes. Again, nothing was expelled. Against her instinct, which fought to eject the intruders on her tongue, she pushed her fingers deeper. They came out covered in something sticky just before she vomited bile. The bitter taste, of acidic death, provoked more retches that expelled only fluids, until she was left dry. Empty. The last thing she'd eaten had been Grace's omelet at breakfast. She'd swallowed the key twenty-four hours ago. If it was too late for it to come out of her mouth, it was on its way to emerge somewhere else. After everything she'd done, Mara wasn't going to allow such a biological complication to release Frank from his responsibilities. Considering how regular she was, in all this time she should have needed to go at least once. It shouldn't be too difficult. She approached a tree by the side of the road. She lowered the denim shorts she'd fashioned to her ankles, and her underwear as well. She rested her back against the pine's trunk, adopting a seated position.

It was much harder than she had imagined.

Diurnal birds that were sleeping in their nests flew up into the darkness, like bats, startled when Mara's initial groans turned into cries of pain that echoed around the mountain.

34.

Grace laid a travel bag on the double bed, like a fugitive preparing her escape luggage. Opening it, she found it full. She overcame the setback by dumping the contents onto the bedroom floor. Emptying a bag to fill it again—her mind wasn't thinking clearly.

"What's going on, Mom?" asked Audrey. "What're you doing?"

"We couldn't hear anything," said Simon. "What's happening?"

The children kept asking questions, but she didn't even have answers for her own. She acted in silence, moving around the motor home with glazed eyes. Frank, who came in after her, touched her elbow in the bedroom.

"Don't touch me!"

Grace couldn't contain her reaction, even knowing her children were present. She was also unable to contain the sob she'd been holding in her throat, a sob that intensified when she saw Audrey's and Simon's faces respond to the way she rejected Frank, as if she no longer loved him, as if it disgusted her to be touched by him. The children had never seen their parents fight like this, not even over the gun, and Grace could almost hear the crunch of something beautiful, something miraculous, breaking in front of her. Innocence. If their parents could stop loving each other like this, what other terrible things could happen in the world now?

"I'm so ashamed," said Grace, voicing this one feeling even though in reality she was being ravaged by others that were worse. "Oh God, I'm so ashamed."

She rubbed her arms, her chest, her face, wanting to get rid of something sticky that enveloped her. She felt trapped by an invisible web, made of all the lies Frank had woven around her, turning her into an insect that doesn't even know why it can't fly off as the spider approaches to devour it. Grace peeled things from her body that weren't there.

"Mom, stop!" Audrey took her by the shoulders. "You're acting crazy. What is it?" Faced with her silence, she turned to look at Frank. "Dad?"

He didn't answer, either.

"Is Mara dangerous?" the girl asked. "She had a knife, we saw it."

Simon hugged his father. He whimpered into his belly, displacing the eyepatch.

"Is she dangerous?" repeated Audrey.

"Yes, honey, she is," replied Grace. "That's why we have to leave."

She continued to fill the bag while Audrey asked why Mara was a threat to them, what she could have against them, if it was all because they ran her over.

"All you need to know is there's a dangerous woman out there and we're going to get away from her. We're leaving. Your father's going to stay here to"—she didn't know what to say—"to fix the RV."

Audrey frowned at the absence of logic in the idea. Simon said that if they were going to escape, they all had to escape together. Grace pulled the boy away from Frank, insisting that Dad was going to stay to fix the motor home.

"But how's he going to fix it?" yelled Audrey. "We've been here an entire day saying it can't be done."

Frank went up to Grace. "Honey, listen to me."

"I said don't touch me."

She linked her hands together behind her back to prevent him from taking them.

"Has Dad done something wrong?" Audrey was beginning to understand. "Dad, did you do something? Why did she cut your face, your arm?"

Grace fought back her tears, waiting for whatever answer Frank was going to give. She wanted to study her husband's face when he lied. To understand why she hadn't detected any revealing signs when he had deceived her day after day. The face that had loved her for years was suddenly an indecipherable enigma. She could no longer be sure what the light in her husband's eyes meant, or what he was thinking when he frowned. The slanted smile that had made her melt might have been covering up appalling truths. For more than a year, Frank had hidden a serial infidelity from her. He had looked her in the eyes after drowning a woman, and Grace had been stupid enough not to see any change in the face she thought she knew as well as her children's. A face she'd observed for a longer time than she'd spent observing her own in the mirror. It saddened her to think of all that wasted time, looking straight at a falsehood without recognizing it.

"I haven't done anything, honey," he replied.

There wasn't a single trace of the lie in his injured features. Frank didn't stutter, his voice didn't tremble. He fixed his gaze on his daughter with the same firmness with which he looked at Grace to tell her he loved her. Perhaps all the *I love you*s Frank had said to her throughout their life together had also been lies.

"So what's going on?" the girl insisted. "Why's she doing this to us?"

"Forget it, honey, we'll talk about it later," Grace said.

She zipped up the bag and left the room, avoiding Frank, telling the children to follow her.

"Mom." Simon grabbed her pants. "You put Dawn in the bag."

She snorted, incredulous. She would have to be out of her mind to put a bottle of dishwashing liquid in the bag. But when she opened it on the dining table, there it was, the orange antibacterial soap with double the grease-cleaning power.

"Are you OK, Mom?"

She nodded, though seeing the rest of what she'd packed was like staring at a depiction of her agitated state: bathing suits, bikinis, the boy's toothbrush, a packet of spaghetti, and five spoons.

"Why do we need a case, anyway?" Audrey sat on the sofa. "We decided we can't walk to find help, the highway's too far. Mom, why won't you look at Dad?"

Without answering, feigning a calm that was cracking under her skin, Grace put the bag's ludicrous contents back where they belonged. The toothbrush in the bathroom cabinet, the spoons in the kitchen drawer. The packet of pasta was entangled in a bikini's straps. She tried to untangle them but knotted them up even more. On the third attempt, she threw the packet on the floor, scattering spaghetti all over the motor home. It crunched when she walked on it.

"No bags, then," she said, as if the decision had always been hers. "Come on, kids."

Frank stood in their way.

"Grace, honey, you're not well."

"Don't you dare tell me how I am." Grace pointed at him with a finger so tense she could have driven it into him. "You're not going to—"

Before she could finish the sentence, her saliva turned so bitter it made her retch. Her husband's condescending expression turned her stomach even more. And his voice, the same voice that would have whispered so many lies to her after whispering dirty words to Mara, churned it until she was unable to resist the urge to throw up. Grace ran to the bathroom and emptied her stomach into the toilet. Kneeling in front of the bowl, through tears of exertion, she glimpsed a single hair, long and black, on the shower pan. It wasn't hers or Audrey's. It could only be Mara's. The sight of the wet hair made her throw up again. She threw up with the jealousy she felt thinking about that hair covering her husband's naked abdomen and with the revulsion she felt imagining the same hair, wet as it was now on the shower pan, under the water in a tub where Frank believed he'd killed her.

From the dining area, her family's conversation reached her in waves: Audrey demanding to be told the truth, Simon defending his friend Earl's innocence, and Frank promising the children the situation was under control and they had nothing to worry about.

"Your mother and I—" she heard Frank say from out there.

"Shut up," Grace whispered in the bathroom. "Shut up, shut up, shut up."

She repeated it again and again into the toilet bowl, trying to insulate herself from her husband's voice, which nonetheless lingered as an indistinct mumble in the distance. The unpleasant murmur of an ocean of lies.

"Shut up!" shrieked Grace.

The intensity of her scream obliterated his mumble and filled her with new energy. She got up, driven by the clarity of one objective: to protect her children. And to do that, she had to get them away from the motor home, as Mara had warned.

"Kids, we're going," she ordered, giving them no option to refuse.

She grabbed Simon's wrist, her daughter's hand. She pulled them toward the door, ignoring Frank's comments. Audrey resisted, pulling her arm away.

"Not until you tell me what's happening! I'm not a child anymore, Mom! You can't drag me wherever you want and ask me to leave my dad without explaining what it is th—"

Grace silenced her with a slap. Her nerves, the urgency of the situation, the volume of her daughter's voice . . . in an instant she found all of these excuses to justify her actions.

"I'm sorry, honey. I'm so sorry."

She stroked the red mark she'd made with a trembling hand that extinguished the anger in Audrey's eyes. Her daughter saw the sincerity her mother felt in her apology, how overwhelmed she was by the situation. And she also understood that whatever was happening was serious enough that there was no time for tantrums or teenage pride. Audrey kissed the hand that had struck her in a gesture of forgiveness that moved Grace. For the first time, she saw the young adult her girl considered herself to be.

"Mom, I—"

The roar of an engine interrupted her.

The light from headlights filled the inside of the motor home.

"A car!" Simon cheered.

Grace elbowed Frank out of the way and got out with the children.

"Is it Mara?" Audrey asked.

"Woo-hoo! Her car's working!" Simon said, as if it was good news. "We can go!"

But Grace headed in the opposite direction. The boy held his free arm out to his father, stretching his fingers out in the air and begging him to go with them. Frank caught up with them and grabbed Simon's hand.

"Don't even think about it. You're staying here," said Grace. "You can fight it out with her. That woman's your problem. Not mine, not your children's."

"Mom, other people's problems are also your own if you really want to help," said Audrey. "To think otherwise is a very selfish way to look at life. I want to help Dad."

"So do I," said Simon.

The car revved its engine, roaring like an animal about to attack. Incapable of looking Frank in the eyes, Grace fixed her gaze on his nose so the rest of his face was out of focus, as blurred as their entire past together was beginning to seem.

"Do it for your children, Frank. Let us go."

The angry beast that was Mara's car threatened them with flashes of the headlights' high beams. Frank let go of Simon's hand.

"I love you so much," he said.

Grace saw the heartbroken expression on his face—the feeling of being left out of the most important team he'd ever belonged to—but she didn't allow pity to control her. She resumed their escape, dragging the children with her, leaving the car and Frank behind. Audrey and Simon complained, kicking up dust and trying to stop her, defending their father. Grace pressed on, diverting them from the route the car could take. She didn't stop until they were safe in the darkness, among the trees by the roadside. From there they saw Frank face Mara.

"What?!" In the motor home's exterior light, the spray of saliva that came from his mouth when he yelled was visible. "What're you going to do?"

"Take you with me," Mara said through the window.

He walked toward the car with his chest puffed out, defiant. Without realizing it, he trampled on Simon's castle, knocking down the tower, the pine cone fortress, the flag made from a leaf.

"Come on!" said Frank. "Do it!"

He kept taunting Mara as he approached her. He added a fist to his intimidating routine, holding it up, tense, his elbow bent behind him. The man drawing on his natural advantage to frighten a woman again. Grace tried to cover the children's eyes, but they swatted her hands away as if she were one of the mosquitoes that besieged them. Neither Frank's bravado nor his physical supremacy was of any use to him when Mara stepped on the gas. The wheels spun, fighting to grip the road's gritty surface. Audrey, Simon, and Grace screamed, fearing the worst, but Frank had just enough time to turn and run. He leapt into the motor home right before Mara crashed into it. The impact knocked the RV door out of position, leaving it hanging from a single hinge.

"I'm taking you!" yelled Mara over the mechanical noise of the transmission.

Frank's response from the threshold was drowned out by the sound of the car maneuvering in reverse, but Grace understood from his gesticulations, pointing at his own head, that he was telling Mara she was crazy. Once the car had regained some distance, it charged the motor home again with a powerful burst of acceleration. It made the vehicle lurch, it even moved it. Inside, things fell, glass shattered.

Audrey leapt from the trees onto the road.

"Mom, we have to help him!" She pointed at the car, which was smashing into the motor home for the third time. "That woman wants to kill Dad."

"Please, honey, you don't understand."

Grace herself was struggling to process what was happening, to comprehend how the peaceful night when she'd been eating hot dogs with her family had turned into an inferno of lies, revenge, and harassment. Simon freed himself from Grace and went beside Audrey. Holding hands, they announced that they were going to defend their father. They escaped in that direction before she could do anything.

After another charge, Mara didn't stop the car. Instead, she kept accelerating against the motor home. The wheels raised columns of smoke and dust, and the smell of burned rubber reached Grace, who was pursuing the children. The car displaced the motor home's nose until it reached the slope on that side of the road. The disequilibrium, added to the instability from the flat tires, made the vehicle tilt. Grace heard Mara's desperate cry over the roar of the engine, which revved itself to the breaking point on a final shove. The children screamed.

"Dad!"

Still some distance away, they stopped to watch the motor home tip onto its side, into the ditch full of undergrowth where Audrey had searched for the cell phones. The ground vibrated, the noise was deafening. A small earthquake in the middle of the forest. The motor home's exterior light flashed as something short-circuited, but it remained on, its new position creating different, strange shadows. Grace reached her children's backs and hugged them, kissing them on the cheeks. They were shaking. She dried Simon's uncovered eye as he asked if Dad was OK. She nodded without knowing the answer, but the sound of Frank dismantling the plastic window above the shower confirmed he was. She pictured him emerging through the hole in the motor home's roof, now a wall. Frank came out from the vegetation brushing off his clothes. Grace sensed that the children intended to run to him. She held them. Mara's attempts to start her car again were limited to fruitless revving, a spluttering exhaust pipe, catastrophic scraping in the transmission. She got out of the car, leaving the door open.

Grace stifled a scream when she saw her clutching the knife.

"Leave my dad alone!" yelled Audrey.

The girl fought to escape Grace's grip, but she didn't let go.

"Kids, please, go," said Frank. "Listen to your mother. Go find help."

"She has a knife, Dad!" yelled Simon.

"Son, you have to go."

Mara, who was on her way around the upturned motor home searching for Frank, used his voice as a guide. She reached the vehicle's rear just as he made it through the last bushes. Finding themselves facing each other, barely three paces apart, they both adopted defensive postures. Frank spoke to the children without taking his eyes off the armed woman in front of him.

"Go with Mom. You have to go with her now. Audrey, Simon, please go with your mother. I'll take care of the intruder." He took a step toward her. "Easy, relax, we're all going to calm down now."

Grace recognized the words he'd used before, when he'd managed to persuade Mara to lower her weapon to outmaneuver her. Mara took the initiative this time, charging Frank as if she were her car and he were the motor home. They rolled together along the road, grunting, panting. Frank catapulted Mara with a kick, and she fell to the ground with a scream. She quickly got up, wiping blood from her lip with her wrist. The children squirmed in Grace's arms.

"Mom, please, it's four against one," said Audrey. "Dad, it's four against one! Let us help you!"

"Get out of here," he repeated. Just as Mara was about to attack again, Frank looked at the trees, at the children. "I love you, kids. Don't ever forget it."

He fled into the forest. Grace understood he was doing it so Mara would go after him, taking the danger away from his family. The branches shook on some of the pines, revealing the route the chase was taking, up the mountain. Simon burst into tears, calling repeatedly for his father.

"Why won't you help him?" Audrey said, without separating her teeth. "Mom, we have to help him. He's our dad."

The way the girl made the argument, as obvious as it was powerful, reminded Grace that not even the world of lies she'd been banished to could destroy certain truths. Her love for her children, for example. Or the fact that Frank would always be the father of those children. And that they would always love him, even if he committed the most atrocious acts.

"All right, but I'll go," said Grace, recognizing all the traces of Frank in her children's faces. "You stay here."

"No, Mom . . ."

"Honey, please, show me you're not a child anymore and cooperate in a real emergency situation. I'm going to help your father, but you have to stay here and watch your little brother. He really is a child, and he needs an adult to take care of him."

Audrey straightened her back, proud to be thought of in such a way.

"OK, Mom." She put her arm over her brother's shoulder. "I'll stay with him."

Grace kissed them both. Then she turned around and faced the thick darkness of the forest through which Frank was running from Mara. It was still possible to determine their position from the moving branches, the pine cones falling to the ground. The motor home let out a mechanical noise like a wail that could have been Grace's. With a hesitant stride, she crossed the road, made her way through the undergrowth in the ditch, and headed up the mountain.

35.

A branch on a bush scratched Frank's face, reopening one of the cuts from the soap. In the darkness, it was difficult to dodge obstacles in time. Blood emerged on his forehead, trickling down his temple and mixing with the sweat that soaked his body. Despite the grueling climb, Mara was still following him at the same speed. Frank was afraid he would be the first to need to give up—making a path through the vegetation meant he was doing some of Mara's work for her.

Now he was truly scared. He considered her capable of anything. More pine trees stood in his way, forming a wall of branches. Too tired to change course, Frank opted to cover his face and go through the curtain of needles. He felt them tearing the skin on his arms. Though he'd taken for granted that he'd find more trees and bushes on the other side, he stepped into a clearing.

It was a semicircle almost devoid of vegetation. Only low grass and flowers carpeted the surface. The forest behind him formed the curved part, and the straighter part turned out to be the edge of a precipice that Frank approached with little steps, his knees bent. The colossal height made his legs stiffen. Frank suffered from the kind of vertigo that's more like a fear of the desire to throw oneself into the void than a fear of heights themselves. Despite the darkness, he could make out the spectacular dimensions of the landscape, the treetops forming a dark, greenish ocean. In the sky—as starry as the one they'd enjoyed last night from the motor home before disaster struck—the same minimal moon as yesterday was shining discreetly. Frank observed it, wondering at its decadent presence. It was almost as if it were saying goodbye to the heavens forever.

Then he smelled the unpleasant aroma and at the same time heard the bubbling, the two sensations suddenly enveloping him. He looked down at his feet. The origin of the sulfur smell and the gaseous gurgle weren't on the ground on which he stood but in the hot springs at the bottom of the precipice.

"We were almost there," he said to himself. "Almost there."

Knowing the motor home had been this close to a place with geothermal activity made him imagine a perfect scene in which his family spent the night at the hot springs, as they'd planned. In that parallel reality, what had happened in the last twenty-four hours was just a nightmare. The fantasy was interrupted when he heard Mara's cry behind him as she went through the wall of pine needles. He was in fact in a nightmare, but the nightmare was real.

"I've got you," she said.

"Come on, give it up." Frank turned around to face her. She was ten paces away. He spoke to her as if she were a child who was an hour late going to bed. "Give it up. What else are you going to do to me?"

"Stab you, if necessary."

Frank snorted. "You're crazier than you seem if you think I'm going to go anywhere with you, or hand myself in. I was this close"—he held the tips of his index finger and thumb almost together in the air—"to getting away with it. I can still do it."

"You ran away from my balcony and you've run until today. But look what we have here: you've run out of ground under your feet." Mara indicated the precipice with her knife. "There's nowhere to run now. It's as if the whole world's sending you a message."

"Running away would've worked if you hadn't come back from the dead." It infuriated him to think of his own clumsiness, the novice's mistake of failing to check that the woman he'd killed was actually dead. "None of this would've happened if you'd stayed dead in your bathtub. Maybe the message the world's sending me is that I have to kill you again. But for real this time." The simplicity of the solution, the ease with which he could rid himself of the problem and experience the same liberation he felt as he descended in the elevator on the night of the hot tub, was overwhelming. "Yeah, maybe that's what I have to do . . ."

Frank walked up and down along the precipice, his stride more energetic the surer he became that his salvation was within reach. Last night, in the tent, strangling Mara had been very tempting. Perhaps it was time to give in to the temptation once more.

"That's what I'm going to do . . ."

He voiced his thought without realizing it, blurting the words out with the rage that grew inside him. Rage at the woman who was intent on ruining his new life. This insignificant woman, this mediocre lover, who thought she had the right to force her truth on his wife and children's happiness, on his own. If killing her was the only way out . . .

"I'm going to kill you!" he yelled into the air. He turned toward Mara with his arms in front of him, squeezing the neck that wasn't there yet. She wielded the knife, feigning confidence, but her trembling hands gave her away. "I'm going to kill you, you crazy bi—"

"Frank!"

Grace's appearance in the clearing subdued Frank's instincts. He stopped dead, still some distance from Mara, when he pictured what his wife was seeing: the man she loved disguised as a grotesque parody of a murderer.

"Frank?" She observed him, as horrified as she was confused. "Who *are* you?"

279

The question, his wife looking at him as if he were a stranger, hurt more than all Mara's accusations, more even than all the things Grace had yelled at him before.

"Do it for your wife, Frank." Mara had regained her composure, the weapon no longer trembling. "Confess and set a good example for your children, show them that taking responsibility for your own mistakes is the right way to behave in life."

"I can't stand the sound of your voice." Frank let out an exhausted sigh—Mara's holier-than-thou attitude exasperated him. "My kids don't have to know anything about what I've done. They won't know about it. I have no example to set for them with anything that's happened here."

He sought confirmation in Grace's eyes that this was how it would be, that they would protect Audrey and Simon from the truth.

"Someday they'll have to know." Grace shook her head. "I'm not going to lie to them like you."

"Shit, Grace, are you on my side or hers?"

"I don't know anymore, Frank. I honestly don't know. You . . ." She stuttered, as if saying words that didn't fit in her mouth. "You . . . you tried to kill her."

"No, Grace," Mara said. "He didn't try. He killed me. He left the apartment believing he'd done it."

Frank bit his tongue to stop himself from saying what he was thinking, but it came out. "And you don't know how much I wish now that you really had died."

"Frank!" Grace shouted.

"You know what?" Mara took a step forward. "At one stage, I even thought dying would've been less painful. A dead woman doesn't have to remember every day how she was left for dead underwater, drowned, forgotten like a bad secret. A dead woman doesn't wake up and discover how insignificant her life must be, her entire life, for a man to think her life is worth nothing. I was just an inconvenience to you, a shameful secret who deserved to die underwater. You don't know how much that hurts. You didn't break my heart, Frank, you broke my soul. Something changed in me forever. Have you ever been so sad you no longer fear pain or death?" With the knife, she traced a bleeding line on her forearm. "I have, since that night. Now the only way to make sense of all this suffering is to see you pay for what you've done."

Frank snorted to dismiss Mara's words. Grace, on the other hand, nodded, wiping tears from her eyes. She approached and rubbed Mara's arm to comfort her.

"This is a joke," he said, unable to believe his wife was taking Mara's side. He turned around to scream his rage into the void. "Unbelievable, Grace! Unbelievable! Christ!"

The immensity sent an echo back to him.

Christ . . . Christ . . . Christ.

At the bottom of the abyss, the water's bubbling remained constant, and the rotten egg smell arrived in waves of growing intensity. The stench of sulfur sparked the image in Frank's mind of hell opening up at his feet, calling to him. Maybe the only way to avoid it was to give in. Maybe Mara had always been right. If his stubbornness had brought him, literally, to the edge of a precipice, maybe it was time to start thinking differently. Or maybe not.

"I'm not doing anything," he decided, turning back. "I'm not going anywhere."

He gripped his waist with his hands.

"Then the video's going on the internet," said Mara. "Your children won't just know what you did—they'll be able to see it. And the police will end up coming after you all the same. I'll have to wait longer to see you pay, but I'll see it."

Frank shrugged, showing indifference.

"First, you'll have to prove the video's real. It's very easy to doctor them these days, there'll be thousands of comments saying it's a fake. And without a real victim, without a dead woman, don't think the police will treat your case with much urgency. At the very least, it'll buy me time. Time to get away. Not to another coast—to another country, if necessary." Though he was speaking off the cuff, his arguments didn't sound completely ludicrous. His plan could work. Bolstered by the logic of his strategy, he took on a triumphant tone. "There's nothing you can do to make me go. You'll have to stick that knife in me, because you have nothing else."

Mara swiveled the weapon in her hand. A breeze came up to the precipice, bringing with it steam from the boiling water down below. Frank saw her tense her eyebrows, her jaw, thinking about something.

"There's nothing you can do," he repeated to her.

Mara attacked Grace as she was searching for something in her pocket—a handkerchief to blow her nose, perhaps. She immobilized her with an arm around her belly, the other hand pressing the knife against her neck. Grace didn't even have time to scream before the weapon cut off her breathing. She just opened her eyes wide, looking down as if trying to check that what was happening was real.

"Don't touch her!"

Frank ran at them.

"Stay back." Mara retreated one step. She pressed the blade's edge against Grace's neck, spilling a drop of blood. "I'll do it if you come closer."

"Frank . . . ," whispered Grace.

"You don't want to hurt her," he said, "not her. My wife hasn't done anything to you. You wanted to help her from the start. It's all my fault, it makes no sense to hurt her. Please."

"You've broken me inside so much I don't even find it hard to hurt other people anymore."

"You don't have it in you."

But Mara pressed harder with the knife.

Grace coughed. Frank spun around, punching his own thighs. He grabbed the hair on his head, pulled it.

"Christ!"

Christ . . . Christ . . . Christ.

"Honey." He begged her for mercy with his palms held together. "I can't go to jail, Grace. I can't ruin my life like this, lose you like this."

"Frank"—Grace cleared her throat against the weapon—"you've already lost us. I'm not going to let you come near the kids ever again."

"Please, honey, don't say that." The anguish threatened to take away his voice. "Oh, Grace, don't say that."

"You have no choice." Grace's voice was clearer when Mara eased the pressure of the knife. "It's not about confessing with her or getting rid of her and coming back to us. We're gone."

"Honey . . ."

He felt his face crumple up, fighting back tears.

"You've lost us," said Grace.

Frank moved away so he couldn't hear her—what she was saying was too painful. He reached the edge of the precipice. The vertigo was so strong his legs shook, but he preferred to face the abyss than the terrible reality Grace presented him.

"You have nothing left to lose," she added behind him.

Her words reverberated in his mind like the echo of his cries around the mountain. *You have nothing left to lose. You have nothing left to lose.* He whispered the last repetition to himself, into the void. "I have nothing left to lose . . ."

The almost nonexistent moon in the sky reminded him of Simon's absent eye.

Frank looked at his arms, one of them covered in blood that was now dry, brown.

"Who am I?"

He repeated the question Grace had just asked him. After twenty years together, his wife had no idea who he was. Maybe he didn't know, either. He'd fooled himself so much that it was impossible to recognize, in the bloodstained person trembling at the top of the precipice, the ideal father and husband he had believed he was. He felt his face, wanting to reaffirm his identity, but all he found were injured, disfigured features. It was as if another Frank, the real one, the one with a deformed and corrupt soul, had physically manifested himself to demand that his ugliness be acknowledged. This degrading image of himself suddenly showed Frank the true gravity of what he'd done. The immensity of the pain he'd caused weighed heavy in his chest.

"Grace, I'm so sorry." His feeling of regret was infinite. "But Mara won't hurt you if I'm not here. I'm the problem, I'm the one who caused all of this. And when this is known, I'm going to continue to cause pain and problems for you and the children." Thinking about his son and daughter momentarily lit up the darkness that was eating away at him inside. "Please, Grace, never tell them anything about what I did."

"Frank, what're you doing?"

"Look at me. I've ended up on the edge of the precipice of my own lies." He looked down into the abyss. "And I'll receive the punishment I deserve: a gigantic tub of hot water. What do you think, Mara? It's a goddamned enormous hot tub. Quite the lesson on karma, huh? And this smell of sulfur . . . I'm going straight to hell for committing the most terrible and ancient sins in existence: adultery and murder."

"Frank!" Grace struggled against the straitjacket that was Mara's arms, that wouldn't let her go. "What're you saying?"

"What else can I do, honey? How else can I avoid ruining your life and the children's? I don't want them visiting their father in jail, if you'd even let them come see me. I don't want them to know the things I've done. What will Audrey say when she knows I tried"—he corrected himself to also honor Mara's pain—"that I killed a woman? I don't want Simon knowing why he lost his eye, his beautiful eye . . . because of me. My God, Grace, I'm horrible."

"Don't do it," said Mara. "Stop running away."

"It's the easiest thing to do." It really did seem so. Maybe running away was all he knew how to do, until the end. "This is . . . cleaner."

He encircled the beautiful landscape in front of him with his arms. The trembling in his legs stopped. The vertigo and his compulsion to leap into the void no longer seemed threatening. He turned to look at Grace one last time.

"I love you, Grace, honey. My only love. I always loved you and I always will. I'm still certain you were meant for me"—he smiled at the memory of the two of them in a car, rewinding the cassette of their song with a pen—"but I don't think I was meant for you, after all. Tell the children I'm sorry, and tell them how much I love them."

36.

Grace started squirming in Mara's arms as soon as she guessed Frank's intentions, but he jumped into the void before she could free herself. Mara stood motionless, unable to react or relax her body's muscles.

"Let go of me!"

Grace unfastened the hands that held her captive, cutting her chest on the blade as she escaped. She crawled to the edge of the precipice— her limbs had lost the ability to hold her up after the chase. Even with four supports, she struggled to keep her balance. Though she wanted to scream her lungs out in a cry that would bring her husband back, only a whisper came from her mouth.

"Frank." It was as if she were telling the abyss a secret. "Please, Frank."

The screams in her chest, in her mind, were nothing more than pants when they left her throat. She touched the wound on her neck to see whether it was causing the loss of her voice, but all she found was a superficial cut.

"Frank," she whispered again.

Her elbows finally failed her and Grace collapsed, her chest on the edge of the chasm, her arms hanging into the void as if, somehow, she could still reach her husband, who had long disappeared into the darkness, so far below, so far away. The cry he let out when he jumped had grown quieter until the bubbling water and the murmur of the sulfuric breeze in her ears were all Grace could hear.

Her tears fell into the void like miniature raindrops. She imagined them dissolving in the boiling, acidic water, where Frank would also dissolve. She remembered what she'd read in the Idaho guide about dangerous hot springs. Earl's stumps, what had happened to his dog. The idea horrified her so much that all the screams she'd been unable to let out now came together in her throat. Grace yelled her husband's name with such force, so many times, that she ended up spitting blood.

She received no answer.

Her delirious mind toyed with the idea of allowing the weight of her arms to defeat the mass of the rest of her body, to let herself fall into the void as well to die with Frank, to flee all her problems, all the pain, like him. Frightened by her own thoughts, she dragged herself backward to escape the influence of the precipice. She cried with her forehead on the ground, the taste of earth mixing with the taste of blood in her mouth.

Mara muttered something behind her.

Grace turned around, saw the moon reflected on the knife's blade. When Mara dropped the weapon, it became a spot of light in the grass, a dim firefly.

"Let me help you." Mara walked toward Grace, knelt and took her elbow. "Come on, Grace, get up."

Grace shook her arm to free herself. She turned around without giving Mara a chance to help and got up by herself without even looking at her. Her hair was covering her face, going in her mouth. She spat some out, coughed.

"Take it easy, Grace. I wasn't going to do anything to you with that knife."

Mara held a hand to Grace's face, perhaps to remove the hair, but Grace stopped it, catching the arm by the wrist.

"Don't touch me, don't touch me again." She shook her head to get her hair away. "I'm very sorry for what my husband did to you, but don't you dare come near me or my family again. Ever."

Grace threw Mara's wrist away as if it were trash. She finished brushing her hair with her fingers, wiped the blood from her chest, and picked up the knife from the ground. Just in case, she threw it into the abyss. Then she set off back in the direction of the motor home, of her children, unable to even think about how she would explain what had happened.

Before Grace left the clearing, Mara let out a sob. She asked the air what she had done. She fell to her knees on the grass, set her backside down, and cried with her face in her hands. Grace's first instinct was to console her, to alleviate another person's—a victim's—agony, just as she would have liked someone to alleviate hers. But she didn't. She thought of Audrey's grief at the loss of her ferrets, of her own suffering when she looked in the mirror and saw her hair falling out. Even if it was being a victim that had turned Mara into an abuser, she was an abuser nonetheless. Peace, true forgiveness, can only be achieved through magnanimity, and magnanimity means being able to overcome suffering without the need to transfer it to anyone else, not even the person who caused it. Grace left Mara alone with her grief. She could still hear her crying as she began the descent through the pine branches.

She went down the mountain at the mercy of the slope, letting herself be carried. Her exhausted brain couldn't even go to the trouble of thinking about whether there was a better way down—all she wanted was to reach her children as quickly as possible. She advanced with her mind blank, a night spirit wandering among the trees. When the upturned motor home's light was visible, she used it as a beacon to chart her course. Pine needles, pine cones, and dry grass crunched underfoot, alerting the children of her arrival before she reached the road.

"Dad?" asked Simon.

Her boy's voice asking for his father crushed her already broken heart. Her sobbing grew louder than her footsteps then.

"It's you, Mom."

She came out of the ditch full of vegetation and onto the road. Her children received her with frightened faces, the girl asking straightaway about the wounds on her chest, her neck. Grace held them.

"What happened?" asked Audrey.

"We have to go find help," Grace replied.

"And Dad?"

"And the crazy lady?"

Grace breathed, not knowing what to say. She felt unable to utter a single word—any response she gave would be equally terrible.

"Is Dad all right?"

She shook her head at the more direct question. She didn't know how to lie, she could only remain silent.

"I'm afraid not." She swallowed. "There's been an accident."

For the time being, she didn't want to explain anything else. What she said could mark the children's lives forever, and her head was in the worst possible state to make such an important decision. Even so, that small amount of information was enough to make Simon start crying. The doctor had managed to save the absent eye's tear gland, so tears spilled from both eyes, until the patch was soaked.

37.

They walked toward the highway. The black sky had gradually turned indigo, and then the light swallowed up the tiny moon. The settling dew brought out the dense pine aroma of dawn, but in the little drops in which Grace had seen sparkling diamonds yesterday, today she saw nothing more than drops. Or tears, the whole forest mourning her misfortune.

After the first few miles, Simon had sat on the ground swearing he wouldn't take another step farther away from his father, and Grace had had to carry him on her back. She listened to him cry on her shoulder until he fell asleep. Now the boy was walking on his own two feet again, holding her hand and his sister's. Audrey had asked a lot of questions at the start of the walk, but Grace's complete silence finally wore her out.

The three of them walked with short steps, the grit crunching under their footwear the only conversation they had until, when they turned a bend, a line of smoke was visible against the pale blue color the sky had taken on. It seemed to be a long way off still, but it was a destination more reachable than the roadside restaurant, which seemed as far away to Grace as Boston, the place where they'd been headed in some other life that was no longer theirs.

"Could it be Earl?" asked Simon.

Grace had thought the smoke would be coming from a camper's fire, but her children's sharpness never ceased to amaze her. It was very possible that it was Earl, though his truck issuing smoke like that worried her, not knowing what Mara might have done to it.

"We don't know what it is," answered Grace. "We'll see."

The possibility of being reunited with Earl inspired Simon to quicken his pace. Grace and Audrey, after exchanging a pessimistic look, also increased their speed, in their case out of fear the man needed urgent help. After the third bend they went around, the three of them were enveloped in a gasoline smell that grew more pungent as they approached. Finally, after cresting a slope, they found the source of the smoke.

It was Earl's pickup.

And, parked beside it, was a family-sized motor home.

Grace blinked to dissolve the mirage. She felt as if she'd been transported back in time, as if a wormhole had taken her back two days, when life had been so different. But even when she rubbed her eyes, this motor home that resembled their own so closely was still there, and so were the two people walking around Earl's truck gesticulating wildly. It was turned over on the road, burned out, with the front and rear windshields smashed. Grace told Audrey to stay with Simon and ran by herself to the accident scene.

The two people turned around when they heard her footsteps. It was a couple, her and Frank's age. They wore shorts and pristine white sneakers, like a cliché of the suburban couple on a summer excursion. They both had polo shirts on, and sweaters around their necks. They stifled a scream when they saw her arrive.

"And what happened to you?" The woman's many bracelets jingled when she held her hand to her mouth. "Another accident?"

Before responding, Grace knelt by the truck and peered into the cab, fearing the condition in which she'd find Earl.

"There's no one there," the man said, turning his head in all directions. "We haven't found anything. We saw the wreck and stopped, but it doesn't look like there's anyone. You weren't in there, were you?"

He asked the question while looking into the distance, as if calculating how far Grace could have flown after the impact. Her appearance must have been bad enough to be in keeping with the consequences of a serious road accident.

Before she could reply, Simon started yelling.

"He's here! It's Earl!"

The boy was waving his arms by the roadside, pointing at something in the bushes. They all ran over. It was a body. Earl. Simon was the first to take off his T-shirt and hold it on a wound on the old man's thigh.

"Are you OK, Earl? Earl!"

The old man opened his eyes. He smiled when he recognized the boy.

"I've been in worse situations." He touched Simon's leg, thanking him for his concern. "At least I didn't lose my hands this time."

He held up his stumps.

"Oh my God. We have to find them." The woman turned around, searching the area. "The hands, we have to find them. They couldn't have gone far, they can still be sewn back on."

Grace stopped her and explained the reality, eliciting a sigh of both relief and embarrassment.

"And what happened to you all?"

"Everything," replied Grace. There was no other word. "Everything happened to us."

Grace asked Earl if it had been Mara who rolled the truck, who cut his leg. The suburban couple looked at each other without knowing what to say.

"She had a knife," Earl confirmed. "She got as mad as an angry bison, she wanted to go back for you."

"She did something to my dad, too," said Simon. "We have to get help."

Earl looked at Grace, inquiring about the seriousness of the situation with his wrinkly eyes. Her slow blink was enough for the old man to understand the tragic outcome that Simon did not yet know.

Earl stroked the boy's face. "You saved me, Simon, you're a hero. And heroes are very strong. Don't ever forget how strong you are. You can do anything."

The man with the sweater around his neck announced that he had just called 911, that help was on its way. His wife said they couldn't wait for the ambulance to arrive, that there was only this road and it would take a long time to reach them, perhaps too long. The smartest thing to do would be to start taking them in the right direction, so the help reached them sooner. It moved Grace to see that it was possible to be good, as the man had already been with his actions, but that it was also always possible to be even better, as the woman had been, sacrificing their own trip to assist a victim.

"Come on, let's get him in."

The couple, Audrey, and Simon surrounded Earl. Grace asked the man for his cell phone. She stepped away from her children, who helped move the old man. She dialed the emergency number's three digits and told the dispatcher what had happened to Frank, and the approximate location of his fall, in case it was still possible to recover his body. She would wait at the point in the road where the first ambulance met the motor home to take Earl. Applying the lesson the woman with the sweater had just taught her, Grace did even better and informed them that another woman had crashed her car in the same area.

"Let's go!" Leaning out of the motor-home door, the woman with the sweater was gesturing at Grace to hurry up. "We're leaving!"

Audrey and Simon waited to climb in with their mother. Once inside, they found two children of similar ages sitting at the table with their seat belts on, except the eldest was a boy and the youngest a girl.

"Did you see the hot waters?" the little girl asked, slotting her tongue into the gap left by a missing tooth as she spoke. "We came to see the hot waters. They're hot."

"No," Grace replied, sniffing. "We didn't get to see them."

"Hot springs, Sophia," her mother corrected her from the passenger seat. "And now we're going to take a little longer to get there, OK? We have to give the gentleman back there a ride."

Grace saw that Earl was lying in the main bedroom. The couple hadn't minded soiling their bed with blood, vegetation, and earth to help a stranger.

"All set?" asked the man, starting the engine.

Grace sat with her children on the sofa, one on each side, Simon without a T-shirt. She hugged them, kissed them on the temples, the tops of their heads. As long as she could repeat that kiss once a day, her life would be filled with meaning. Audrey interlinked her fingers with those on Grace's right hand, and Simon did the same with her left. They both rested their heads on her shoulders. The motor home set off, rocking them. Through the kitchen window, Grace watched the wooded landscape pass by. She distanced her mind from worse thoughts by listing the conifers Simon studied: Western white pine, ponderosa pine, Douglas fir, western hemlock . . .

The woman with the sweater took her husband's hand on the armrest, just as Grace had done two nights ago, holding on to Frank so he would guide her toward the future. In the couple at the front of the motor home, with their two children of similar ages, Grace saw a family portrait as ideal as her own had been two days before. When her and Frank's had also seemed like the perfect marriage.

38.

Grace had been waiting for the children to go back to school for weeks. Restoring their routine would help reestablish some of the normality they'd lost at the start of the summer. She did up her robe as she was preparing breakfast—the mornings were already cold in early September. She still opened the wrong cupboards, still searched for the cereals and bowls in the wrong place, her brain still accustomed to the layout of the house they had left with Frank and to which they never returned. Though they'd gone back to Seattle—neither she nor the children found any reason to leave the city they felt was their true home—Grace turned down the offer from Frank's company to move them back into their old house, accepting a smaller one in the same area. Like Frank after the accident with the gun, Grace didn't feel she could live in a house with a hole in it from the bullet that cost her son an eye. Now that she knew the truth, that hole, even repaired, would always remind her of the handgun her husband bought to protect himself from the lover who was breaking into their home to pressure him, and whom he ended up killing in a hot tub before running aw—

Grace halted the obsessive train of thought that began with the hole in the wall and always ended the same way, in disaster and emotional pain. That was why it would have been impossible to live in the other house. This one was sufficient for the three of them—in fact, the kitchen was bigger, and that was why Grace kept opening the wrong cupboards and drawers when she made breakfast. As soon as the children finished and left for school, she would record her first video in two months for her YouTube channel. She'd already arranged the set and prepared herself mentally to face the camera. One day she'd tell her subscribers the true story of what had happened. She had always been very honest with them, and she had no intention of changing. But for the time being she preferred not to address the subject. Through a piece in the local newspaper, one of those stories about lost tourists or hikers who end up burned or dissolved in hot waters they hadn't given enough respect, some followers leaked the news on social media that the husband of Gracefully—many of them called her by the name of her channel—had suffered a fatal accident in the mountains, and all that was recovered were some bone remains. Grace planned to maintain this version of events by default until she felt ready to tell the truth. Just as she'd shared her marital happiness to serve as an example and encourage people to aspire to perfection, now she would share all her pain, shame, and suffering to serve as an example of how to face up to the toughest setbacks that life hides from us.

The microwave beeped when the milk had finished warming.

Grace took away the finger she was rubbing against her eyebrow and called the children.

Audrey was the first to arrive, less dressed up than one would expect of a nervous girl about to start a new school year. But she always wanted to show herself as she was—she felt comfortable in her own body, confident about what she wore, and she didn't need adornments or to trick her classmates by making more of an effort for the first impression than she would later on. Grace knew her daughter wanted to be as true to herself on the first day as she would be on the last.

Audrey, unlike Gracefully's subscribers, *did* know what really happened on the mountain. She made Grace tell her not long after the events, arguing that she had every right to know the truth about her father. Grace told her one night, the two of them crying with their hands interlinked on the kitchen table, drinking cups of hot chocolate that she made following the recipe from one of her videos. She even put marshmallow pieces in, as if the white candy could somehow combat the bitterness of the world, make the darkness of reality a little lighter. Audrey, the young teenager belonging to a generation many adults mocked, demonstrated that she was more grown-up than her own mother when she asked to see a therapist. For these young people, long gone was the cliché of a mother recommending a psychologist to her daughter and the girl rebelliously rejecting the idea, arguing she wasn't crazy. That didn't happen anymore. Today's teenagers were mature enough to know how much therapy can help, and they could talk about mental health without fear or reservations of any kind.

Audrey knew that with professional psychological help she would be able to accept the bad her father had done, a bad that had to be confronted and acknowledged but that shouldn't be the only thing to which Frank's memory was reduced. Audrey wanted to be able to remember all the good things about her father, of which there were many, almost everything. She refused to allow the bad to eclipse the good, as it did in so many other situations in life, when in reality the bad is almost always smaller and less powerful than the good. Even at sixteen, Audrey spoke about people as complex beings, full of conflicting feelings, and she argued that it made no sense to condemn such a quality in others when we all have this complexity within ourselves. The only coherent approach is to accept the contradictions in others the way we accept our own. Grace was left speechless when she heard her little girl talk like this. She even felt envious of the open mind with which Audrey was able to cope with what had happened. What most surprised her was that she was the same girl who sang Taylor Swift in the shower and still cried watching *The Fault in Our Stars*. Perhaps it showed that criticizing the cultural references of subsequent generations is a very superficial reading of their reality.

Grace herself didn't feel as mature as Audrey. She was still struggling with the despair that had overwhelmed her since the incident on the mountain. It was the opposite for her than for Audrey: she could barely remember the old Frank she had loved. Every time she thought of him, as she did every day, at all hours, all she felt was fury, sadness. Hate. For everything. For the deceit, for the gun, for Simon's eye, for jumping off the precipice as if there was no other way out. Grace knew it wasn't fair to only remember Frank for the bad things, that in twenty years, he hadn't just lied and cheated on her with another woman. He had also made her happy, very happy, during the same twenty years. As Audrey said, allowing the bad in the last part of their marriage to eclipse the good in all the parts that went before it—much more important ones—would be a mistake, an injustice, a terrible road to go down for her and for humanity in general. The Frank who leapt into the abyss was the same Frank who recorded a Jewel song for her twenty times on the two sides of a cassette. But Grace couldn't see it that way yet. She would have to keep working on her anger, on her capacity for forgiveness.

Simon walked into the kitchen, trim and neat, smiling even though he was more nervous than Audrey about the first day of school. Opening both eyes, he asked Grace if his classmates would notice which one was fake. With complete sincerity, she answered no. The first time they implanted the prosthetic eye at the hospital—in the end, he completed his treatment where it began—Grace was so surprised at how realistic it looked that, for a second, she thought a miracle had restored her son's eye, that it had all been a strange nightmare from which they were finally waking. She even felt Frank's hand grab her from the empty chair beside her, asking her why she'd suffered so much these last few months when nothing had happened, when everything was fine.

Simon still believed his father had fallen off the precipice accidentally when he was running away from the crazy lady, as he still called Mara. As far as he knew, she was nothing more than a stranger they crossed paths with, one who wanted to harm them for the hell of it, because she was a bad person. And the crazy lady had to be a bad person if she'd made his father fall into the void.

Grace never heard from Mara again, and Earl didn't want to have anything to do with her, either—he didn't even report her for assault. When Grace asked him why, he replied that she would be punished by a different kind of justice more fitting than any invented by man, and that he would rather just be grateful to her for pulling him out of the truck. If she hadn't done it, he said, he would be a cloud of ash flying among the pine trees right now, and his wife would have to kill the stinkbugs all by herself each summer. Earl had already written two postcards to Simon by this time, demonstrating everything he could do with no hands. Grace had sent him a photo of the boy with his new eye not long ago, and Simon was eager to receive his response.

Audrey spilled the milk when she poured it in her cup—maybe she wasn't as calm as she seemed.

"You're going to do great, everyone's going to love you," Grace told her, certain of what she said. "It's impossible for them not to love you. And who knows, you might meet your senior-year sweetheart today, the man in your life."

"Or the woman in my life. Mom, when are you going to ditch your heteropatriarchal ideas?"

"All right, all right, the person in your life," Grace corrected herself.

"Much better." Audrey cleaned up the spilled milk and finished filling the cup. "*Person* is the best word to describe one another: genderless, ageless, everything-less, just humanity and personality, which is what we all have in common."

"Mom, are you sure her classmates are going to love her if that's how she talks?" Simon blurted out.

Audrey was the first to laugh, and Grace and Simon joined her.

They all fell silent at once when they heard a strange sound in the living room. Or perhaps it had been on the rear porch. Simon was unconcerned, but Audrey and Grace exchanged worried looks, both of them ascribing the same terrible explanation to the noise. Grace was struck by a wave of anxiety, a carbon copy of the ones she experienced on the nights they heard noises in the house when Frank was still there.

"Don't move," she ordered the kids.

She took her cell phone from her robe pocket.

She dialed 911 without making the call, listening to the silence in the house.

"What is it, Mom?" Simon asked.

She instructed him to be quiet with a finger on her lips.

The next time the floor creaked, Grace tapped the green icon on the screen. She held it to her ear, ready to announce she had an intruder in her home. But before dispatch answered the call, there was a particular noise, like a whistle, that made Audrey hold a hand to her chest. Her features untwisted her worried expression to form another look closer to expectation. Then they heard a peculiar pitter-patter.

"No way."

Audrey's expectation was turning to joy. More whistles, which in reality were high-pitched whines, were audible along with the patter of scurrying feet approaching the kitchen. Two little snouts with whiskers appeared in the doorway.

"It's them!" Audrey yelled. "It's Hope and Joy!" Her ferrets scampered into the kitchen and ran straight for her. They climbed her legs, the table's legs, they jumped onto her chest. They sniffed their owner's face as if covering her in kisses to celebrate their reunion.

"You came back!"

Audrey hugged the restless animals, which went around her neck, investigated her belly, stole cereal from Simon's bowl.

Moved by her daughter's reaction, Grace paid no attention to the voice in her ear, asking her what her emergency was. It asked the question again just as, through the window, Grace saw a bush move near the backyard entrance.

Mara had just been there.

When the voice asked the question for a third time, Grace had to decide whether she could forgive Mara. Whether her justifiable initial intentions and the goodwill of returning Audrey's ferrets could be enough to begin to repair the damage that woman had caused, or whether she would continue to live in fear and resentment. Before answering, Grace looked at her daughter, at the pure joy flowing from her smile. She also looked at Simon, who was stroking the ferrets with tenderness, telling his sister he always knew they would come back home to her.

She hung up without saying anything.

She decided to accept Mara's peace offering, and to let love and trust be the values that prevailed over hate and suspicion. She thought that, with little gestures like hers—the simple act of interrupting a call born from resentment—the pain in the world might slowly be reduced.

Grace left her cell phone on the countertop, next to the photograph in which she and Frank were rewinding a cassette with a pen, an image that Simon still used to talk to his father. Then Grace sat with her children, allowing the ferrets to climb on her body as well, the first time she'd ever let them do it. Somehow, the animals' reappearance had restored her faith in the future, because she realized that if Hope and Joy could come back, many of the things she lost under the water could also return.

ACKNOWLEDGMENTS

Seeing my books translated into English is a dream that, since *The Light of the Fireflies* was published, has continued to be fulfilled with each of my new novels. A beautiful dream I still haven't woken up from thanks to my translator, Simon Bruni—a perfect replica of my voice in English—and my brilliant editor Elizabeth DeNoma; spectacular covers by artist David Drummond; and, of course, the tremendous AmazonCrossing team, whom I was lucky enough to meet in Seattle recently. With each new project, I feel that all of them—from production to design, from the copyeditor to the audiobook's voice-over artists—look after and present my stories in the best way possible.

ABOUT THE AUTHOR

Paul Pen is a bestselling Spanish author whose four novels have been translated to English, German, Italian, Russian, and Turkish. His book *The Light of the Fireflies* has sold more than one hundred thousand copies worldwide, and his debut novel *The Warning*, which is soon to be published in English for the first time, was adapted to the big screen in 2018. Motion pictures of *The Light of the Fireflies* and *Desert Flowers* are also in development, the latter scripted by Pen himself. In his capacity as scriptwriter, Pen is working on a forthcoming Netflix series. The author returns in fall 2019 with the international release of his new novel *Under the Water*, bringing his unmistakable brand of literary suspense to readers around the globe.

ABOUT THE TRANSLATOR

Simon Bruni is a literary translator from Spanish, a language he acquired through "total immersion" living in Alicante, Valencia, and Santander. He studied Spanish and Linguistics at Queen Mary University of London and Literary Translation at the University of Exeter.

Simon's many published translations include novels, short stories, videogames, and nonfiction publications, and he is the winner of three John Dryden awards: in 2017 and 2015 for Paul Pen's short stories "Cinnamon" and "The Porcelain Boy," and in 2011 for Francisco Pérez Gandul's novel *Cell 211*. His translation of Paul Pen's novel *The Light of the Fireflies* has sold over one hundred thousand copies worldwide.

For more information, please visit www.simonbruni.com.